Truth or DARE

KINGSTON BROTHERS NUMBER 2

BESTSELLING AUTHOR
ISABEL LUCERO

Truth or DARE

KINGSTON BROTHERS NUMBER 2

CILLIAN

Over the buzz of my gun and the rock music playing lightly in the background, comes the grating voice of a woman who accompanied her boyfriend for his tattoo appointment only to talk shit about his choice of tattoo.

"I mean, I just don't get it. Why do you want to get a tattoo of a woman? I have to look at it all the time because it's on your arm."

"Well, Jan, let me blow your mind real quick. Maybe, just maybe, the tattoo isn't for you."

I press my lips together in an effort to keep from laughing. My client—Dasan, exhales just as his girlfriend huffs, and I keep working.

The tattoo is of a striking woman smoking a cigarette. The smoke and hair wisp and whirl around her, creating a pretty cool border around her face.

"Is this one of your ex-girlfriends?"

"Oh my God, no! He drew her up!" Dasan explains, gesturing to me with his other hand.

Jan looks at me with pursed lips. "Did you?"

I give a single nod. "Yep. She was born from my own imagination."

She harrumphs and Dasan sighs. "Sorry, dude."

I just smile and continue to do my job. It's not the worst experience I've had in this shop.

"Are you apologizing for me?"

"Oh Lord. Jan, why don't you go down the block. Have a drink. I'll come find you."

I tune them out as they continue to bicker back and forth. I'm almost done anyway, and luckily, he's my last customer.

Earlier, I texted my girlfriend, Zoe, asking if she wanted to come hang out at my studio once I was done here, but as usual, she declined.

For the past several months things haven't been going so well with us, and for a while, I assumed everything would end up okay, because while we always fight, we also always make up. We always had sex to fall back on. I think maybe that's why we put up with each other. The sex is pretty good. We fight, then we fuck, and we're happy. However, it's only temporary. And lately, we haven't been doin' much fucking.

"All right, man. That'll do it," I say, wiping off a mixture of ink and blood from his arm. "Wanna take a look before I wrap it?"

"Yeah."

Dasan climbs out of the chair and makes his way to the floor-length mirror between my chair and the next. He rotates his arm, getting a good look at all the detail, then smiles. "I love it. Thanks, Cill."

"No problem."

When he sits back down, I clean and rub ointment over the fresh ink before wrapping it up.

"Oh good. At least I won't have to look at it when we go home," Jan says.

I lift my eyes up to look at Dasan, and notice he's rolling his.

"Just for a couple hours," I tell him. "Then let it breathe."

After Dasan pays and I clean up my station, I head to the back to find Wes.

"Hey, man. You done already?" he asks, looking up from his sketch.

"Yeah. How long you think that's gonna take?" I ask, nodding to his drawing.

He tilts his head, inspecting the work. "I don't know. Another hour at least. The guy came in earlier wanting to make some changes."

"Okay, well, unless you have a walk-in, feel free to close up when you're done."

Wes stands up and stretches his arms above his head. "All right, dude. Thanks. Fuck, my back is killing me. Been hunched over too damn long."

"I told you to take a break."

"Breaks are for the weak," he says with a laugh, scratching his inked up left bicep before

reaching into the mini fridge for a Coke. His tattoos cover his entire left side—from neck to ankle. I'd know because I did every single one of them for him.

"Looks like you're taking a break now."

"Fuck off. You're distracting me."

I laugh as I turn and leave. I pull out my phone and tell Zoe I'm heading to my brother's bar if she wants to meet me there for a little while, but she doesn't respond.

Since King's Tavern is only a block and a half away, it doesn't take long to get there. It's Saturday, and close to eleven, so it's fairly busy, but I spot an empty seat next to my brother's girlfriend, London.

"Hey, Lo," I say, dropping into the stool next to her.

"Oh, hey!" she responds cheerfully. "You just get off work?"

"Yep. Decided to grab a drink before heading to the studio."

"Drinking and painting. Does that work well for you?" she asks with a giggle.

"Willing to try anything to get the creative juices flowing."

She frowns, tucking her blond hair behind her ear. "Still struggling?"

"I'll be fine."

"What about juices?" Midge asks, spinning in her stool next to London.

I've known Midge since elementary school. This small town makes it to where you basically know everybody, or at least know of them.

"Creative juices," London repeats. "Cill's lost his mojo."

Midge slides out of her seat, her black boots hitting the floor with a thud before waltzing around London. "I'm sure whatever you've been working on is great. Why don't you show it to us?"

I make a face. "Not gonna happen. It's definitely not ready."

"Yeah, but you said that about the last piece and then you ruined it with black paint before anybody could see it. Maybe you're just way too critical about your own work."

"Nah, it was shit."

Midge rolls her eyes. "Whatever, man. What if I want to procure your services?"

I furrow my brows, judging her choice of words. "Procure my services?"

She puts a hand on her hip. "You know, hire you for some work."

I squint my eyes at her. "What would you need to hire me for?"

"My mom's birthday is coming up, and I have an idea for this amazing painting. I think you'd do such a great job, and I don't know any other artists, and it's for my mom. Are you really going to say no to a painting for my mom?"

She keeps her tiny little hand on her hip, cocking it to the side and looking at me with her wide, doe eyes. Midge knows I love her mom. She was there for me and my brothers when we lost our parents, always reaching out to ask if we needed anything. And then, of course, there were all those times I spent at their house. She treated me like one of her own, and honestly, I'd do anything for her.

"Fine. I'll do whatever you want, but I don't wanna talk about it now. All I want is a beer."

Midge bounces on her toes with a wide smile stretching across her face. "I'll go get that brother of yours." I think she's going to walk over to where he's standing, but then she yells, "Hey, bartender! How about some service over here, huh?"

Royce's head snaps in our direction, but when he sees the three of us, he cracks a grin. "I'm coming, I'm coming."

"Where's Zoe?" Midge asks.

"I'm not sure," I reply, pulling my phone from my pocket to check if she responded to my text yet. "She didn't want to hang out at my studio, so when I decided to come here, I texted her to let her know, but she hasn't written back yet."

I put the phone on the bar, and the girls share a look before focusing on me.

"What?"

"Nothing," they answer simultaneously.

"Sorry, bro," Royce says, popping up with a beer in his hand. "Busy night. What's goin' on?"

5

"Not much," I reply, taking the beer and swallowing down a large gulp. "Just got off. Figured I'd come have a drink before heading to the studio."

"I'm not even gonna ask how it's going," he replies with a small shake of his head and the tiniest of smirks.

He's been asking how my painting has been going but I keep giving him the same answer. Absolute shit.

He talks to London for a little while, and Midge makes her way over to me.

"So, are you and Zoe currently together? I know y'all like to break up every few weeks. I can't really keep up," she says with a short laugh and small smile.

"We just got back together a couple weeks ago."

She snorts and rolls her eyes. "You guys are crazy."

I chuckle as I bring the beer to my lips. "Guess I'm used to it."

"So, about this painting." She holds up her hand when I open my mouth. "I know you said you didn't want to talk about it, but you have your beer, so shut up. I'm looking to be a little drunk soon, so if I don't say it now, who knows that I'll even remember this conversation."

I shake my head. "Okay, go."

"My mom spent many summers at her parents' house at Lake Erie. She hasn't been back in so long but she talks about her time there pretty often. My grandparents still own it, but I don't think they make it up there too often. Usually it's rented out. Anyway, I'd love to have you paint that house and general scenery. Cill, it's so beautiful. It's right on the water, and I know you can make it look spectacular. Mom would love it."

Midge's eyes lit up as she was talking about it, and now they're staring at me, pleading. Like she really thinks I'll say no.

"Lake Erie, huh?"

"I know it's a few hours away, but I'll check with my grandparents and see if it's free, and you can stay there if you want. It would be the perfect place for you to maybe get your mojo back."

I contemplate it. It's not a bad idea actually. "Yeah, okay. Sounds good. Just let me know if it's available, and then I'll make sure to take some time off from the shop."

Midge lets out a high-pitched squeal. "Eeee! Thank you so much, Cillian!" She wraps her arms around my neck and squeezes.

"Yeah, yeah. You're choking me."

She gives me another squeeze before placing her hand on the side of my head and pushing.

"Don't be a baby."

"What's all the squealing about?" London asks.

"Cill's gonna stay at my grandparents' place on Lake Erie and paint a picture for my mom."

"Wait," London says, her face turning serious. "You mean to tell me we could've been staying at a house on Lake Erie this whole time and you're just now telling me it exists?"

Midge cackles. "Sorry. I don't think about going out there."

"Oh my God, I hate you."

"No, you don't. Maybe we can head up there too. Just for, like, a day or so, cause Cill needs the alone time so he can—"

"Masturbate?" Royce chimes in.

I give him the finger.

"No," Midge continues. "So he can create a masterpiece."

I hear Royce mutter something to London, and I'm pretty sure it was "masturbate" again. Asshole.

"That'll be so much fun!" London chirps. "We can have a nice weekend out there."

I finish my beer and slide some money toward Royce. "I'm outta here. Gotta go try to be creative."

"Try masturbating first," Midge says. "Just kidding! I'll let you know about the house."

I shake my head. "All right. Bye, guys."

I check my phone again once I'm outside, but there's still nothing from Zoe. I walk to the studio I rent out a couple blocks from my tattoo shop and hope when I get there I'll be able to create something I'm proud of. But I can't stop wondering why Zoe hasn't responded to me.

2

MIDGE

"I FEEL BAD. I THINK WE SHOULD TELL HIM," I TELL LONDON.

"I don't know. I mean, I guess I get that, but I don't want to be the person responsible for breaking his heart."

"Fuck that. We're not responsible. Zoe is!"

"Are you sure you saw what you think you saw? Maybe it was innocent?"

I scoff. "I saw her tongue literally in someone else's mouth. Her literal arms around someone else's neck. She was literally, basically humping this guy in public."

"Okay, okay. Stop saying literally."

"But for real. Literally. She's cheating on him."

"Maybe we can tell Royce and he can tell him."

I shake my head and take a sip of my drink. "Nah. I'm his friend, and I'm the one who witnessed it. I should tell him."

London frowns. "Well, good luck with that. I hope he doesn't take it too hard."

"Me either, but at least he can escape to Lake Erie for a while and get away. I need to call my grandparents tomorrow so I can make sure nobody's already in it."

"I still can't believe you didn't tell me about this house," London pouts.

"I'm sorry," I say, wrapping my arms around her and leaning my head against hers. "I promise we'll go more than once this summer. You forgive me?"

"Mmm," she leaves me hanging for several seconds. "I guess."

I playfully smack her as I pull away, and we both start laughing. After we finish our drinks, London spends some time saying bye to Royce, so I grab my phone and scroll through Facebook. Ava, a friend from school, posted some pictures from a night out she had recently, and something in the background of a couple of them catch my eye. After I zoom in and study the two pictures some more, I realize I'm seeing an unmistakable couple of photos of Zoe and the guy she's cheating on Cillian with.

In the first picture, Zoe is looking up at this guy and smiling. The tips of her fingers rest inside his upturned palm, like they were either beginning to hold hands or just letting go. In the second picture, she's moved in closer and rested her head on his shoulder.

I get that it's nothing concrete, and she could even try to talk her way out of these, but I know what I saw two days ago. I may not have pictures, but Cillian will have to believe me, because he knows I'd never make that up. And now, here she is being so brazen to be out in public with this guy, holding hands and cuddling up. Doesn't she realize how small this town is? Someone is bound to see her, just like I did in front of that restaurant.

Just as I was getting out of my car to head inside for lunch, I spotted her and some tall guy in a suit at the corner of the building having a quick goodbye make-out session. She disappeared around the corner as the guy went the opposite way, and I was left standing there wondering what the hell I just saw.

Now that these photos are online, someone else may see them, so I need to tell Cill as soon as possible. Especially now that I know they aren't on one of their little breaks.

"You ready?" London asks.

I hand her my phone. "Look at this photo and the next."

She takes it and slides her thumb back and forth as she studies the pictures. "Are they having a bachelorette party?"

"No, look in the background."

Her thumb swipes across the screen several times, and then she brings the phone closer to her face before her eyes widen. Her jaw drops as she looks at me. "Is that Zoe?"

I nod once. "Yep."

"And that's obviously not Cill."

"Hell no."

"Oh, my God! You have to tell Cill now! What if he sees these or something?"

I take my phone back and drop it into my small, black purse. "You think I should tell him tonight? Wait till tomorrow? It's almost twelve-thirty."

"I don't know."

"I guess I'll send him a text. Maybe he's still at his studio."

She nods her head and sits down in front of me, so I take my phone back out and type out a quick text.

Midge: *Hey, you busy?*

Surprisingly, he responds almost right away.

Cillian: *Just staring at a blank canvas.*
Midge: *Studio?*
Cillian: *Yep.*

"Okay, he's at his studio," I tell London.

"You heading over there?"

"Yeah," I say with a nod. "Just gonna get it over with."

"All right. Well, I'll probably just go stay in Royce's apartment upstairs and wait for him to get off. Take a Lyft. Don't walk."

"Don't worry. I'll be safe," I say with a small grin.

"Text me later."

"Okay. Bye, girl."

As soon as I'm outside his studio space, I start to get nervous. I've never been the bearer of bad news before.

I know Zoe, because we went to school together, but we've never been friends. You know how sometimes you just don't click with people, and it's not really for any specific reason, except that you hate everything about them? Well, that's how I feel about her. She's always annoyed me. Her voice, the way she twirls a lock of hair around her finger when she talks, and how she always changes who she is depending on who she's around.

I'm aware she's not too fond of me either, but I'm fine with that. However, Cillian is my friend, and has been since elementary school, and I need to tell him what I know. Not because I hate Zoe, because if he were with anybody else, he'd still deserve to know the truth.

With a deep breath, I rub my palms over my jeans and then knock. Cill's studio has two large windows on either side of the door, but he's blacked them out, so nobody can look in. I can understand that. People are constantly walking down this road, and I wouldn't want them to be able to watch me either.

When he doesn't come to the door, I pound even harder. Finally, I hear the thud of his boots hitting the floor as he approaches.

The look he has when the door is yanked open would probably scare most people away. Not me, though.

"It's about time. Jeez. I could've been abducted out here," I say, pushing past him.

His face changes. The scowl is replaced with a grin. "Nobody'd abduct you, Midge. And if they did—"

"They'd bring me back? Yep. My mom used to say that all the time."

He smirks and shoves his paint covered hands in his pockets. "What're you doing here?"

I don't bother walking around and trying to get a look at his work, because I know he wouldn't want that. Instead, I move to the front corner where there's a couple foldable chairs.

"I just wanted to come talk to you," I reply, my stomach tightening at the thought of potentially breaking his heart.

"Okay," he says, dragging out the word like he's confused. "You never come here."

"I know." I allow my eyes to roam over the small room. The fluorescent lights are bright, but besides his painting necessities, these two chairs, and beer and soda cans, the room is empty. The harsh lights highlight the bare walls and the flickering one in the corner makes me uneasy. I don't know how he can spend so much time here. "I think you need a new studio."

He laughs and sits in the chair next to me. "Oh yeah? Why's that?"

"Well, I don't know. It's drab. There's no color in here. Nothing. For an artist, this is like purgatory. And that fucking light is driving me insane."

Cill grins at me. "I see."

"Anyway, that's not why I'm here."

He settles into his chair, leaning back and letting his long legs stretch out in front of him as he watches me. "Figured not. Must be important. What's up?"

"Well, uh," I start, gazing around the room for something to focus on besides his face. "I thought you should…well, I wanted to tell you that…um."

"Midge."

"Yeah?" I answer, looking back into his eyes.

"Spill it."

"Zoe. She's cheating on you."

After the words are out, I pinch my lips together and hold my breath. I continue to stare at his face, unsure of what his reaction will be, but ready for anything. The change is nearly imperceptible. Had I not had my eyes glued to him, I wouldn't have noticed the slight widening of his eyes, though it was brief. His jaw clenches, and I can nearly see all the thoughts he's having flash behind his eyes.

Cill sits up and leans his elbows on his knees. "With who?"

I shake my head and offer up a pitiful frown. "I don't know who it is."

"You saw them?"

I nod once.

"Did she see you?"

"No. They were…well, do you want to know?" He thinks about it for a second and then nods. "They were making out

14

in front of Lucio's. I was going in for lunch, and I guess they were just leaving."

He's nodding his head while clenching his fists. "What's he look like?"

"Oh, pft. Awful. I mean, really, Cill. Zoe is stupid for cheating on you. This guy looked stuffy and boring. A plain, tan suit and hair that had way too much gel in it. You're a thousand times better than that guy."

"Sounds like everything I'm not," he replies, lifting up his tattooed arms and gesturing at his jeans and T-shirt. It's amazing how cheating can make even the best looking people feel insecure. Cillian is beyond hot, and more than that, he's such a good guy.

"Seriously, Cill. This is not about you. She's dumb and I don't know, blind? You're great. Really."

He shakes his head. "Does anybody else know?"

I bite down on my bottom lip. "Well, that's kind of why I wanted to tell you tonight. I saw some pictures Ava Delvechio uploaded, and Zoe and this guy are in the background of a couple of them. I think it's just pure coincidence, but with all the tagging people do on Facebook, someone else may see them. Small town, you know? Word will spread fast."

"Just fucking great." He stands up and knocks the chair down in the process. "I gotta call her."

"Yeah, of course," I say, getting up and grabbing my purse. "I'm sorry, Cill. Really. You don't deserve this."

"Thanks for telling me. I can't say I'm surprised, but...I don't know. I guess I didn't want to think she'd actually cheat on me."

I walk behind him and pat his shoulder. "I'm gonna go. I'll see ya around."

He runs his hands through his hair, pushing it back, but keeps his fingers interlocked on the top of his head. "Yeah, okay." When I get to the door, he says, "Wait, it's late. Let me get you home."

I shake my head. "No, please. Don't worry about me. You have other things to worry about. I'll head over to the diner a couple streets over and call a Lyft."

He rushes over to his painting corner and grabs his keys and phone. "Come on," he says, walking past me and opening the door. "I gotta get home anyway."

I quietly follow behind him until we get to his motorcycle. Normally, I'd probably have something to say about riding on this thing, but not right now. He hands me his helmet and straddles the bike.

"Arms around my waist. You'll be fine," is all he mutters as I try my best to look like I know what I'm doing as I try to fit the helmet over my head.

"Um."

"Come here."

I take a couple steps and stand there as he helps secure the helmet. He cracks the tiniest of grins when he's done, so I'm sure that means I look funny, but I don't fight with him about it. I just climb behind him and wrap my arms around his middle.

The bike roars to life, making me jump a little, and then we're off, traveling the nearly empty roads until we get to my place. The ride only takes about fifteen minutes, and to be honest, I'm glad we were on his bike, that way we didn't have an uncomfortable silence between us the whole way.

I manage to get off the bike fairly easily, but removing the helmet doesn't come gracefully. My hair gets caught somewhere inside, and by the time I pull it off, my hair's all over the place.

"Thanks for the ride. And sorry about…everything."

He nods once as he easily puts the helmet on. "I'll talk to you later."

I wave and watch him drive off before I enter my house. For some reason, seeing Cillian like this makes me feel sad. I just want to go inside and eat some ice cream from the container and then fall asleep.

So that's what I do.

3

CILLIAN

ZOE NEVER RESPONDED TO ANY OF MY TEXTS. I DECIDED I didn't want to let her know that I was made aware of what she's been up to via text message or voicemail, so after many unanswered calls, and texts that were never responded to, I stopped trying.

It isn't until nearly noon on Sunday when the phone rings and her face lights up the screen.

"Hello?"

"Hey."

She doesn't even sound like she wants to talk to me, like she's only calling because she's aware I've been trying to get in touch with her since last night. I remember the days when she'd call and sound happy, even giddy to talk to me. I always knew when she was smiling over the phone. Her voice would be high and flirty. I don't even remember when that stopped.

"You been busy?" I question, trying to keep my anger and frustration tamed. If I tell her now, she'll never agree to see me, and the minute I question her, she'll hang up and we'll never have the conversation we need to have.

"Not really. Well, I guess. Last night I was out with Stacey, and we went to this bar. My phone was in my purse all night, and by the time I looked at it, it was already dead. I just plugged it in before I went to sleep, and woke up not too long ago."

The fact that she's trying to thoroughly explain why she didn't see my texts or try to get in touch with me before I even have to ask seems telling. She's covering her ass already, because she knows she's in the wrong.

"I see. Stacey, huh?"

"Uh-huh. I told you about Stacey."

"New girl who works with you. I remember."

She's silent on the other end, and while all I want to do is yell *I know you're fucking someone else!* I don't.

"You at home?"

"Where else would I be?" she asks with a chuckle. I don't know if I'm thinking too much into it, but she sounds nervous.

"I'm not sure." I swallow down my anger. "I want to take you to lunch, so I'll be over there soon."

"Wait!"

I hang up and stomp my way into the garage. Zoe only lives about twelve minutes away, but I'm sure I can cut that in half.

It takes eight minutes for me to get to her apartment, but it takes her fifteen minutes to get there herself. I watch from across the street as her little black Jetta pulls into her garage. She was in such a rush, I'm sure she didn't see me.

I only wait about thirty seconds before I get out of the Jeep and stride across the street and up to her door. When she opens it, she's flustered—her cheeks stained red and her hair in disarray.

"Hey," she says, out of breath.

"Were you working out or something?" I question, wondering if she's going to lie.

She looks down at her floral blouse and jeans—obviously something she wore last night while she was out. I'm sure there's a pair of heels somewhere between her garage and front door that she kicked off.

"Oh, no. I was just about to get in the shower, so I kind of jogged down the hall to get to the door.

"Shower?" I lift a brow. "You're already dressed."

"Yeah, well…" she trails off, choosing to shrug and laugh it off. "Anyway, where do you want to eat?"

"Actually, do you mind if I come in for a minute?"

"Sure." She pulls the door open wider and I step inside, looking around like I'm going to find evidence of her affair somewhere in the room.

I drop onto her pale-yellow loveseat and outstretch my arms across the back. She eyes me warily before sitting in a black accent chair to my left.

"So, what's up?" she asks.

"What *is* up?" I throw back at her.

"I don't know. Why are you acting weird?"

"I'm just wondering why you're lying to me."

"Lying to you?" she screeches. "What the hell are you talking about?"

I tilt my head, surprised at how fast she's ready to defend herself, even though she knows she just got done lying to me a minute ago.

"You weren't about to get in the shower."

She rolls her eyes. "Yes, I was!"

"You just came home."

She hesitates. "No. I've been here."

"Really? So, that wasn't you who just came flying down the street and into your garage?" She doesn't answer. "I was outside, Zoe. You were so caught up in your bullshit, you didn't even notice."

She opens her mouth to argue, but there's nothing to say, so she presses her lips together as her neck and cheeks begin to flush.

"Did you even come home last night? Or is this the first time you've been home since you were out with Stacey?"

She takes a deep breath and then lets her shoulders drop. I think she's about to confess.

"Okay, fine. I got way too drunk last night and ended up passing out in the car on the way home, so I stayed with Stacey. I was just too embarrassed to tell you how fucked up I was."

I take a minute to study her. She's pretty good. Had I not seen the photos Midge texted me, or heard Midge's story, I might've believed her. But I know better now.

"Really?"

"Yes, Cill. Jeez."

Zoe gets up from the chair and marches to the kitchen. She probably doesn't want me to be able to study her face and see the lies dripping from her mouth.

"Okay," I state, getting up and following her to the kitchen. I pull my phone from my pocket and pull up the pictures I saved. After placing the phone face up on the counter between us, I look into her eyes and say, "Who's this?"

After huffing her annoyance, she picks up the phone and sees the zoomed and cropped photo of her and whoever this guy is. I watch as her emotions take control of her face. Shock flashes behind her eyes before embarrassment and anger redden her cheeks. When she looks at me, fury simmers beneath the surface of shame.

"Are you following me?"

"Really, Zoe? That's the first thing you're gonna say to me? Who the fuck is this guy?" I demand, swiping the phone from her hand and holding it to her face. "Who is he, huh? You seem awfully close."

"You're crazy," she says, turning her back on me and going to the sink to wash off a plate that had been left behind in there. "I'm not doing anything in that picture. That's someone I know from work. We happened to run into each other. It's not a big deal."

I have to keep myself from slamming my phone on the counter. Instead, I ball my free hand into a fist and hit the table hard enough that the glass decorative dishes clatter.

"Stop fucking lying to me, Zoe!"

She spins around, eyes wide, mouth agape. "I'm not!"

"My friend saw you and your other fucking boyfriend making out in front of Lucio's. Okay? So just fucking admit it already and get it over with. I don't believe shit you're saying."

Zoe scoffs and turns her back on me again. I imagine it's because she doesn't want me to see her *oh shit, I've been caught* face. "I can't believe you'd accept some story a friend told you over what I'm saying to you now."

"Well, I've known this person longer than I've known you, and nobody would lie about seeing you making out with some guy. The same fucking guy in these goddamn pictures!" I yell, holding the phone up again.

She turns around and leans against the counter, staring at me. We study each other for what feels like forever, and then she finally breaks.

"Fine. It's true."

"Why would you do this?"

She laughs a humorless laugh. "Are you kidding me?

You're never around. You're always at work or at the studio. You don't want to spend time with me, Cill."

"You're invited to my brother's house every fucking Sunday. I always invite you to come to the studio with me, and I've even been asking you out, but you keep turning me down."

"I'm not talking about for the last month when you've been trying to put forth more effort."

"That's how long you've been fucking this guy, huh? Jesus Christ, Zoe," I say, running my hands through my hair.

"We've been drifting apart for a while now, Cill. You know that."

"Then why do we keep coming back together? If you've been unhappy, why do you keep coming back to me?"

She shrugs, looking down at the floor. "I don't know. Familiarity."

I turn around and walk into the living room. When I face her again, she's got tears welling in her eyes.

"I'm sorry, Cill. I am. But you care too much about creating your art. I don't want to hang out with you in your studio all night."

"I don't go every night. I've invited you out on dates, told you to come to my brother's bar, but I think you checked out a long time ago. I don't think you even saw what I was trying to do for you. But my art is my life. You don't know what it does for me."

"Then I guess I don't know you as well as I thought."

"I guess fucking not," I say on a breath. "Jesus, Zoe. I guess we're finally done for good."

She shrugs and a tear spills down her cheek. "I didn't want it to end like this."

"Then you should've ended it the right way," I say and then storm out.

4

MIDGE

"So, what happened? How did he react when you told him?" London asks.

I take a sip of my Coke and then pick up a huge slice of pepperoni pizza from Antoni's, which is one of our favorite spots to eat at. "He was fairly quiet. Angry. But he didn't explode. Not the type, you know? But you can tell he was hurt."

"At least he believed you."

I shrug. "Why would I lie? Cill knows me, and it sucks to see that happen to him. He's a good guy, you know?"

London nods. She didn't grow up here in Gaspar, but now that she's with Royce, she sees his brothers often, and I know she adores them.

"You haven't heard from him yet?"

I shake my head as I swallow down my food. "I doubt he'll reach out. I'm sure they already talked, but I hope he was smart enough to dump her ass and not give her another chance."

"Royce hasn't mentioned anything about it, so I don't even think he's told his brothers yet."

"Maybe his ego is bruised. Cheating on someone can really do a number on their self-esteem. I was thinking about this when I told him. Cillian is hot as fuck! I mean, come on, he walks in the room and everybody looks. He's just one of those people. There's no way he should ever feel like shit about himself, but when someone chooses to fuck you over like that, it hurts."

London frowns, and I know it's because she's thinking about what happened to me a few years ago. My lovely boyfriend at the time, Matthew, decided to cheat on me, and to make matters worse it was with a woman who worked with me, and who he knew I didn't like. For a while I didn't think my heart would ever heal, and my confidence went down the drain. It was awful. It took me a long time to figure out it wasn't about me. He was just a dick.

"Maybe you can talk to him," London offers. "You're not a bullshitter, and you know what he's going through. Tug on that common thread and let him know what you know."

I nod. "Maybe I'll text him later."

"Good." London focuses on her food. "Now, let's plan this lake house trip."

I send Cillian a text at six-thirty, not really expecting him to respond, but wanting to reach out anyway. I started and deleted three different messages before settling on one and pressing send.

Midge: *Hey. How's everything?*

I'm sure he'll know what I'm referring to. I put my phone

down on the couch and get up to look for something to eat in the kitchen.

My house was built in the sixties, but it doesn't feel that old. The kitchen is nice and big with plenty of counter space, and more cabinets than I need, but I'd rather it be too big than too small. My underused dining area sits off to the right of the kitchen with a small table and two chairs. I mainly use the table for work purposes and eat on my couch.

I open the fridge and realize it's probably been two weeks since I went grocery shopping, and since I loathe being in the grocery store, I tend to only buy enough food to last a week.

The pantry is nearly as bare, with some chips, canned goods, a couple boxes of cereal, and a half-eaten carton of cookies. I go back to the fridge, thinking something will have changed from two minutes ago. I pick up the gallon of milk only to be disappointed in the small amount left. Not even enough for a decent sized bowl of cereal.

"Fuck it." I grab my keys and decide to head to McDonald's.

As soon as I grab my phone, it goes off. Cillian responded.

Cillian: *All good. Thanks again.*

Men. Never giving us the details until we wrench it out of them.

Midge: *So, you're okay?*

I want to ask more. I want to ask if he broke up with her. I want to know if she tried lying about it. I want to know if he told her it was me that told him, and if I need to worry about a crazy bitch coming to fight me. But I also don't want to come off as nosy as I am. Jesus McChrist, can't men just spill out all the deets without us begging for them?

Cillian: *I'm fine. Just about to head over to Elijah's.*

Oh yeah. Sunday. The day they all get together for dinner. I know Zoe went a few times, and London's been going since her and Royce got together. I think it's nice that the brothers still make time for family. Which reminds me, I need to talk to my grandparents.

Midge: *Okay. Enjoy!*

The three little dots pop up in the bubble, but after a little while they go away. I swipe to my contacts and call my gramma while I look for my wallet. She answers immediately.

"Hey, Gramma. It's your favorite granddaughter."

She laughs. "I was just about to call your momma. What're you up to, girl?"

"Just heading out to get some food. I really need to go grocery shopping."

"Make sure you lock your door."

"Yes, ma'am," I reply, flicking on the outdoor light before locking the door behind me. "Is Mom in trouble?"

Gramma laughs again. "Isn't she always? No, I was just gonna ask her to swing by tomorrow to help me with a little project."

"Making more birdhouses?"

"All done with the birdhouses, and I'll tell you what, those little birdies love them."

It's my turn to laugh. "I bet they're very grateful."

"Yeah, yeah. I know you're not fond of birds like your gramma."

"One pooped on me!"

"Oh, so they're all bad?"

I shake my head as I laugh and open up my car door. "Anyway, I'm about to start driving, but—"

"Well, get off the phone, baby."

"Gramma, I'm not driving yet. Just sitting here, looking at my house. Still safe in the driveway."

"Oh. Okay then. Don't forget to wear your seatbelt."

"I know. But hey, I wanted to ask about the lake house."

"What about it?"

"Is anyone staying in it right now?"

"I don't think so. Let me ask your granddaddy. Winston, is anyone staying in the lake house right now? Winston!" I hear my granddad mumble something in the background. "The lake house. There's no tenants there, right?"

After a little more back and forth between them, she gets back on the phone. "Child, I don't know when he became such an old man, but I swear he can't hear anything I say."

"Maybe it's just selective hearing," I say with a chuckle.

She scoffs. "I don't think we're scheduled to have anyone in there until August, so this month is free. You tryin' to go up there?"

"I have a friend who needs to get away for a bit, but also is gonna paint a picture of the house for Mom."

"Oh, she'd love that. She's always been so fond of that little house. I don't know why she doesn't visit more often."

"She blames work. So, it's free the rest of the month?"

"Yep."

"Great. I'll get the keys soon. Thanks, Gramma."

"Of course, baby. I love you. Be safe."

"Love you, too!"

I end the call with a smile on my face. Now I can call Cillian and let him know the lake house is free to use for the rest of the month. I'm happy that I'll be able to do something for him that will hopefully make him feel a little better.

5

CILLIAN

"WELL, IT'S OVER FOR GOOD," I ANNOUNCE AS I WALK INTO Elijah's kitchen.

Both he and Royce turn and gaze at me with confusion. "What're you talkin' about?" Royce asks, tearing off a piece of a roll and popping it into his mouth.

"Me and Zoe. It's done."

Royce chuckles and turns back to whatever's cooking on the stove. Elijah keeps studying me.

"You good?" E asks.

"Y'all will be back together in a couple weeks," Royce drawls. "You've broken up, what, seven times?"

I toss my keys onto the island and lean my hip up against it, crossing my arms. "Not happening this time. She was cheating on me."

Royce spins around, his bright green eyes going wide as he looks at me. "No shit?"

"No shit," I mutter, stealing a roll from a dish on the counter. "Some stuffy guy in a suit."

"You know him?" Royce questions.

I shake my head. "Nah."

"Sorry, man. That's tough," Elijah says. "Want a drink?"

"Yeah, that'd be good. You know, I thought something was going on with her. All the signs were there, you know?" I shake my head. "Whatever. It's not like it was the healthiest relationship. You're right, we broke up too often."

Royce's lips draw down into a frown. "But still. It's fucked up. You deserve to be pissed."

Elijah comes back in and hands me a drink.

"Oh, I'm pissed. She could've just broken up with me, but I'm not gonna go into a depression over it. Shit happens, right?"

My brothers continue to look at me, not saying a word, like they think I'm feeding them bullshit before I break down and cry. But the truth is, I'm not going to mourn our relationship. It wasn't the best. Yeah, I'm mad about what she did, but it's not like I want her back.

"All right, well, dinner is about done," E announces.

"What is it?" I ask, peeking over their shoulders to get a look at the stove.

"Balsamic chicken and potatoes."

"Yum."

"Set the table," Elijah orders.

I roll my eyes at Royce who smirks in response.

"Where's Lo?"

"She'll be here for dessert. She was on the phone with her mom when I talked to her last."

I nod, and right before I sit down, my phone rings.

"It's Midge," I say before answering.

"Hey, what's up?"

"Hey! I have some good news for you."

"Oh yeah? What's that?"

"The house on the lake is free for the rest of this month. I hope you're ready to take some time off from the tattoo shop and get away, because it's happening, baby. Whoo whoo!"

I laugh. "Was that an impersonation of a train? That was awful."

"Oh shut up. Didn't you hear the rest? The lake house? Getting away? A break from work?"

"I heard. Thanks, Midge. I'll check my schedule at work and get some time off, then I'll let you know."

"Cool. I'll let you go since I know it's dinner time. Call me!"

She doesn't give me time to respond before she hangs up. I put my phone down and look up to see my brothers staring at me.

"What?"

"Time off? You're taking time off?" Royce questions.

"That doesn't happen often," E chimes in.

"I know. Midge wants me to paint something for her mom, and she thinks getting away will be good for me. Something about getting my creative juices flowing again."

"Well, that's nice of her."

"Well, she's getting something out of it," I say.

"You may end up getting more out of this little trip than you think," Elijah states.

I shrug. "We'll see. It will be nice to get some new scenery."

"Lake Erie?" Elijah questions.

"Yeah."

"Nice," Royce mumbles around a mouthful of food.

I don't stick around too long after dinner this time. I'm determined to try to get some painting done, so after we've finished our food and cleaned up, I say bye to my brothers and drive to my studio.

With a long and gentle stroke, cerulean blue streaks across the canvas, creating the beginnings of a darkening sky. Once the sky is complete, with shades of blue, yellow, and orange coming together to create a vivid sunset, I start working on a dying tree set in the foreground.

I take a few steps back to inspect the work-in-progress, then grab a bottle of black paint and squirt it over the entire thing.

"Absolute shit."

I take the ruined canvas and transport it to another easel next to me, and then grab a new one from the floor. I pull my stool up and stare at the blank canvas, waiting for something to come to mind. I haven't painted a piece I've been proud of in almost a year. My brothers have tried telling me they've looked fine, but I know I can do better.

The last one I loved was showcased in an art show in Philadelphia, and sold within the first hour. It was an oil painting of a woman, her body angled to the left with her chin pressed against her bare shoulder and her eyes looking up and straight at you. Her hair was flying forward, as if the wind was blowing from behind her, but within the strands of hair were thoughts I believed this woman was having.

I am brave.

I am strong.

I am not my past.

I am capable.

I am driven.

I am damaged, but I am surviving.

I do not need your pity.

I do not seek your approval.

There were more messages hidden in the splashes of color

that created her hair. It was as if the wind were blowing her thoughts through the strands. I don't feel like I've created anything quite as powerful since then.

Then again, I've been struggling with my relationship with Zoe, and I think that's what's taken a toll on me. I've been constantly on edge and stressed out. I don't remember the last time I felt truly, one hundred percent happy. And perhaps that was because of the rollercoaster that was my relationship.

However, now that it's over, I'm hoping things will start changing. Based on the ruined picture to my right, I'm not one hundred percent sure, but maybe this trip to Lake Erie will help.

I decide to call it a night, because I just don't feel like I'm in the right headspace to create anything. I'd just be wasting supplies.

I gather my keys and wallet and take a quick look around the sparse room. Midge is right, this isn't the best space to be creative. Maybe I should paint the walls and fix the flickering light at the very least.

After locking the place up, I hop on my motorcycle and ride the short distance to my tattoo shop, Work of Art. Since it's closed, it's the best time to pop in and take a look at my schedule.

Once inside, I lock the door behind me and keep the lights off so nobody thinks we're open. I turn on the computer and go into the schedule. The only time I can really get away with taking off is the last two weeks of the month, and that's only if I can convince Wes, Khalil, and Bree to cover some shifts for me. I don't have appointments scheduled for those weeks, since I'm only supposed to be here for walk-ins, so it should be okay.

I put in ten days off in the computer and plan to talk to the other workers tomorrow to confirm. On my way out, I pull out my phone and call Midge.

"It's way too late to be calling me, Cill. Unless, of course, you're hurt or dying," she says as soon as she answers.

"Oh shit." I pull my phone away from my ear and look at the time. It's nearly one-thirty in the morning. "Sorry. I didn't even realize what time it was."

She yawns. "Yeah, yeah. What's up?"

"Oh, I was just calling to tell you I put in for ten days of leave at the end of the month."

"Oh, good. Well, London is already making plans to stay up there for a weekend, so we'll probably head up next weekend, and then right as we're leaving, you'll be coming, so I can hang back and show you around a bit before we leave."

"Sounds good." I pause, leaning against the front of my building. "Just you and London? Or is Royce going?"

"You know what? She'll probably invite him. Great. I'll be the third wheel."

I laugh. "Why don't you make it a big thing? Invite Jon and Daniel to go too."

"Then I'll be the fifth wheel. That doesn't help."

"Oh. I guess you're right," I say with a chuckle. "Maybe I can meet you guys up there Saturday night. I might be late, and you'll have to be fifth wheelin' it Friday, but that's all I can offer."

She's quiet for a beat. "Mm. I guess that could work. I'll figure out all the details and let you know."

"All right. Well, I'll let you go back to sleep. Sorry for waking you."

"No worries. Just don't let it happen again."

I let out a short chuckle, then the call ends. She's crazy, but at least she makes me laugh. Then again, she always has.

6

MIDGE

AT THE END OF THE WORKDAY, LONDON COMES INTO MY office with a grin on her face. "How bad is it that I'm already dreaming about our lake weekend?"

I look up from some loan paperwork. "Not bad. Unless you're actually dreaming about it. Then that's weird."

"I dreamt I went skinny dipping in the lake," she says with a laugh.

"Oh God. Please don't do that."

"Oh shush." She sits in the chair opposite my desk. "So, is it okay if Royce comes?" she asks, biting down on her thumb nail.

I twist my mouth at her. "Figured he'd be coming. I talked to Cill last night and he suggested inviting Jon and Daniel, too. Then he'll try to make it late Saturday."

London goes quiet as I'm cleaning my desk off and putting files away. When I look up, I notice her watching me while trying to keep from smiling.

"What?"

"You talked to Cillian last night? And he's coming to the lake house?"

I roll my eyes. "It's not whatever you're thinking."

"Okay."

I pin her with a look. "Don't say okay like that."

"Like what?" she asks, feigning innocence.

"The way I said it when you tried denying the fact that you liked Royce."

She cracks a smile. "You've already admitted that you think Cill is hot."

"All the Kingston brothers are hot."

"Yes, but now Cill is available."

"Newly available. Hooking up with him now would be a mistake."

"Now? But maybe later?"

I avoid her smirking face and get up from the desk. "Lo."

"I see you trying to keep from smiling," she says, getting up to follow me. "Just admit you wanna ride him into the sunset."

I bust out laughing. "Okay, fine. I've always been attracted to him. Who wouldn't be, right? But we're friends."

"So? That's even better. You have a foundation. History."

"But wouldn't it be weird?" I ask, making a face. "That's like me and you hooking up."

London throws her head back with a loud cackle. "Not really, ya weirdo."

"Anyway, I don't know why we're talking about this. He's coming to the lake house to do me a favor."

"Yeah, do you the favor of giving you a taste of his dick."

I gasp. "I think I'm rubbing off on you."

London shrugs, tossing her blond strands behind her shoulder. "I'm just saying."

I grab my purse and head for the door. "Let's get the hell out of here."

"Okay, but don't get off subject."

"Look, the fact that we're friends would maybe come in handy if we were trying to start a relationship, but if we just hook up, then it becomes weird every time we're around each other. And we're not talking about relationships."

"Why not?"

London and I wave goodbye to Daniel before we leave the bank. "Because he just got out of one. Are you not listening?"

"Okay, let's say that's not the issue. Would you be willing to be in a relationship with him? It's been a while since you've been in one."

"I know, and I've liked it that way. Less heartbreak."

"I don't think Cill would break your heart."

At our cars, I turn to face her. "Two things. Cill isn't even into me like that. And I've had a thing for him for years. He has the ability to hurt me more than anybody else. I can't let that happen. We have to stay friends."

She stares at me from across the top of her car. It's no secret I think Cillian is sex-on-a-stick. I've said as much dozens of times. I think I've only alluded to my childhood crush on him, but now she knows.

Her lips turn down as she tilts her head, and I know she's giving up for now. "Okay. Talk to you later?"

"Yeah. Later." I give her a smile to let her know I'm not upset, and then I climb into my car.

Instead of going home, I go straight to my grandparents' house. I have to drive down Main Street, and end up taking a quick peek down Sycamore when I drive past, and spot Cill's motorcycle parked in front of his tattoo shop.

The rest of the fifteen-minute drive is spent thinking about what it would be like to hook up with Cill. Damn London. Okay, I won't lie, it's not like this is the first time I've thought about it, but it has been a while. Like, almost two years. He's been in a relationship, and we've been casual friends who see each other from time to time. There's never even been a moment, you know?

At no time have we been pushed up against each other, and the world quiets down around us as we gaze into each other's eyes. There's never been drunken moments where we stumble into a room together, laughing about nothing, then start making out.

We've always been one thousand percent friends. Nothing more. Maybe it's because I've never gotten a vibe from him. Usually, if there's a vibe, I'll take my shot. I'm not a shy girl. I'm not a prude or worried about being called a slut for having a sex life. But Cill's never led me to believe he likes me more than a friend, so I've left it alone.

London's crazy. Cill isn't coming to the lake house to give me a taste of anything, so I might as well stop thinking about it.

When I pull up to my grandparents' house, I spot Gramma kneeling in the garden, pulling weeds. She's wearing this funky little straw hat that makes me laugh.

Their home was built in the fifties, though they moved into it about twenty years ago, since they wanted to down-size. Gramma hated having a big house with no kids in it, so now they have a pale green, three-bedroom place that they love.

I pull up their long driveway and park in front of the detached garage, then walk back toward the house.

"Well, hey there, pretty girl," Gramma says, slowly getting up. "Gramma's getting old," she complains.

"Ah, but you don't look a day over thirty."

She swats me in the arm. "You're full of shit. Just like your momma."

I laugh and give her a hug. "Garden looks nice."

ISABEL LUCERO

"It's a labor of love. Come on. Let's go inside and get some lemonade."

We walk to their small deck and enter through the sliding glass doors that lead into the kitchen.

"I'll get it, Gramma. You sit down."

She sounds a little out of breath as she makes her way to the living room. "Thanks, dear. You know your way around."

I grab a couple glasses from behind their new white cabinets and grab a pitcher of lemonade from the fridge.

"I love the new look in here," I say, admiring the subway tile backsplash, and updated cabinetry and countertops.

"Yes, well, it was time to go. We probably should've done it years ago. It's not like we're gonna be here much longer."

"Don't say that," I chide, bringing the lemonade into the living room. "You and Granddad are in good health and shape. You'll likely be around another twenty years or so."

Gramma takes a sip. "I can't imagine living to be ninety. Just take me out and shoot me."

"Gramma!" I say with a laugh. "You're awful."

She chuckles. "Oh, you know me. Anyway, how ya been?"

"Pretty good. Workin' during the week and drinkin' on the weekends."

"Well, at least you're working and playing. Can't do just one. Any men in your life?"

"Oh, just one for every day of the week."

Gramma laughs. "Yeah, right. That's too much work."

"Not really looking for a relationship."

"How old are you again?" she asks.

"Twenty-seven."

"Ah, well you have some time then."

"Where's Grandad," I ask, looking around.

"The old man's taking a nap."

40

I giggle. "Oh."

"So who's this friend that's going up to the lake house? I noticed you were vague and didn't mention the sex of said friend. Safe to assume this friend is male?" She raises her brows at me.

I snort. "Yes, it's a man. No, it's not a boyfriend or lover. It's Cillian. You remember him? The Kingston brothers?"

"Oh, yes. The tattooed one?"

"Yes, the tattooed one," I reply with a laugh.

"It's a shame what happened to their parents. Nice family. The boys grew up well."

"Yeah."

"Well, let me grab those keys for you," she says, pushing herself up from the couch with a groan before slowly walking down the hallway.

I finish my lemonade and wash out the glass before Gramma returns, holding out the keychain.

"Here you are. The place should be clean, but there won't be food or anything."

"That's fine, Gramma. I really appreciate this. I'll make sure it's ship-shape when we leave."

She smiles. "I know you will. Have fun."

I slide the key ring onto my finger and give her a hug. "I'll call you later, okay?"

"Sounds good. Drive carefully."

I crane my head and glance over my shoulder as I walk out. "Always. Love you."

"Love you."

7

CILLIAN

AFTER GOING TO WORK ON MONDAY, I GOT EVERYTHING figured out with my employees, and finally got the official confirmation that my leave is good to go. I mean, I'm the owner, but I'm not such a dick that I'll do what I want and screw over my employees, so making sure they're good with their extra workload is important.

I'm actually starting to look forward to this trip now. Wes, the good guy that he is, even offered to work more tomorrow so I could head to Lake Erie tonight instead. Well, he's also getting paid a little more, so there's that.

Since I'm a procrastinator, I'm throwing some clothes in a duffle bag before I jump in the jeep and start the three-hour drive. I guess I should invest in some decent luggage, but I don't travel often, so I never felt the need to have actual suitcases.

Most of my wardrobe consists of jeans and t-shirts. My job doesn't require me to dress up, so I don't have many suits. I actually only have one. When I've had my art displayed at galleries, I'll put on a suit, or at the minimum a pair of slacks and a button up.

My phone rings as I'm putting together my shaving kit, so I walk to the bed and see that it's Midge.

"Hey, girl. What's up?"

"Oh, not much. Just drinking."

"Hey, Cill!" I hear multiple voices yelling in the background.

I laugh. "Who's that?"

"London, Jon, and Daniel."

"Ah. Where's Royce?"

"He's coming later because he refuses to leave the bar before he has to."

"Sounds about right."

"Anyway, Jon was looking up restaurants for us to eat at, and you know Jon, he has fancy taste."

"I'm classy, darling," I hear Jon say in the background.

"Anyway, his classy ass picked a restaurant that has a dress code. So keep that in mind when you're packing."

"Doing that now. I guess I'll pack my button up and black slacks. Or does it have to be a fucking tuxedo or some shit?"

She laughs. "I don't think so. If they don't let you in, we'll blow off the rest of the gang and go eat at Taco Bell or something."

"Sounds good to me."

"All right. Well, we'll see you tomorrow."

"Yep. See you then."

I decide not to tell them that I'll actually be up there late tonight. They'll all probably be wasted by the time I get there, but oh well. I can catch up fast.

After I toss the phone back on the bed, I pull out my dressier clothes and hang them over the closet door. I won't shove them in the bag so they don't get wrinkled.

As soon as I'm done packing, Royce sends me a text.

Royce: *Hey, dude. When are you heading up to the lake?*

Cillian: *Probably within the next hour or so. Why, what's up?*

Royce: *Just wondering if you wanted to ride with me, or let me ride with you.*

Cillian: *When are you gonna be ready to go?*

Royce: *I can be ready within an hour. I already have a bag packed upstairs. It's kind of busy, but Chad, Luna, and Lennox say they can handle it.*

Cillian: *I'm sure they can. You're the psycho who thinks he needs to be behind the bar 24/7.*

Royce: *Oh, fuck off.*

Cillian: *I'll swing by when I'm done doin' the shit I gotta do. Your ass better be ready to go too.*

Royce: *Yeah, yeah.*

After I throw my luggage into the back seat of my Jeep, I make sure I get rid of any food that'll go bad, and take the trash out.

My house is only a few blocks from Elijah's, so I'll have him swing by once or twice—not because I think anybody will break in, there's mostly retired folks around here, but just to take my mail inside and make sure nothing springs a spontaneous leak.

Unlike Elijah's neighborhood, which is the neighborhood we grew up in, mine is a newer development. These houses sprung up around eight years ago, and I bought mine five years ago. Normally, a twenty-one-year old wouldn't be able to purchase a home, but when my parents were killed in that car accident, they left us all a generous amount of money.

Elijah, being our guardian, helped me with the process, and in the early years, had a key of his own to stop by whenever he wanted. I think he was aware that I'd be having parties since I was twenty-one and able to purchase alcohol, but they were never too out of hand. Yeah, my house was trashed afterward, but not damaged. And the neighbors never complained about noise.

Now that I'm damn near twenty-seven, my crazy party days are over. I guess I grew up quicker than most. I went a little crazy after Mom and Dad died, but I was fifteen and already pissed off at the world. I'm surprised I didn't give Elijah a mental breakdown. Royce and me both.

Elijah really encouraged my talent as an artist. When I said I didn't want to draw anymore because Mom and Dad would never get to see it, he told me that Mom and Dad wouldn't want me to give up something I loved and was so good at.

Mom bought me my first sketch pad, Dad took me to art galleries, and Elijah picked up the baton when they died and made sure I was never without supplies. He always wanted to see what I was painting or drawing, and he made sure I went to college and honed my craft by taking classes.

While losing my parents at such a young age was completely fucked up, I'm glad that I at least had my brothers. Royce, Merrick, and I will never be able to thank Elijah enough for giving up his freedom to make sure we grew up okay.

Royce owns his own bar, I own my own tattoo shop, and Merrick is on the verge of becoming a world-renowned rock star, and my oldest brother lives alone in our parents' house with a dog named Sugarfoot that his ex left behind when she left him. I feel like he deserves so much more, but he swears he's content with his job at the college and the array of women he cycles through.

My phone dings with a text as I'm about to climb into my Jeep.

Royce: *I'm waiting.*

I settle behind the wheel and start it up. It won't take me long to get to his bar, and then we'll be on the road, and hopefully I'll be on the way to getting my shit together.

8

MIDGE

"I NEED TO SLOW DOWN OR I'M GONNA BE FUCKING PASSED out before midnight," I announce, putting my glass down on the coffee table.

"Slow down? What's that?" Jon questions, looking between London and Daniel. Then he downs the rest of his drink.

"Oh, pft," I mutter, waving my hand through the air. "You're bigger than me. You can handle more."

"Darling, I'm petite," he says, putting his hand on his hip. "You're acting like I'm some three-hundred-pound gorilla."

"Definitely not," Daniel murmurs into his neck, grabbing him around the waist and pulling him into his chest.

"Ugh. No lovey love crap. I'm single! Hello!"

Jon gives Daniel a quick peck before turning around. "So, change that."

"I don't have anyone right now," London chimes in. She's lounging across the light blue couch, her legs hiked up over the back cushions.

"Right now, but soon Royce will be here, and I'll be the lame fifth wheel with nobody to make out with. Which probably means I should stop drinking. Drinking only makes me want to jump someone's bones, and I don't think anybody here is willing to let me do that."

Jon and Daniel scrunch their faces and hastily shake their heads as London lets out a cackle.

"We should go out! There's bars around here, right? Maybe the love of your life is right around the corner."

I walk to the kitchen and grab a package of pop tarts from the pantry. "The love of my life better not be in some skeezy bar right now."

London rolls her eyes when I plop down next to her on the couch. "So judgmental. You know, I met the love of my life in a bar."

"Yeah, but it's not skeezy."

"Okay, so we won't go to a skeezy bar."

"Ugh." I break off a piece of the Pop-Tart and toss it into my mouth. "I don't really feel like going out right now."

"Then shut up, stop complaining, and drink with us!" London hops off the couch, almost hitting me in the head with her long legs, and then pulls me up with her. "Who knows when Royce will even show up. You have me. Those two can disappear into a room all they want, but me and you ain't going nowhere but drunktown. Eat your stupid Pop-Tarts and get ready for a shot. Royce has been teaching me some things."

"Ooh. I love his drink making skills," Jon says.

"Then you're gonna love this new one," she states, grabbing the plastic shot glasses we bought from a liquor store nearby.

"All right, all right, let me go to the bathroom first."

As I'm in the bathroom, the music gets a little louder, and the three musketeers out there start laughing about something. Once I'm done washing my hands, I grab my phone from the bed and think about texting Cill. I don't even know why. All these years we've been friends, and I never really texted him. Especially once we were out of school. We'd see each other around, but we'd never make plans to hang out or anything like that. But recently, the urge to talk to him comes more frequently.

I throw my phone back on the bed and tell myself it's a bad idea. I don't need to get involved with Cillian Kingston. For one, it would mess up our friendship. Royce and London are together now and I don't want things to be awkward for everyone. I'd just be a rebound, and since he's newly single, I'm sure he's ready to enjoy bachelor life.

"All right, give me a shot!" I announce as I walk back into the living room.

London has a cheeky smile when she passes them to us.

"She didn't let us see what she put in them," Jon says.

"Uh-oh."

"Yeah," Daniel agrees.

London giggles. "Bottoms up."

And after that shot, things become blurry.

9

CILLIAN

WHEN I PULL UP TO KING'S TAVERN, ROYCE IS ALREADY outside, leaning against the building with a duffle bag at his feet. With a nod in my direction, he slips his phone in his pocket and hoists the strap of his bag over his shoulder and jogs over.

"'Bout time."

"Please. Get in and shut up."

He tosses the bag in the back and climbs in next to me. With a big grin on his face, he grasps my shoulder and shakes me. "You excited or what?"

I pull away and head toward the highway that leads us out of town. "Well, you are."

"I don't vacation often."

"I know."

"Neither do you, so liven up! At least you'll be out there longer than the rest of us."

"I'm definitely ready to be there. I think it'll be just what I need right now. I keep worrying I'm gonna run into Zoe and this dude she's fucking with. Goddamn small towns."

"I feel ya. Me and London ran into Hunter. It was, well, interesting."

I laugh. "What happened?"

"We were walking down Main Street, talking and laughing and shit like that. At one point I pulled her into the alcove of that old theater because nobody was around and we were just fuckin' around, you know? Anyway, we step back onto the sidewalk and Hunter's there."

"Shit," I say with a chuckle.

"Yeah, so we both just stop and she says hi and asks him how he is, but the air around all three of us is vibrating with awkwardness. He looks us both up and down, clearly holding onto some anger and hurt feelings. But I start getting mad that's he's sizing me up. I mean, come on, what man is gonna like that shit? But I get it, he's mad that his girl left him for me."

I laugh. "Uh-huh. Probably doesn't even know you had been asking her to do that for a while."

"Probably not. Anyway, I put my arm around London and smile at him. He doesn't like that." Royce chuckles. "Not at all. Meanwhile, he hasn't even said anything! So I start guiding London around him, and as we're passing him, he says something like *'this is what you want?'* Man, I about lost it. I moved away from London and stepped up to him, but then London's pulling on my arm and trying to diffuse the situation. I think my parting words were, *'you're damn right this is what she wants and she gets it every fucking night.'* You know, something petty like that."

"Fuckin' crazy, man. He didn't say anything else?"

"Nah. Can't wait for that to happen again," he says sarcastically.

"Well, I don't think I'd fight this guy, whoever he is. I

don't have that kind of emotion, so I guess that means I was already kind of over that relationship."

"Yeah, because love makes you a crazy person."

"I did love her, but somewhere along the way, shit changed. I don't know. Fuck it. I'm ready to be at the lake, do some drinking with you guys, then relax and start painting again."

"Fuck yes!" he yells, reaching over and shaking me again.

My phone vibrates from inside the cup holder. "Can you check that?" I ask him.

"It's from Midge. She says, not looking forward to being the fifth wheel. Why are you coming so late? Everyone will be making out tonight and I'm all alone. Why don't...never mind."

"She said why don't never mind?"

"Shit's a little misspelled. I sense some drunk texting going on here."

I smile and shake my head. "She thinks I'm coming tomorrow night. She knows you and Lo will be together and Jon and Daniel, so she wants me there to keep her company."

"To keep her company? Or keep her company?" He questions, changing his voice the second time around.

"Don't start."

"What? I'm just asking."

"We're friends."

"Okay, but remember that one time when—"

"No," I cut him off.

Royce tosses his head back, laughter floating between us. "You remember. You told me you wanted to kiss her when you were over at her house."

"I was a horny teenager. I wanted to kiss everybody."

"I know you like her."

"Of course I do. So do you. We've known each other for a long time."

"Yeah, but y'all were especially close in high school."

"Do I need to point out how long ago that was?"

"So you don't think she's cute? Funny? Interesting?"

"That's irrelevant."

"Is it?" he says with a laugh. I shoot him a look and he raises his hands. "Okay, okay."

"You hear from Merrick recently?" I ask, changing the subject.

"You know, it's been a while. I think he's busy with the tour."

"Yeah. I think they'll be ending that tour with a stop in Cleveland. We'll have to go."

"Shit, he better stop ignoring us then and give us some backstage, VIP tickets."

"I'll try to call him tomorrow."

The next couple hours go by fairly fast with me and Royce talking and laughing non-stop.

"I wish Elijah could've came." I say. "I think he needs a break more than all of us."

"I know. I mean, it's summer. He doesn't have to work. Did he tell you why he couldn't come?"

"Nope. Just said he had plans already."

"A woman?"

"Fuck, I hope so," I say with a laugh. "That man is wound tight."

"Now that you're single, you gonna be lookin' for someone to—"

"Not looking. We're almost there," I say seconds before the Google Maps lady announces my last turn.

I pull up to the house and park in the driveway. Since it's

dark, I can't get a feel for what I'll be painting, so I'll scope out the area tomorrow.

Royce and I grab our bags and start heading toward the front door. As we get closer we can hear music and laughter.

"Sounds like they're having a good time," he says, ringing the bell.

It doesn't take long before the door is yanked open. The second Midge sees me, she screeches and jumps into my arms. Luckily, she's a tiny little thing or we would've went cascading backwards.

"I'm so happy you're here!"

I spot Royce over her shoulder smirking at me before he lets himself inside.

MIDGE

"You're here! I thought you were coming tomorrow," I say after I drop from Cillian's arms and take a few steps back.

"I was able to come early and wanted to surprise y'all."

I smile. "I'm glad. Jon and Daniel have been making out every chance they get."

"Hey!" the two men protest from the living room.

"And now that Royce is here, I'm sure he and London will be doing the same. Yuck."

"Why yuck?" London asks, pulling away from a kiss with Royce.

I roll my eyes and grab Cill by the wrist. "Let me show you around real quick so you can start drinking."

"Sounds good," he replies.

"So, kitchen and living room here," I point out as we walk through them. "You know those losers," I say, gesturing to Jon, Daniel, and London. "I'll show you the rooms and you can choose which one you want to stay in. There's four. Two have king-size beds and the other two have two full-size beds in each room. I imagine you'll want one of the king-sized beds because you're, well, big. But whatever."

Cillian laughs. "Yeah, show me the king-size rooms."

"Why are you laughing? You laughing at me?" I ask, glancing over my shoulder and looking up at him.

"You're just extra chatty when you're drunk."

I roll my eyes. "Whatever. Okay, well, one is downstairs and one is upstairs. Preference?"

"Not really."

"Well, I'm already walking to the one downstairs. You can drop your shit off in there and if you want to change rooms later, you can."

He laughs again. "Okay."

"Here it is. The window actually faces the lake, so you'll have a nice view during the day. The master bath is right over there. Towels and everything you need should already be in there. Umm. What else?" I murmur, tapping my finger on my lips.

Cillian chuckles and gently squeezes my upper arms while looking into my eyes. "Midge. It's fine. I'm just gonna use the bathroom and then I'll be out there and ready to drink."

A soft sigh emerges from my lips before I give him a grin. "Okay. I'll just wait out there then."

"Okay," he replies with a lopsided smile.

I make my way back into the living room, but spot the group in the kitchen.

"Oh, you're back," London says with a stupid grin. "Wasn't sure how long you'd be gone."

"Oh shush," I say, glad nobody else is paying attention. "What're y'all doin'?"

"Royce is making us drinks," Jon answers excitedly, clapping his hands together.

"You ever get tired of making drinks for people?" I ask.

"Nah. I love it. Where's my brother?"

"Bathroom."

"All right, well I'm making double shots for us since we're late to the party."

"Somebody say double shots?" Cill says when he enters the room.

"Right here, bro," Royce answers, handing him a glass with dark liquid. "Me and you have some catching up to do."

"All right."

Cillian takes the drink and he and Royce clink their glasses together before swallowing down two shots' worth of liquor.

"Okay, now what does everybody want?" Royce asks, making a variety of drinks for everyone.

London pulls me aside and raises her eyebrows. "So, Cill looks good tonight."

I tilt my head. "Uh-huh. Aren't you with, who was that again? Oh right, his brother?"

She smacks her lips. "I'm just saying. Don't you agree?"

We both look over at him as he stands in the kitchen talking to the guys. He does look damn good. And in that brief moment when I threw my body against his, he felt damn good too. Somehow Cillian's able to make jeans and a T-shirt look runway ready, and all that ink covering his body makes me want to strip him down and study each and every piece.

"Yeah," I finally answer on a breathy sigh. I peel my eyes from Cillian's tall frame and connect with London again. "He's a walking wet dream, but—"

"Why're y'all being all secretive over here?" Cillian asks, walking up to us with a drink in his hand. "Did you say something about having a wet dream?"

"What?" I feel my face flush. "No."

He smirks. "Right. So what're y'all talkin' about? Royce?" He rests his arm on my shoulder as he looks at London.

London's eyes flicker to mine before meeting Cillian's. "Oh. Yeah."

"He in trouble already?"

She laughs. "No, nothing like that."

"That's good." He removes his arm from my shoulder and shifts to face me. "I can't wait to see this place in the daylight."

London makes her way back to Royce in the kitchen, leaving me and Cill together in the living room.

"Oh, yeah. It's beautiful. I'll show you the grounds when we get up. Which will probably be in the afternoon."

"Definitely. How's the water out there?"

"It's nice, pretty smooth usually. The grass slopes down, leading into a rocky area before you hit the water. It looks better than I can explain," I say with a grin as I tuck my hair behind my ear.

"You gonna go swimming with me?" he asks with a flirty smile. No, not flirty, just friendly.

"You want me to go swimming? With you?"

"Well, you don't have to sound so thrilled," he says with a laugh.

"Sorry," I say with a small giggle. "I didn't mean it like that. Yeah, sure. We can go swimming."

He eyes me curiously with a tiny grin on his face as he brings his glass to his mouth. "Okay."

"Okay."

"Hey, Midge!" London calls. "We're doing shots. Come on."

I look back up at Cill and find he's still watching me. My

stomach does a flip as my entire body warms up. "Guess we should join them."

When we get to the kitchen, London and Royce are whispering and laughing near the fridge before turning around.

"Okay, we're doing body shots. Me and Royce will obviously be paired up, and Jon and Daniel too. So, I guess that means y'all are stuck together."

I widen my eyes at her and mouth *what the fuck?* She giggles and gives me a shrug. I know she's just getting me back for when I tried making her take a body shot off Royce.

"That works," Cill says calmly. "Who's first?"

London raises her brows at me, giving me a smug grin. "I think you should take a shot off Midge, since you still haven't had much to drink."

Cillian shrugs like it's no big deal. "Okay. Royce, give me a shot of Patron. You got some salt and limes?"

London happily gets what he asked for and places them on the counter between us. Cillian finally turns and looks at me. "You ready, shorty?"

I put my hands on my hips. "Hey. I am not short. Just because you're a giant."

He laughs. "Of course not. You're the perfect size."

I find myself smiling. "Whatever."

I squeal as Cillian picks me up and places me on the counter. He smirks. "See. The perfect size."

I roll my eyes and attempt to appear all cool and collected while there's a million butterflies taking flight in my stomach and heat coursing through my bloodstream like lava.

His eyes roam across my face, and then he steps to the side and eyes my neck and chest.

"Preference?"

My pussy is what I want to say, but instead I just shrug

and act like I'm completely unaffected. "Your choice. Doesn't matter to me."

He arches a brow and does another once-over, this time glancing at my exposed legs. All I'm wearing is a pair of black shorts and an off the shoulder gray T-shirt, so there's plenty of skin to choose from, but usually people stick to the neck area, so I'm assuming that's where he's going. I'll just have to do my best not to moan when he does it.

I glance over my shoulder and spot Royce and London giggling about something. Probably this situation. Great, now I'm going to have both of them trying to push me toward Cillian. Doesn't Royce think this is a bad idea? I'm going to have to talk to him. Jon and Daniel are looking at something on Daniel's phone, not really paying attention, so I look back at Cillian.

He hands me a lime wedge. "I'll let you put this in your mouth."

"Gee, thanks." I want to tell him he can put something else in my mouth, but whatever.

He smirks, then bends down and licks a tiny patch of skin right...on...my...thigh. Mostly the top, but very close to my inner thigh. And I almost shove his head between my legs. Jesus McChrist, I have got to keep it together.

Cillian sprinkles some salt over the moistened skin, grabs his shot glass, and gazes into my eyes. "Ready?"

Probably should've asked me that before licking my thigh, but what can you do? "Yeah, sure."

I hope I'm pulling off this nonchalance stuff as well as I think I am. He grins. Christ, I probably moaned those words out.

Cillian leans down to lick the salt off, but this time he's much more thorough about it. His warm tongue caresses my thigh as he makes sure to lick off every salt crystal. He even administers a second lick in order to get it all. I'm ninety-eight percent sure I make a noise. A moan, a gasp, a curse. Something comes out of my mouth, but I'm intoxicated by the alcohol—and even more so by the man—that I'm not even sure what's happening.

He stands up and takes the shot while watching me, and when I run my tongue across my lip, I realize I need to put the lime wedge in still. Once it's between my lips, his large hands find residence on the counter on either side of me, and then he leans forward and takes the wedge into his mouth.

His lips barely touch mine, but it's enough to know I'm utterly screwed. His eyes penetrate mine in a gaze so intense, I shiver. Hell, maybe that's me remembering what his tongue feels like on my skin.

I'll never forget this moment for the rest of my life. I'm going to bed thinking about this moment, for sure. Cillian Kingston has just started something that I'm not sure I'm willing to let come to an end.

I swallow and lick my lips again. "My turn."

CILLIAN

I SUCK THE JUICE FROM THE LIME AND WIPE MY LIPS WITH THE back of my hand, as I watch Midge slide from the countertop. She puts her hand on the middle of my chest and pushes, making me take a small step back.

Jon and Daniel hoot and holler, but when my eyes look over Midge's head and meet the gazes of London and Royce, I know I'll be hearing shit from both of them. Royce's bright green eyes are wide and I can tell he's holding back a laugh. London's jaw is practically on the floor with eyes as wide as Royce's.

Okay, maybe I took the body shot a little too far. Sure I could've put the salt on her forearm or some shit, but where's the fun in that? This is a party, right? We're all trying to have a good time. I don't think Midge minded. In fact, with the way she's looking at me right now, I have a feeling she's about to enjoy returning the favor.

Royce wasn't off base before. I liked Midge in high school. A lot. I always felt she was way too cool to ever be with me, but we were friends, and I was happy with that. She talked to me about her boyfriends and boy problems, and that's when I knew I was in the friend-zone.

But we're adults now, and we're both single, and lately I feel like she doesn't look at me like that tall, gangly kid from school. She looks at me like she wants to see more, and I'd be lying if I said I wasn't intrigued.

I was shy and nervous back then, but a lot of things have changed.

"Your turn, huh?" I ask, stepping close to her as I put the lime wedge back on the table.

Her breath hitches as she looks up at me. "Yeah," she breathes. "Fair's fair."

"Oh, God. Please don't make him take off his pants so you can lick his thigh," Royce murmurs.

Everybody except me and Midge laugh. We're too busy staring at each other. I raise an eyebrow. "Where do you want me?"

Midge does her best to appear unaffected, but I know better. She clears her throat. "You can stay where you are."

"But I'm almost a foot taller than you."

"I'm aware," she says, turning around and pouring another shot. "Take off your shirt."

Everybody goes quiet. I don't hesitate. I reach behind me and pull the shirt over my head and toss it on the counter.

"Oh, Jesus," Jon mutters.

When Midge turns around with the salt in hand, her eyes widen slightly as she takes in my ink covered chest and stomach. Her tongue glides across her bottom lip swiftly before she meets my gaze.

"Preference?"

I give her a lopsided grin. "Lady's choice."

She tries to keep her smile in check, but I see it. She

reaches back for a wedge of lime and squeezes some of the juice right between my top two abdominal muscles.

I inhale sharply and she gazes up with a grin on her lips.

"Cold," I say.

"Mmhmm."

She sprinkles the salt over the juice, but most of it falls to the floor. Midge then hands me the lime to put in my mouth.

Without wasting any time, she licks the salt and lime juice mixture from the ridge between my abs and swallows down the shot. She's too short to reach the lime, and I could make things easier by leaning down enough so she can grab it, but I don't. Instead, I grab her by the waist and lift her up, and she wraps her legs around me. With her arms over my shoulders, she gives me a quick look before taking the lime between her lips. We don't stay like that for very long, and before I can say or do anything more, she slides from my arms and back to the floor.

"Who's next?" she asks after clearing her throat and giving me one last glance.

The rest of the gang look back at us with curious and confused faces, but London speaks up.

"Royce is. You want me to lay across the table, baby? You know, like old times?"

And just like that, the conversation switches, and people start asking London when she was lying across a table.

I grab my shirt and pull it back on, then head into the kitchen where Midge hands me a drink.

"Thanks."

She smiles, her cheeks flushed, and then clinks her glass against mine. "You're welcome."

After everybody does their body shot, and scarfs down some chips and cold dip, we all spread out and do different things. People filter in and out of the house, sometimes going to the back for fresh air. London and Midge disappear somewhere in the house for a while, leaving all the guys in the living room watching TV.

London comes back and snatches Royce off the couch and they disappear out back while Jon and Daniel go to the kitchen to find something else to eat.

"Hey there," Midge says, sitting on the coffee table in front of me with a bottle of Rum in her hand. "Drunk yet?"

"You tryin' to take advantage of me?"

She giggles. "Not sure I could overpower you."

"I could let you."

"You're crazy," she says with a laugh. "Drink?"

I grab the bottle from her hand and take a swig. "Where'd London and Royce disappear to?"

"Probably to their room," she says, rolling her eyes.

I glance over at Daniel and Jon in the kitchen. They aren't paying attention to us, because they're too busy making out. "I think they'll be going to their room soon, too."

Midge looks over her shoulder to see what I'm talking about.

"Get a room!"

"Okay," Jon says after pulling away from Daniel's mouth.

"You don't have to tell us twice," Daniel states with a smile, pulling Jon by the hand.

Midge looks back at me. "Well."

"Just us now."

"Yeah."

I lean back into the soft couch cushion and stretch my arm across the back. I kick my right leg out and wait for Midge to say something.

"Why are you looking at me like that?"

"Like what?" I ask with a grin.

"Just, like you're doing."

"I'm not looking at you any differently than normal." At least I don't think I am. The alcohol is definitely running through my system now, and I don't know if I could control my face if I tried.

Midge gazes around the room, like she's looking for a conversation topic to jump out at her. She's not normally like this, and I'm assuming the body shots have something to do with the fact that she's acting strangely around me now.

"What's up?" I ask her.

"What? What do you mean?"

"You're being weird."

She laughs. "No I'm not."

"You're acting like you don't know how to talk to me."

She ducks her head and tries to tuck a piece of hair behind her ear, but it falls forward again. "But I am talking to you."

I take a minute to think before I come up with a plan. "Let's play Truth or Dare," I say.

"Really?"

"Yep, but if you choose truth, you have to actually tell the truth. No lies."

"Okay," she agrees.

"I'll go first. Truth or dare?"

"Truth," she replies hesitantly.

"Do you regret the fact that we did body shots off each other?"

It only takes a couple seconds before she answers. "No."

"Your turn."

"Truth or dare?"

"Truth."

"Are you sad about your breakup?"

"No. Truth or dare?"

"Truth."

"Are you drunk?"

"Not really. Truth or dare?"

"Truth."

She thinks about it for a while. "Are you happy to be here? Like, at the lake house?"

"Yes, for more reasons than one. Truth or dare?"

"Dare, because one of has to be brave enough to say it."

I cock a brow at her, my lips curling up at one end. "I dare you to tell me what was going through your mind when I licked the salt off your thigh.

She bites her lip. "Uhh."

"Come on. Be brave."

She rolls her eyes. "I choose to drink."

"That wasn't part of the rules."

"Everybody knows those are the rules."

"Fine," I say with a chuckle. "So much for being brave."

Midge takes a tiny sip from the bottle. "Oh, shut up. Truth or dare?"

"Truth."

She makes a face, mad that I didn't choose dare. "Is it true that now that you're single you're gonna be out being a man-whore?"

I widen my eyes before I bark out a laugh. "Haven't really thought about it. Guess I'll go with...no?"

"You don't seem so sure."

"Can't be sure about something I haven't thought about. Which one will it be this time?"

"Truth."

"Is it true that you want me to do another body shot off of you?"

She swallows and then her lips part. "Umm. I mean, I wouldn't say no, because it's not a big deal or anything."

I use my left leg to pull the coffee table closer, and Midge lets out a squeak at the sudden movement.

I lean forward, my arms resting on my thighs, and look into her dark brown eyes. "So, that's a yes?"

She eyes my lips before meeting my gaze. "Yes."

Midge doesn't say anything for a while. "Oh. Truth or dare?"

"Dare."

I'm inches away from her mouth and all I want to do is lean in and kiss her. I hope that's her dare. Please let that be her dare, because I'm struggling to keep my hands to myself.

"I dare you to touch me."

My heart races inside my chest. "Where?"

"Your choice."

My hand travels slowly from her knee to her thigh, and stops at the spot I licked salt from—right at the top. I squeeze the soft flesh in my hand, my fingertips coming to a stop right under the material of her shorts, and my thumb resting on her inner thigh. If I moved it up just a fraction more, I'd be touching something else entirely.

Midge's breath comes in heavy pants now, and there's no mistaking the way she's looking at me.

"Truth or dare?" I ask, my hand still firmly in place on her thigh.

"Dare."

"I dare you to tell me what you want me to do next."

She licks her lips and I give her thigh another squeeze. She glances down, watching my fingers graze across her skin.

"Everything."

MIDGE

BEFORE I CAN TAKE ANOTHER BREATH, CILLIAN MAKES HIS move. He reaches out and pulls me from the table and places me on his lap.

I spread my legs and straddle him as his large hands move from my hips, and go up my sides before he places them on either side of my face and brings me in for a kiss.

His lips are warm and soft, and his tongue tastes like liquor. I wrap my arms around his neck and grind myself against him. Cillian groans, then grabs a handful of my hair and tugs. My head goes back, exposing my neck to him. I moan when his tongue traces a path from the base of my throat all the way up to my chin, and then his tongue slips past my lips again.

I can't help but grind against him again when I feel his growing erection underneath me. Heat floods my entire body, and I'm ready to rip every piece of clothing off when Cillian, who appears to be on the same wavelength, pulls my shirt over my head, leaving me in my strapless bra.

"Fuck, Midge," he groans, cupping each breast in his hands and squeezing.

I arch my back, loving having his hands on me.

A noise in another room followed by laughter startles us both.

"Room?" he asks.

"Yeah."

I climb off of him and grab my shirt from the floor and make my way to the bedroom he'll be staying in while he's here. It's closest to us, and far away from everybody else.

Once inside, I turn around and watch as Cillian closes the door behind us. He stalks me like a predator. With each step he takes toward me, I take a step back. He rips his shirt off and then starts unbuttoning his pants. My heart races in my chest as I study him. He's massive, both tall and built. Good Lord, what's waiting for me behind the zipper on those jeans? My legs hit the mattress, leaving me with nowhere else to go.

Before Cillian drops the jeans, he reaches into his pocket and throws his wallet on the bed, and then he moves to undo my shorts. I sit on the edge of the mattress, my body pulsing with excitement as he pulls them off and drops them on the floor.

I can't believe this is actually happening. I'm struck stupid, unable to be my normal, confident, take-control self. This is Cillian. My friend from school. And he's running the show.

Everything about him is overwhelming, but in the best way. He makes everything smaller. This room feels tiny with him in it. This king-size bed feels like a twin. He's going to ravage me, and I can't fucking wait.

The only light in the room is coming from the moon shining into the open window, but I can still see the dark intensity of his eyes. The way they're roaming over my body makes me break out in goose bumps even though my body is on fire for him.

Cillian moves closer, and I lie back, allowing him to climb over me. I spread my legs and let him settle in between them as he kisses and nibbles on my neck.

"Cillian, please," I beg, needing more.

He groans before his hand travels down my stomach and slips under my red, lacey panties.

I gasp and bite my lip as his fingers slide over my clit and slip into my warm and wet center.

"Fuck," he grunts, penetrating me slowly with two fingers.

"Ahh," I moan, squirming below him. I'm so turned on I'm afraid if he keeps playing with me, I'll come before I get to feel him inside me.

Cillian rolls off of me and gets off the bed. I watch as he grabs his wallet and pulls a condom out, then I stare at the ceiling, breathing like I just ran three blocks. Before I know it, my panties are being ripped down my thighs and Cillian's crawling back over me.

As I'm thinking about how I missed seeing his cock, I feel it at my entrance.

"Oh shit," I breathe.

"You ready?" he asks.

The way he asks makes me wonder if I should be scared. I nod my head and pant out a *yeah*, and then he plunges in.

"Holy shit."

I feel him smile against my cheek. Dude is packing!

Something feels different. Have I never been with a guy with a big dick before? I thought I had, but Holy Christ.

Cillian thrusts into me, spreading me wide around his cock. I reach around him, digging my nails into his back while I call out to God. Not that I want to be saved.

He moves back, resting on his knees, and then he hooks his arms under my legs and leans back over me.

With my legs up higher, and the angle he's coming in at, I feel his cock hit that perfect spot. The spot most men never find. The spot Cillian found in no time . The G-spot.

"Oh, God. Oh, God. Oh, shit. Oh my God," I chant.

Cillian grunts. "Your pussy feels so fucking good. God, Midge. You're so wet."

"Mmm," I moan, unable to speak words.

He keeps his stroke strong and steady, hitting that sensitive spot over and over. The sensation is out of this world. I feel the orgasm building, and I know it's going to be glorious.

"Please don't stop. Don't stop," I breathe.

"I'm not stopping, baby," he mutters.

I grab onto his biceps, feeling the muscles flex.

"Oh, God."

He grunts. "Yeah."

"Cillian. Oh my, God."

"Fuck yeah."

The pressure. The overwhelming pressure. I swear I can feel tears at the backs of my eyes.

"I'm...about...to…"

I don't even get the last word out. No need to. I'm coming like I haven't come before. Maybe ever. I can't think straight. This moment is heavenly. It's perfect. I scream and squeeze his arms as the orgasm overtakes me.

As soon as the wave is over, Cillian changes positions, letting my legs drop. He braces himself on his forearms and continuously thrusts into me hard and deep.

A symphony of curses and groans enter my ear as he buries his head in my neck, seeking his own release.

"Oh fuck," he grunts.

"Yeah," I breathe. "Yes, give it to me."

"Fuck."

His pace picks up, and then with one hard thrust, going as

deep as he can, he comes with a roar. He continues his movements, but slower this time, still emptying himself inside me.

"Jesus Christ."

God, I don't want this to be done. I want another round. And then another. I need to explore more of this man. I need to be satisfied like this more than once.

Slowly, Cill pulls out and rolls to the side. We both lie there trying to catch our breath. I pull the edge of the comforter over to cover most of my body. I chance a glance over at Cill and find him pulling the condom off his massive length.

I watch as he ties a knot in the condom, and almost miss the fact that he has— "A piercing? You're pierced?" I ask stupidly. He obviously is, because I'm looking right at it.

Cill chuckles as he sits up and plants his feet on the floor. "Yep."

"I knew something was different."

He laughs again, then gets up to throw the condom in the small trash can near the door. "Want to use the bathroom first?"

"Go ahead."

He struts to the bathroom, fully naked, his cock still standing at attention, and I enjoy the show. His muscles are defined, even through the ink. His body is slicked with sweat, and I still want nothing more than to lick him all over. But I wouldn't limit myself to his stomach this time.

Once he closes the bathroom door, I push back the covers and get up to find my clothes. I hold them against my body, covering what I can, before the door opens.

"All yours," Cill says as he emerges from the bathroom, stark naked still.

I try not to ogle him, but Christ, what is a girl to do when presented with such a work of art? "Thanks."

He gives me a cocky smirk.

After I pee and clean myself up, I get dressed again and then head back into the room, unsure of what sort of awkward hell I'm about to be in.

Cillian's partially dressed now, wearing a pair of lounge pants that are hanging dangerously low. He's digging through his bag for something, his back to me. I don't know what to say, so I just slowly walk around until he sees me.

Cill smiles. "Hey."

"Hey."

"Just looking for my bathroom stuff."

"Ah."

Awkward silence. Do we discuss what we just did? Do we say that this won't ruin our friendship? Will that be a lie? Gah! This is why this probably wasn't the best idea. I told London it would be weird. But alcohol makes people lose inhibitions, and make decisions they normally wouldn't. Especially when it comes to sex. Alcohol equals horniness. It's science.

"So, I'll see you in the morning? Or afternoon, probably," I say with forced laughter. "I'm pretty worn out."

Cill turns and looks at me with a grin emerging on his face. "Yeah, me too."

I smile. "All right. Uh. Yeah, see ya."

Then I spin around and rush out the door, feeling like the dumbest broad on Earth. But also, the most satisfied.

13

CILLIAN

I WAKE UP TO MY DUMBASS BROTHER JUMPING ON MY BED, and a slight headache.

"Hey, bro. Get up. It's almost one o'clock already, and we're all ready to go to lunch."

"Get the fuck off me," I croak, pushing him away.

Royce laughs. "Long night?" I don't bother responding. "Well, get your ass in the shower and get dressed. The girls are starving, and they're likely to start stabbing people soon. You have fifteen minutes."

He shoves my head into the pillow before he gets up and leaves, slamming the door behind him. Ass.

If it was just him, I'd take my sweet ass time getting ready, but since there's a group of people who want to eat, I guess I should hurry. I didn't think I'd be the last one to get up. I guess the mixture of alcohol, and some late night sex really knocked me out.

Sex.

With Midge.

Fuck, it was good. Shit got a little awkward when she left, and I don't know if she's already told London, and if

London's told Royce, which means I'll be getting looks all day. Oh well, fuck it. People have sex all the time. I'm sure everyone else in this house had sex last night.

I get up, grab some clothes, then head to the bathroom. As I'm in the shower, I can't help but think about last night. I can still remember what her tight, wet pussy felt like around my cock.

My dick starts to harden, so I reach down and give it a few slow strokes. Jesus, I wish she were here with me right now.

"Five minutes!" Royce yells from the other side of the bathroom door.

"Fuck off!"

I stop fucking around and finish my shower. Knowing I'll be around Midge all day with the memories of last night still fresh in my head, I'm sure my cock will have a hard time staying soft.

When I turn off the shower, I quickly come to realize that there aren't any towels in here. I search through the cabinets, but only find washcloths and different kinds of soap.

With a grin, I grab my phone from the back of the toilet and text Midge.

Cillian: *Hey, there aren't any towels in here.*
Midge: *Oh, sorry. I thought I had put some in there. One second.*

A minute later there's a knock on the door. Still fully naked, and dripping wet, I crack the door open just enough to reveal half my body.

"Oh. I didn't realize you had already showered," Midge says, looking up and away while she shoves a stack of towels at me through the door.

I chuckle as I pull the door open a little wider in order to take them from her. "Royce has been rushing me. Something about the girls getting stabby soon if they don't eat."

She laughs, still refusing to look at me. "Oh. Well, here you go."

"Hey," I say, resting my hand on top of hers as I grab the stack of towels. "Look at me."

Midge turns her head and looks into my eyes. "What's up?"

"You good?"

She nods. "I'm good."

"About last night?"

"Last night was good," she answers with a smile.

"We good?"

Her smile widens as she nods. "We're good."

"Okay. I'll hurry up then."

"Yeah, do that," she says before spinning around and walking away.

After I'm dry, I throw on a pair of black jeans and a white T-shirt, then slip on my black boots and head into the living room.

"Fucking finally," Royce says.

I flip him off. "Sorry, everybody else."

Everyone laughs, and I don't notice London looking at me any differently, so maybe Midge decided to keep what we did to herself. Until I talk to her again, I won't tell Royce either. Honestly, I don't want to hear his shit.

"Okay, we're going to this nice little place about a block away. They serve breakfast all day, but they have a bunch of shit to choose from," Midge says, swiping her purse from the counter.

Outside, the wind blows just enough to keep you cool under the bright rays of the sun. We left through the front door, so I still haven't seen the lake. Midge told me that the back of the property backs up to the water.

I glance over my shoulder to take a quick look at the front of the house I'll be painting. I was expecting a quaint cottage-type house, and though this house appears to have been here a while, it's fairly big. I can definitely see families coming here for the summers and having a good time.

On the right of the pale blue house, is a cluster of large trees that creates plenty of shade. The front yard is perfectly manicured with bushes and pink and red flowers blooming in the garden area.

"You comin'?" Midge asks, the only one of the group who hung back.

"Yeah, sorry. Just tryin' to get a look at the place."

"The back is what sells this place," she says with a smile. "I'll show you when we get back."

"Cool. Yeah, I still haven't even seen everything inside."

"It's a nice place. My grandparents have upgraded a few things over the years."

We stay a good ten feet behind everyone and talk like we didn't just have sex twelve hours ago. Everything seems normal, so that's good.

"I expected it to be louder around here," I say with a laugh. "You know, lots of kids running rampant."

Midge giggles. "Not around here. Not too much anyway. Marblehead has less than a thousand people. Tourists, retirees, but it's not a huge party place. You'll definitely have some peace, especially when we all leave," she says, angling her head over her shoulder with a grin.

"I'll make sure to enjoy the company while I can then," I say, returning the smile.

We watch each other for a little while before she turns her head. "Oh, you have to go to the lighthouse. And there's a couple galleries here, too. One has some beautiful blown glass, and they offer classes. There's some fantastic oil paintings of the lake and the lighthouse." She shrugs. "You might be interested."

"Yeah, for sure. I'll check it out."

The group up ahead stops and looks back at us. "This it?" Jon asks, pointing to a restaurant.

"Yeah," Midge replies.

Once inside the somewhat small and outdated restaurant, the waitress seats us after pushing two square tables together. We all take a few minutes to decide what we want, and about twenty minutes later we're all scarfing down a variety of cheeseburgers, seafood, and fried chicken.

"You guys have to try their donuts," Midge says. "They are the best!"

"I'm already eyeing a piece of pie," London says.

"No! Donuts!" she reiterates. "They're famous for them."

"Fine, I'll try some donuts," London says with a laugh. "Psycho."

"So, did everyone have a good time last night?" Royce asks, looking at everyone with a smile on his face like he knows what everyone did.

"We did," Jon says quietly, knocking his shoulder into Daniel's. Daniel smiles in response.

London rolls her eyes playfully, and me and Midge take a quick glance at each other before taking a bite of our food.

"Oh yeah, it was fun," Midge mumbles around her food.

"I haven't drunk that much in a while," I say. "We doin' the same thing tonight?"

While the question is aimed at the whole group, I make sure to look across the table at Midge when I ask it, then I glance around at everyone else.

Midge coughs, then takes a sip of her Coke, but a flush crawls up her cheeks.

"Ooh! We could have a little bonfire out back, right?" Jon asks Midge. "Didn't you say there was a little set up out there?"

She swallows down her drink. "Yeah, the back is made for entertaining."

"And we can get in the water!" London squeals.

"That means no classy restaurant tonight," Midge tells Jon.

Jon seems to contemplate this for a second. "I guess I prefer backyard drinking with you guys."

"Guess you're not as classy as you thought," she jokes.

Jon fake flips his non-existent long hair then turns to talk to London excitedly about our plans for tonight. Royce and Daniel talk about taking a canoe out on the water, and I stop paying attention to their loud chatter and focus on Midge.

I nudge her foot under the table until she looks up at me. "Do we need to go to the store or anything? Get some food?"

"Yeah, that's probably a good idea. We only bought drinks and small snacks yesterday. You'll definitely need some food in the house. Plus, tonight we can cook on the grill."

"You know how to grill?" I ask, raising a brow.

"You say that like it's something hard to master. It's cooking outdoors. Of course I can grill."

I raise my hands in defeat. "All right, sorry. I'll just supervise."

She purses her lips at me. "Pft. I'll put you to work."

"Oh really?"

"Mmhmm. You're not just gonna be sittin' pretty while I do all the work."

I chuckle. "Yes, ma'am."

She rolls her eyes while her lips curl into a smile. She looks down at the rest of the table. "Donuts to go? I'll probably order a couple dozen. Believe me, they'll go fast."

"Sounds good to me," London says.

"What're we up to next?" Daniel questions, looking at Midge.

"Umm. Well, me and Cill were just saying we need to go to the store for some food. I'm thinking we can grill for dinner, then just stay out back to drink and swim," she says, looking at London. "But I can do that on my own. Y'all should go out to the beach or something."

"We don't wanna leave you behind," London says with a frown.

Midge waves her off. "I've been here and done that a thousand times. I'll be fine. You guys go enjoy it. I'll get the food and make sure everything is marinating before we cook. Maybe even take a nap," she says with a laugh. "Don't worry about me."

"You sure?" London asks.

"Positive."

Once we're paid up and Midge gets her donuts, we all start the walk back to the house so everyone can get in their swimsuits, and so Midge can get her car.

After Royce puts his swim trunks on, he comes into my room and throws a small, pink backpack on my bed.

"Cute."

"Fuck off. It's London's."

"Right. What're we supposed to bring? Towels?"

"Jon and Daniel have the towels. London's bringing snacks and sunscreen. So, just put on your trunks and let's go."

I go to the bathroom to take a piss and change, and come

out to hear Midge yelling out her grocery list to see if anybody wants anything else.

"Oh crap, I think I need to get stuff for the grill, too. I'll have to double check the garage, but I'm not sure if we have propane."

"That'll be pretty heavy," I say, squeezing into the doorway next to Royce. "Plus, since I'm gonna be staying here, I'll be needing more stuff, so I might as well just go with you. You shouldn't have to carry all this shit on your own."

"It's really fine. They have carts, and I'm not as weak as my delicate frame may suggest," she responds, resting her hand on her cocked hip.

"Right, of course," I reply with a grin.

Everyone stands around looking at each other, not sure what to say.

"Cill will be here for another week, anyway. He doesn't need to go to the beach with us," Royce says, slapping me on the back and giving me a smile like he's doing me a favor. "Just let him help you, Midge."

"Seriously, I can do it," she says, being stubborn.

"Okay. Well, I'll just go to the store on my own then. Maybe I'll see you there," I say, turning back to the room so I can change back into my jeans.

Midge scoffs and London laughs. When I exit the bathroom dressed and ready to go, Royce is sitting on my bed with a stupid smile painted across his face.

"You and Midge will have some time together while we're out."

"We will be shopping and getting dinner ready for all of your asses."

"I'm sure you'll have some free time, though."

"You're being ridiculous," I state, even though I've had a

similar thought cross my mind. We'll have the house to ourselves without the worry of being caught or heard if we decided we wanted round two.

"Whatever, man. I'm out. I'll see ya later."

"Yep. Have fun."

He throws a grin over his shoulder as he walks through the door. "You too."

After I grab my phone, wallet, and keys, I wander into the living room looking for Midge. I hear the screen door shut, so I dart toward it, and spot Midge sauntering down the walkway toward the driveway.

"Hey! Wait up!"

"I told you I can go by myself," she replies, not looking back.

"And I told you I have to go to the store anyway. You're just gonna let me get lost?"

She spins around, her hair flying in the wind. "Oh, come on."

I grin and rush over to the passenger side. "Cool. Let's go."

She laughs. "You're annoying."

"You're stubborn."

She shrugs as she starts the car up. "Yep."

14

MIDGE

WE START OUR DRIVE TO THE GROCERY STORE IN comfortable silence. He gazes out the window, checking out the scenery, and I quietly hum along to a song playing through the speakers. We're only five minutes away from the store when he speaks up.

"I haven't told Royce."

I stay silent for a couple seconds. "I haven't told London either."

"Why? Don't girls tell each other everything?"

I shoot him a look. "Stereotypist much?"

"Uh, Royce told me a little story about you and London having full-on, detailed conversations about your sexual escapades."

Heat rushes to my cheeks. "So, boys talk too?"

"Touché."

"Anyway, yes, usually I tell her about all my escapades. But I don't know, this is different."

He shifts in his seat, facing me. "How so?"

I tighten my grip on the wheel. "Uh, you're Royce's brother? We're childhood friends? It has the potential to get messy. I don't want her to know and start thinking one thing, then when shit dies off, everyone feels uncomfortable when we're around. If they don't know, they don't get uncomfortable."

He's quiet for a little while. "Okay, so we don't tell anybody."

I pull into the parking lot and find a space up front. When I put the car in park, I turn my head and study him. He's so damn good looking it makes no sense. His elbow is propped up near the window and his fingers rest against his temple as his dark eyes stare intently into mine.

"Deal. We won't tell anybody what happened."

His lips curl up on one end. "You say that like it was a one-time thing."

My stomach flip flops and heat spreads across my chest. "Wasn't it?"

He leans in, his hand coming to push a lock of hair away from my face. His tatted knuckles graze my cheekbone. "I have a feeling it could happen once or twice more."

I bite down on my lip. "Just once or twice?"

His eyes flicker to my mouth before meeting my gaze again. "You yourself said this would die off."

Guilt coils in my stomach. "Seems to be the case for me."

He shrugs. "Every relationship ends until you find the right one."

"I haven't been in a relationship in a while, and I like it that way. I'm not about getting my heart stomped on."

"I'm not in the business of stomping on hearts, so..."

"So this is what? Friends with benefits?"

He smiles. "Sure."

"And we won't tell anybody?"

"No, we don't have to tell a single soul."

"And we won't let this ruin our friendship?"

"Definitely not."

He leans closer, his lips a hairsbreadth from mine.

"And when things die off, no hard feelings?"

"No hard feelings." He speaks the words against my mouth.

"Okay," I breathe. "Those are the rules, then." I lick my lips, grazing his in the process. "One more thing."

"What's that?" His lips ghost over mine when he talks.

"No falling in love."

He smiles. "Good luck."

Then he slides his tongue across my lips, parting them with ease. He swallows my moan as he delves deeper into my mouth, massaging my tongue with his. His hand wraps around the back of my neck, pulling me in closer, and his other hand squeezes my hip. I start getting too turned on to be in the front row of a parking lot at a grocery store, so I force myself to pull away.

"We're not in the right place for that kind of kiss," I say, out of breath.

"Then let's hurry and get back to the house," he answers with a mischievous grin, before leaning in and planting another kiss on my lips.

He pushes the door open and steps out. Through the passenger window I notice him trying to be as inconspicuous as possible as he adjusts himself. I chuckle to myself before I get out of the car and start toward the store.

To make this a quick trip, we each get our own cart and split up to get what we need. Twenty minutes later we meet up at the registers and check out.

"What'dya get?" he asks, peeking into my cart.

"Hamburgers, hotdogs, and wings. Keepin' it simple. I also got some chips and more stuff to drink. How about you? Get everything you need?" I glance into his cart and see a variety of food, some Gatorade and energy drinks, and a pack of condoms.

When I look back up at him, he's already watching me with a grin. "I got all the important stuff."

"Based on that box, looks like you're planning on more than once or twice. You know I leave the day after tomorrow, right?"

"Do you think you can only have sex once a day or something?"

I playfully roll my eyes. "We have other people in the house."

"Makes it more exciting, right?"

As I think about it, I smile. "Maybe."

"And we'll eventually be back in town together, so I'll probably need a few boxes."

I shake my head with a smile firmly planted on my face, but I don't say anything because I'm up next to check out. The old woman smiles at me before doing a double take at Cillian behind me.

She looks startled before he gives her a charming smile and a nod. She returns the smile. "You find everything you need?"

"I think so."

"You visiting?" she questions.

"Yeah. My grandparents have a house here, so we're just taking a little vacation."

"Oh, that's nice." She glances at Cill again. "You guys together?"

"Oh, no, we're just friends," I say with a laugh, and maybe too quickly.

She gives me a polite smile. "I meant are you paying together, dear."

"Oh." I laugh, feeling my cheeks heat up. "Sorry."

"We'll be paying separately," Cill answers. "And we just broke up." He gestures between me and himself, frowning. I widen my eyes at him, wondering what the hell he's doing.

"Oh, well, that's too bad," the woman replies.

"Yeah, she said something about me being too much to handle or something. But we rode up here together, so I can't leave until she does."

The cashier eyes me with light blue eyes, her wrinkled face wrinkling even more between the eyes. "Yes, I'm sure that's a bit uncomfortable for you both. Maybe things will work themselves out."

She busies herself ringing up my items, and I turn to Cillian and mouth *stop*. He smiles.

"Well, I'm not sure," he says, looking at me. "What did you tell me last night? That something felt different about me?"

My eyes nearly pop out of my head as I stare at him. He's talking about when I found out he was pierced. Luckily, the woman would have no idea what he's referring to.

I turn to the woman and roll my eyes. "Men."

She cracks a smile and continues doing her job. When I look back at Cill, he gives me a wink.

At the car, I smack him in the arm. "You ass."

He laughs. "What? You did say that."

I shake my head as we start piling bags into the trunk. "Anyway, about that. Didn't that fucking hurt? I can't even imagine."

"It has benefits."

"Can't be beneficial to you."

"Sure it is. It increases the sensation, but I'm a generous man. I did it for others. It really helps hit that sweet spot. You know what I mean," he says, a hint of humor laced in his tone.

I look over and find him watching me with knowing look. He knows it worked last night. I laugh. "Yes, how nice of you. What kind is that?"

"It's called king's crown."

"I see."

As we finish loading the car, my mind flashes back to last night and the brief moment I saw it. Too bad it was dark. I wish I would've gotten a better look at it. But maybe I'll get the chance after all.

When we're back in the car, I ask, "So, it's like in...or I mean, is it through...never mind." I shake my head, blood rushing to my cheeks.

Cill laughs. "You want me to whip it out so you can see for yourself?"

Yes. "No!"

"It's not through the hole, if that's what you were gonna ask. It's through the ridge up top."

"Okay, it's okay. You don't have to explain."

His chuckle is low and deep. "I'm not embarrassed."

"I see that. I was just curious."

"I'm sure you'll get a closer look at some point. At least I hope so."

I sneak a peek at him and find him smiling. He's getting a kick out of this. I might as well have some fun, too.

"Oh, well, I don't do blow jobs. I guess I should tell you that now."

His smile disappears really quick. "Oh. Okay. That's, yeah, that's fine."

"Yeah, I think so," I reply, keeping a straight face while I look back at the road ahead. He's quiet for a long while, and I can't hold it together any longer, so I sputter out a laugh when I see him looking forlorn as he stares out the window.

"What's funny?"

"You. You look so depressed. I was just fucking with you."

As I'm cracking up in the seat next to him, he shifts to face me. "Wow, that's cold."

"Well, call it payback for being a weird ass in the grocery store with that poor old lady."

He chuckles. "Fine. We're even."

Once we're back at the house and the car is unloaded, Cill puts away the groceries while I prep the food for dinner tonight.

By the time everything is done, it's about four o'clock. Since I don't know how long the rest of the gang plans to stay out, I'm unsure of how much time me and Cill have alone in the house, but I want to take advantage. However, I don't want to come off as horny and desperate as I am.

Cill smiles at me from across the kitchen like he's reading my mind. "Come on," he says, holding his hand out.

I walk toward him and put my hand in his. He closes his fingers around mine and starts walking to his room. A smile spreads across my face as I follow him, and he turns around and catches me. I'm rewarded with a low chuckle.

15

CILLIAN

IN THE ROOM, I KICK OFF MY BOOTS AND UNDO MY JEANS, allowing the black boxer briefs to peek through. I remove my shirt and toss it with the rest of my stuff on the floor, all while Midge stands nearby, watching with rapt attention.

"Your turn."

"But you're not done yet," she replies, gazing down at my crotch.

"And you're fully dressed."

I step closer, studying her face while my hands go to the button of her shorts. I make quick work in popping it open and unzipping the zipper before pushing them over her hips and down her thighs before they fall to the floor.

I go to lift up the green and white striped top she's wearing, but she starts to reach up and says, "It's a halter. You have to untie it."

"Let me do it," I reply, turning her around.

"Once this is off, I'm basically naked. And you still have your jeans on," she says softly.

"Don't worry," I say, pulling apart the bow at the back of her neck. "You'll see all of me soon."

With the bow untied, the shirt falls loosely around her. I push down my jeans and remove her shirt completely. I press myself up against her back and while my right hand reaches around to cup her breast, my left hand travels past her hip and cups the soft flesh of her ass. Thank God for thongs.

"Mmm," I moan into her ear. "I love how soft your skin feels."

My right hand moves down across her quivering stomach, and then travels further south where my fingers slide over the soft material that's keeping me from finding out how wet she is already.

I play with her pussy through the fabric in soft, slow strokes, teasing her gently while my mouth plants kisses on her neck.

"Cillian, please," she begs, her body trembling.

"Get on the bed," I command. "On your hands and knees."

Midge crawls onto the bed, looking sexy as fuck in nothing but that black thong. As much as I love it, it has to go. I pull the material down her thighs, and she lifts up one leg at a time to allow me to take them off completely.

With that done, I drop down behind her, plant my hands on her ass, and let my tongue slide out and taste her.

"Oh, my God!" she gasps.

Her pussy is already wet for me, but I continue to devour her. She drops her chest to the bed, pushing her ass up into the air even more, and gives me a better angle to lick more of her. My tongue glides over the clit, slides through her wet folds, and penetrates her warm, tight hole.

"Jesus Christ," she pants.

I get up and give her ass cheek a quick squeeze and light smack. "Roll over."

She obeys, quickly getting to her back. Her legs are

spread apart for me, and my eyes go straight to her glistening pussy.

"Goddamn, you're sexy," I growl, pushing my underwear down and reaching for the newly purchased box of condoms that I put on my nightstand.

She brings her knees together and lays them to the side to get a good view of me. Before I rip open the wrapper, I grab the base of my dick and give it a few languid strokes while I watch her watching me.

She captures her bottom lip between her teeth and makes a noise in the back of her throat. I inch my way closer, pushing her legs apart as I kneel between them. I continue to stroke myself, because I can tell she likes it. Once or twice, her eyes flicker up to mine, but then she's back to studying my cock in my hand.

Because I can't wait any longer to be deep inside her, I rip open the package and sheathe myself with the latex. I grab my shaft and slowly put the crown of my cock into her wet entrance. I watch as her tight pussy stretches around my girth, then I thrust all the way in.

"Holy shit," she breathes.

I lean over her body and she spreads her legs apart even wider, welcoming me in. My thrusts are long and deep, and because nobody is here, her moans are loud and uninhibited.

She ping-pongs between grabbing at my arms and digging her fingertips into my back. She squeezes me with her thighs and then cries out my name.

I lean back, slowing my movements, and pull almost all the way out. I grip my cock and slide it up and over her clit, teasing her. I dip the crown of my cock back inside, coating myself with her arousal and then slide back up to her clit.

"God, Cillian. Please," she begs, breathless.

"Please what?" I ask, continuing to tease her.

She breathes heavily, her eyes squeezed shut. "I need it. Please."

"Mm. I like you like this. Needy for my cock."

I slowly slide back into her, filling her to the hilt.

"Ah! Yes!"

I stay on my knees, and push hers farther apart as I keep my strokes slow and deep. I bring my thumb to her clit and rub circles over the engorged bundle of nerves.

"Fuck. Yes."

She clenches around me, arching her back and curling her toes while steadily chanting, "Yes, yes, yes."

I shift and plant my left hand firmly on the back of her thigh, pushing down until her knee is nearly touching the mattress. This brings her ass up off the bed, and allows me to penetrate deeper.

Her tits bounce with each thrust, making my cock throb even more. She brings her hand to her right nipple and pinches it between her finger and thumb.

"Fuck," I growl.

"So good," she moans.

I push her other leg back, spreading her wide. "Rub your clit," I command through heavy breaths.

She quickly obliges, reaching down with her right hand and rubbing circles over her clit. God, the sight of her playing with herself spurs me on.

"Fuck yes."

"Oh, God," she calls out, her hand quickening. "Oh yes, give it to me."

I slam into her, giving her every fucking inch. Her arousal splashes between us, and her skin flushes red. Her body tightens up, and I know it's coming.

"That's it," I grunt. "I'm ready for it. Come for me. Come all over me."

As if my words helped push her over the edge, she yells, "Oh, God! Oh fuck! Yes!"

And then her pussy contracts around me in wet pulses. I slow my movements and look between us. Evidence of her orgasm coats my cock and drips onto the bed.

"Christ," I groan.

Her body twitches as the aftershocks hit. "Oh, my God." She chokes the words out while gasping for air.

"Goddamn, you got my dick so fucking hard."

I lift one leg up, holding onto her thigh while I push in and out of her soft, slick center. My orgasm edges closer with each thrust. My balls tighten as my climax mounts. I worry my thrusts are too vicious, too hard, but then Midge cries out in pleasure. The orgasm rips through me, and I grunt and curse as I ride it out.

"Jesus Christ," I pant, sweat dripping from my temple.

"Yeah," she agrees on a breath.

I take my time to pull out, not yet ready to be free of her tight warmth.

She lies there, sweat slicked and out of breath, and sexy as hell.

"You are a vision. If I could paint you like this, I would."

She laughs, bringing her legs together and turning to the side. "Please don't. I'm sweaty and gross."

"I think I'd title it *Satiated*."

"Stop," she says with a laugh.

"So, how much time do you think we have before everyone gets back?"

She opens her mouth to answer, and then we hear voices.

"Shit!"

MIDGE

I HOP OUT OF THE BED, SCURRYING TO FIND MY CLOTHES AS Cill quickly rips the condom off and pulls on his underwear and jeans.

"Shit, shit, shit," I mutter, pulling my shorts up over my ass, not bothering trying to find my underwear. "Find my panties and stash them!" I whisper harshly.

As I'm trying to tie the halter around my neck, I hear the front door open and the voices get louder.

"Just go to the bathroom," Cill says, pulling his shirt over his head.

"I can't go into your bathroom! Why would I use your bathroom? They'd be suspicious."

"The other bathroom is across the house."

"I know!"

"Hello? Guys?" London calls out.

I widen my eyes in a panic, staring at Cill, hoping he has a plan.

"Maybe they'll all go upstairs to their rooms. They have to shower, right?"

I roll my eyes and hurry to his bathroom. "Tell them

you're about to shower and you don't know where I am."

"Why would I shower twice in one day?"

"Oh, my God!" I basically only mouth the words. "Say something before they come in here."

I watch as he walks to the door to his room. "Hey, have fun?"

"So much fun!" London responds. "Where's Midge?"

I plaster myself against the wall behind the bathroom door, hoping he can come up with a good excuse.

"I don't know. I came in here and fell asleep. She may have done the same."

"Maybe. I gotta get in the shower, though. My skin feels all dry and sandy."

"You took a nap?" I hear Royce question. "Like you're a toddler?"

"I was fucking tired, man. Why don't you go shower with your girl and leave me alone."

"Good idea."

I hear footsteps racing up the stairs, and sag in relief. Hopefully I can sneak out of the room and get to mine before anybody comes down.

Cill peeks around the door with a grin on his face. "I'm a pro."

I roll my eyes. "Whatever. Move, so I can hurry and get to my room."

I quietly step into the hall and listen for voices. When I don't hear any, I inch toward the living room and then run as quickly and quietly as I can, on my tip-toes, getting to my room on the other side of the stairs.

Cill's low chuckle floats across the room, so I make sure to turn around and give him the finger before I slip into my room and close the door.

Before London can come check on me, I strip out of my

clothes, realizing I didn't even zip or button my shorts. That would've been a dead giveaway if I ran into someone. I find my favorite Rolling Stones shirt. It's been worn no less than a thousand times, it's almost threadbare, but it's so damn comfortable. I find a pair of underwear and some shorts made out of an old pair of ripped blue jeans, and pull them on. Now I can go to the bathroom to freshen myself up.

I slip my cell in my back pocket, and once in the small bathroom across from my room, I send a message to Cill.

Midge: *You find my panties?*

He doesn't respond right away, so I do my business and get a washcloth and soap to clean up my lady parts. I wipe away some smudged mascara and grab my makeup bag from the back of the toilet to reapply some lipstick and powder my face. After I comb through my nearly, shoulder-length black hair, I'm satisfied that nobody will be able to guess what we were up to.

Cillian: *I have them.*

Good, now I don't have to worry about Royce going in there and finding them. I exit the bathroom and start heading toward Cill's room since nobody is downstairs yet.

Standing safely in the doorway, I call out to him. "Psst."

His head pops out of the bathroom. "Psst? Really?"

I glance over my shoulder. "Shush. Give me my underwear," I whisper.

"Your what?" he responds loudly.

"Oh, my God, shush!" Another glance behind me. "My panties," I say quietly, gesturing to my vagina.

Cillian smirks. "I thought they were a souvenir."

"What's wrong with you?" I whisper yell, looking behind me once more. "Just give them back. They're my favorite pair."

"My favorite, too."

I'm about to take a step into this room when I hear footsteps traveling down the stairs. "Midge!" London squeals. "We had so much fun, but I missed you."

"Yeah, extra tooth paste should be in the cabinet," I say awkwardly to Cill. He chuckles.

"Forgot his," I say to London, rolling my eyes and walking into the living room. "So, it was fun? What'd you guys do?"

She starts telling me about their adventures, meanwhile my heart thunders in my chest and my mind keeps replaying my time with Cillian.

It's going to suck not being able to talk to London about this. I have to tell someone about his massive, pierced cock! I have to let somebody know how surprised I am by how good he is in bed.

I don't know why I'm surprised, but I am, and I need to get all these things off my chest, but I can't tell her. I can't risk making things awkward for the whole group. Because let's be honest, I'm his rebound and he's just another guy I won't want to be in a relationship with because I'm a damaged, bitter bitch.

Yeah, men are good for sex. Well, some. Sometimes they can be good for conversation. Are they good at not being assholes and completely breaking your heart, trust, and confidence? Eh, not so much. At least that's my experience with them.

Cillian is a really nice guy. He's funny and easy to be around. He's great. But I'm not in a relationship with him. People always change once they're in a relationship.

We always meet the best representation of somebody first. The side of themselves that says and does everything they think the other person wants to hear or see.

Oh, you hate horror movies? Me too!

Oh, you hate when people chew with their mouths open? Same!

Oh, you've been cheated on? I'd never do that! I respect women.

And it goes on and on. Meanwhile, she comes home to him sitting on the couch watching Freddy Leatherface Vorhees with a mouth full of chips as he talks to some other woman on the phone.

Yeah. No thanks.

I snap out of my thoughts when Cillian struts into the living room. I quickly glance up at him, but then I focus on London.

"Sounds like you guys had a good time. I mean it would've been better with me there, because I'm a party in a bottle."

She laughs. "I can't wait." London peeks over her shoulder, watching Cill go into the kitchen. "So, how were things here?" she whispers.

"Fine. I got the wings marinating, and the burgers and hot dogs will be easy. We already had propane, so I didn't have to worry about that. I'll probably start cooking around six."

She gives me a pointed look. "Not what I was talking about. You and Cill? That whole body shot thing?"

I wave her off. "Drunkenness is what that was."

Cill comes in to save the day. "Hey, Lo. Did you get Royce out in the water?"

"Barely," she replies, rolling her eyes. "But he's getting in the damn lake with me later."

"Oh, am I?" Royce says, coming down the stairs, hair

still wet.

"You are," she replies with a flirty grin. "Or else."

Cill drops down next to me on the couch with a water bottle in his hand. "Water?"

"I'm good."

Though I am thirsty, but the drink I want is a tall glass of Cillian fucking Kingston. It doesn't matter that I just had a taste of him not that long ago. Now that I know what he's working with, I need more. I need to come up close and personal with that cock. I want to know what it feels like to lick around that piercing.

"If you're gonna try to play it cool around everyone, you're probably gonna need to stop staring at my dick."

I snap my head up and find Cillian grinning, his arm slung across the back of the couch, and his other hand bringing the water bottle to his lips. A quick look around the room lets me know London got up to meet Royce near the stairs where they're speaking quietly to each other.

"You should probably learn to whisper better," I say in a hushed tone.

"You whispering is gonna draw attention."

"You saying I'm staring at your dick is gonna draw even more attention." I mouthed dick as to not perk up anybody's ears.

Cillian shifts slightly, casting a gaze toward Royce and London before removing his arm from the back of the couch and running his hand over his cock. He presses down, highlighting the fact that the thick beast is laying against his thigh.

"What were you thinking about?"

I peel my eyes away and shift further down the couch. "Nothing."

"Don't lie."

"I wasn't. I just zoned out."

"You want to touch it?"

More than anything. I purse my lips at him. "No."

He grins. "Liar."

I try to hide my smile. I need to end this conversation. Cillian Kingston is mischievous.

"Where's Jon and Daniel?" I yell over my shoulder to Royce and London.

"Still showering, I think." Royce replies.

I push off the couch and walk to the kitchen. "Well, I'm gonna start cooking. I'm starving. So I'm taking the meat outside, along with a bag of chips to snack on. Y'all gonna come with?"

"I'm coming," London chirps, spinning away from Royce and coming to the kitchen. "What do you want me to take out?"

"Grab this dish," I say, handing her the one filled with hamburgers and hotdogs. "I'll grab the wings and chips."

"You need help with the grill?" Royce asks.

"I'm good. You can just come out and be pretty."

Cillian coughs. "What about me? Can I just be pretty too?"

I barely give him a glance as I walk behind the couch and head to the glass doors that lead to the back. "Who said you were pretty?"

"Ohh!" Royce yells, laughing at his brother.

I hear Cillian get up and follow behind me. "I'm pretty sure someone did. Recently too."

Oh Lord. I choose to ignore him.

Stepping outside onto the covered patio, I pass the little seating area with two wicker chairs, a matching loveseat, and small coffee table with tempered glass. Two large, potted plants sit on both sides of the sitting area, up against the stone wall.

The grill sits around the corner, along with a table and two chairs. Out at the edge of the grass are four large maple trees, with a hammock tied between the middle two. Just past them, the property drops off about a foot, and becomes a rocky beach before you get to the water.

"It's so serene out here," London murmurs, standing at the edge of the patio and looking out toward the water.

"Yeah, it's beautiful."

I place the wings down on the table and flip the lid of the grill. London turns around and brings the rest of the food. "And a hammock? God, I could stay here forever."

Cill and Royce come around the corner, laughing about something.

"So, what do you think?" I ask Cill. "Think this will be good for you?"

He turns and puts his hands in his back pockets, gazing out at the water that appears to go on forever. "This will definitely make an amazing piece of art."

"Just wait until the sun goes down. It sets right over the water. It's gorgeous."

"I'm gonna go yell at Daniel and Jon and tell them to bring their asses out here," London says, marching back to the door.

I get the grill going while Royce and Cill wander around the back, walking toward the water. Soon, I hear Jon and Daniel talking, then spot London running out toward the water where she jumps on Royce's back.

Daniel pops around the corner. "This is a beautiful place, Midge. I can see why your family's kept it so long."

I smile. "My great-grandparents bought this way back when. This whole covered patio wasn't here. The trees were smaller. No hammock. No picnic table around the side, and no built-in fire pit near the water. My grandparents, and later, my parents helped spruce this place up. Some of the rooms inside have been updated a bit, but I like that it has some old school charm too."

"Is this beach area private?"

I nod, placing some wings on the grill. "Yeah, we have this little area to ourselves."

"Nice."

"My mom met my dad up here. They have the cutest little love story. She has so many memories that involve this place. That's why I want Cill to capture its beauty in a painting for her."

"I bet he'll do a great job, and I'm sure she'll love it," Daniel says with a warm smile.

I throw on some hotdogs on the other side of the grill, then close it up and sit down with my bag of chips.

Jon calls Daniel away so they can go explore some of the property, and I watch from my chair as Royce and London attempt to get into the hammock together. It's pretty comical.

"Hey there, shorty," Cill says, sauntering his way toward me.

"Pft. I'm fun-sized."

"I'd say so," he replies. "I've had plenty of fun."

My stomach does a somersault. "Yeah, well, no more fun tonight. Too many eyes around."

"I thought we established that that makes it more fun," he says, sitting in the chair next to me.

"My heart almost jumped out of my chest today when they came home. Not the most fun I've had."

"I'll show you how fun it can be."

Fire travels through my veins, heating up my body. "How are you gonna do that?" My voice comes out breathy.

"You'll see."

CILLIAN

AFTER WE STUFF OURSELVES FULL OF FOOD, WHICH WAS DAMN good, everybody gathers around the picnic table on the side of the house, and Midge brings out Uno and a regular deck of cards.

Me, her and Daniel are squeezed together on one side, while Royce, London, and Jon sit across from us.

"Plus four, sucka!" Midge shouts as she slams the card down.

"I had one card left!"

"Exactly. I can't let you win."

I pull my four cards and the game keeps going. I nudge her knee with mine, but she slams hers back as a warning. I smirk and take a sip of my drink. My right hand moves under the table and my fingers spread across her thigh as I give her a gentle squeeze. I feel her tense up briefly before she resumes what she was doing.

"Fucking stupid red cards. Who chose red?" Royce asks, mad he has to pull from the deck.

"Oh, don't be a baby," Midge responds, throwing down a

red card. "I have like half the deck in my hand, thanks to somebody." She aims her comment at me.

"It's not my fault." I reply, grazing her inner thigh with the tips of my fingers.

She shivers, and when London looks at her, she says, "Cold chill."

"It's hot though," Royce chimes in.

"I don't know why it happens, leave me alone." She clamps her thighs together, but ends up trapping my hand between them. I rotate my wrist and press my fingers against her pussy.

"Your turn." She chokes out the words, clearing her throat afterward.

She widens her legs just enough to free my hand. I look at my cards and put one down.

"Why don't you ever have to pull from the deck?" Royce asks.

"Guess I'm just lucky. Don't be a sore loser. London, did I ever tell you how much of a baby your boyfriend is when it comes to games?"

She laughs and looks at Royce who's pinning me with a look in the hopes of making me shut up. It won't work. "I don't think so."

"Well, back when we were younger, if anybody was beating him at a game, no matter what game it was, he would swear up and down we were cheating. If we weren't cheating, then the game was 'stupid' or he'd suddenly have to leave, just so he wouldn't lose."

"It's called being competitive," Royce says, picking up another card. "Nobody likes to lose."

"When he'd be playing a video game, if he was about to lose, he'd shut it off and start over," I say with a laugh.

Royce flips me off. "You wanna tell stories?"

I smile at him, unafraid. "Go for it."

"Ooh, I love stories," Jon says, leaning in for something juicy.

"Cillian would stay up watching scary movies, even though Mom and Dad would tell him not to, and he'd scare the shit out of himself so much that he'd be afraid to go to his room alone. He would stand in the doorway trying to talk to one of us while he was changing like it would keep him from being eaten by monsters or some shit."

Everybody at the table laughs. "Dude, I was like eight."

"I thought Freddy Krueger killed my parents one night," Midge says. "My stupid older cousin made me watch a marathon, and then my parents left, and I guess I felt like they were taking a really long time to get home, so I'm sitting on the couch, staring out the window, waiting for them. I see these three cracks in the wall and convince myself they were Freddy's scratches. So I'm sitting there with tears in my eyes, convinced he got my parents," she says with a laugh. "Then they show up and I'm trying to wipe my tears and act like everything is fine. Stupid scary movies."

We all crack up, and everybody takes turns telling somewhat embarrassing stories about their childhood while we finish the game.

Once it's over, we head inside to get some drinks.

"Anyone doing any body shots tonight?" London asks, her eyes bouncing between me and Midge as her lips curl into a smile.

"No body shots tonight," Midge answers.

"Aww, party pooper," London teases.

"You can do them all you want," Midge replies. "I'll take my shots from the shot glass."

"Wow, you're boring," I say, knowing it'll get a rise out of her.

Midge whirls around and pins me with a look. "Oh yeah?"

I nod, my smile growing. "Yep."

She points at me. "I'll remember that."

We all gather around and take our first shots—out of shot glasses, and then we get our drinks and venture back outside. There's four Adirondack chairs on the grass facing the lake, so we pull two of the wicker chairs from the patio and bring them out.

Everyone kicks back and enjoys their drinks while taking in the view. Small waves crash against the rocks, and the night sky brings a slight breeze that cools the air around us.

"God, I don't want to go back home," London muses. "It's perfect out here."

"It really is," Jon says. "We need to make these trips more often."

After London finishes her drink, she strips out of her shorts and shirt, revealing her bathing suit, and lures Royce to join her in the water. Jon pouts at Daniel and convinces him to go in as well.

"You gonna go in?" I ask Midge, who's sitting two chairs away.

"Probably not, because I'm so boring."

I throw my head back and laugh. "Aww. I was just messin' with ya."

"Mmhmm." She brings the plastic cup to her mouth and takes a sip.

"What if I go in? You won't come in with me? Looks like they're having some fun," I say, looking to the rest of the group.

"Go ahead," she gestures to the water.

"You don't have to pretend you don't want to be around

me when nobody else is here, you know?" I stand up and take a couple steps toward her.

"Who says I'm pretending?" she counters, tilting her head up and looking at me.

"Oh, is that right?"

She grins. "Yep."

"I think you're full of shit."

Her smile widens. "Okay."

I take my shirt off and throw it on my chair. Her smile falters. "I think you're trying to convince yourself you don't want to be around me as much as you do."

Midge takes a drink and stares out at the water. "You can think that." Her voice has lost some confidence.

I kick off my shoes and start undoing my pants. Her head swivels back toward me and her eyes watch my hands work.

"I think you wish you were alone with me right now."

I take my pants and throw them on the chair with my shirt. I'm left standing in only my boxer briefs. Midge tries to look me over without moving her head.

"I think maybe you're full of yourself," she replies.

I step closer to her and take the drink from her hand and place it on the grass. "I think you want to be full of me."

I pick her up and throw her over my shoulder and march toward the water. She squeals, getting the attention of everyone else. They all cheer as Midge smacks me in the back.

"Put me down!" she screeches. She tries to act indignant, but she ends up laughing. "I hate you so much."

I take advantage of the dark and distance between us and the group and move my hand up from the back of her thigh where I'm holding onto her, and squeeze her ass cheek before sliding it back down. "No, you don't."

"Can I at least take my clothes off before you dump me in the water?"

I place her on her feet at the edge of the water. "I'm not gonna say no to you taking off your clothes."

"Ha-ha," she says dryly, pulling her shirt off to reveal a teal colored bikini top. "I have a bathing suit on, you perv."

"I'm the perv? You've been eyeing my cock all day."

"What? No, I haven't!"

Walking backwards, I take a few steps toward the water while she pulls her shorts over her hips. I run my hand over the length of my dick briefly, but long enough to get her attention.

"There you go again."

"Ugh! You tricked me!"

I laugh and then make my way toward the rest of the group. A few seconds later, I hear water splashing behind me. Before I can turn all the way around, Midge uses both hands to shove water at me.

"Hey! This water isn't exactly warm."

"Aww, worried about a little shrinkage?" she says with a faux pouty face.

With a smug smirk, I say, "Shrinkage would just give me an average sized dick. I'm not worried about it."

She scoffs and sloshes past me. I scoop her up from behind, cradling her in my arms as I dip her in the water. She squeals, her voice high and thin as the water hits her back and covers her stomach and chest. I'm sure to keep her head above water, because I don't have a death wish.

"You got me all wet," she growls through her grit teeth.

"I promise to get you really wet later," I say, raising my brows. She narrows her eyes at me. "Oh, come on, we're in the water. You were gonna get wet anyway, plus, you started it."

When I place her on her feet, she gives me a once over as she walks past. "You're gonna pay for that, Mr. Kingston." Her words drip with sex, threat or not, I'm already turned on.

"You promise?" I growl.

She ignores me, because now the group is getting closer.

"Wow, she's gonna kill you, Cill," London says.

"Nah. I'm sure I'll survive."

Royce shakes his head, laughing. "You did that same shit to her at the pool when we were teenagers."

The memory hits me all at once and I start laughing. "Oh yeah."

Midge faces me. "So, now you're gonna pay twice."

Jon and Royce let out a pair of *oooh's*.

"Well, at least he didn't dunk you all the way under like last time," Royce points out.

"Whatever. I'll get you back. Just wait."

A half hour or so later, all of us are out of the water and drying off with the towels Daniel went inside to get. Midge comes out with stuff to get the fire pit going, and London emerges with a pitcher of blue liquid.

"What is that?" I question.

"My own creation." She glances at Royce. "Okay, maybe I had some assistance. But it's basically vodka, rum, pineapple juice, and…" She looks to Royce for help.

"Blue curacao, sweet and sour mix, and Sprite."

"It's a fishbowl punch, but we don't have a fishbowl, so it's a pitcher," London says, holding up the pitcher.

"Well, it sounds delish," Jon says, holding out his cup.

London pours everyone a cup full of the drink and Midge gets the fire going behind us.

"All right, people. Bring your chairs around the fire," Midge says. "We can tell ghost stories or something," she finishes with a laugh.

"There's no such thing as ghosts," Daniel mutters.

"Yes, there is!" Jon counters.

Daniel rolls his eyes like he's had this argument before.

"Or maybe not ghost stories," Midge says.

I settle into my chair, choosing to sit next to Midge this time. Jon and Daniel continue to debate about whether ghosts are real or not, and London sits sideways on Royce's lap, talking quietly about something.

"Why don't you tell me a little about this place," I say. "Something about your mom's experience. It'll help with the painting process."

She sits back in her chair and holds the cup on her knee. "Okay, well, when my mom was young, probably about seventeen, she came here with her parents for the summer. That wasn't out of the ordinary, but that year, my dad was here," she says with a smile. "He didn't live close by. I think it was over eight hours away, but they had one month together that summer, and that's how their story began."

"You can't end it there. What else happened?"

Midge shifts in her seat, sitting cross legged, and perks up excitedly as she tells the story. She's so damn cute.

"Well, they wrote each other letters during the year. They still have some of them to this day, locked up in a little box. Anyway, they were pen pals. They updated each other on what was going on in school and whatnot. They made a few phone calls when they could. My dad's parents were strict, and didn't really allow him much freedom, so he did what he could.

"When the summer was approaching, Mom told Dad to convince his parents to come back here again. He made no promises, but said he'd do the best he could. When my mom came up here with my grandparents that summer, she waited to see my dad. She walked into town and hoped to come across him. She had sent him the address to this house with instructions to mail any letters during the summer here, so she'd get them. But no letters ever showed up. She tried calling his house, but nobody answered. It was like he had disappeared. She was devastated."

I furrow my brow. "Doesn't sound like the happiest love story."

"What love story doesn't have complications? There's always an obstacle. Sometimes more than one, but it's getting through them and over them that makes the story a love story. Plus, I'm here, so obviously it has a happy ending."

I smile. "You're right. Continue."

"So, Mom spent the summer moping around, broken-hearted. She didn't think she'd ever see him again."

"But."

She grins. "But, she did see him. It wasn't until the following year though. She didn't receive another letter from him. Her calls went unanswered. She had given up and actually started dating someone else. But when the summer came around, she was here."

"Was your dad here?" I ask, completely sucked into the story.

"Shush. Just wait. So, Mom is out with a couple friends, doing who knows what, and when she gets back home, she checks the mail and finds a letter addressed to her. There's no return address, no stamp, just her name. She opens it up and finds a letter from my dad. All it says is *I've missed you. I'm sorry.*"

"That's it?"

"That's it," she says with a smile. "But then, there's a

knock on the door, and it was my dad. Mom throws herself into his arms, crying. Dad explained that his parents got a divorce. It was messier than that. His dad was abusing his mom, and one night, his mom grabbed him and they fled. He hadn't told my mom about his family problems, because he was embarrassed, but yeah, he and his mom left and moved even farther away. He didn't have Mom's number memorized, or her address, and the letters he was able to take with him, were just letters. No envelopes."

"Wow."

She nods and takes a sip of her drink. "Yep, so they spent the whole summer together that year. My grandparents let him stay with them, in another room, of course. Because Dad didn't come with his mom. He came alone."

"Wait, so he came back here by himself, in the hopes of seeing your mom?" London asks.

Me and Midge both glance around and realize everybody's listening to the story.

"Yep. His mom had to work and couldn't afford to take a summer vacation. My dad was eighteen at that point, so he used the little money he had saved from his after-school job, drove this old, beat-up car to get here, and hoped for the best."

"Aww, that is so romantic!" London says.

"He found the house, saw my mom leave, popped the letter in the mailbox and waited for her to get back."

"But your grandparents let this stranger into their house for the whole summer?" Daniel questions.

Midge laughs. "They had met him the first summer they met. They were inseparable, so he was always here, and when they weren't here, they were off somewhere together. Mom had cried to my gramma about Dad. She knew the story. So when he showed back up, and Mom was deliriously happy, they allowed him to stay. My grandparents have always been pretty lax on stuff. Plus, Mom was nineteen."

"Wait, didn't you say your mom had started dating someone else?" Royce asks.

"Yeah, she had. It was new, but the moment she saw my dad, that relationship ceased to exist. Dad was it."

"Aww," Jon and London sing together.

"And they've been together ever since. They spent the next two summers up here, and then they were focused on school and work and having me, so their time up here came sporadically. It's been years since they've been now, but this place holds so many memories for them."

"That's awesome," I say.

"Yeah, I love their story."

"Maybe you'll have your own story start here, too," Jon tells her.

She rolls her eyes a little. "Probably not. All right, let's drink."

MIDGE

AT MIDNIGHT, I'M DAMN NEAR DRUNK. THE LIQUOR HAS loosened my tongue and heightened my sex drive. If nobody finds out about me and Cill tonight, it'll be because they're also drunk and can't see what's right in front of them. However, Cill seems to be doing his best to maintain the ruse.

"Who else wants to take body shots off of Cillian's abs?" I yell, raising my hand high in the air.

London giggles, also drunk. "What happened to no body shots tonight?"

"People can change their minds," I say with a shrug.

Cill casually drapes his arm around my shoulders, just like he has in the past, just like any friend would do. There's nothing romantic or sexual about it, yet my heart hammers against my ribcage at the contact.

"I don't think Midge needs anymore shots," he says with a laugh. "As much as I'd love to take my shirt off for everyone."

Royce scoffs. "Keep it on. Please."

"Hater. I told you I could give you a little artwork. It'll make you more interesting to look at naked."

Royce gives him a smug grin. "I don't need ink to be more interesting to look at. Especially naked. Huh, babe?" His glassy eyes meet London's.

"Can we stop talking about people being naked?" I whine.

"Why don't you call that one guy?" London says. "The last one you went out with. Didn't you say he was nice?"

Cillian drops his arm and moves to the kitchen. "I mean, I guess he was nice. But, I'm not really interested."

"Whyyyy?" London asks. "You said he was good in bed."

My eyes grow in size. "Shhh."

London waves her hand through the air. "Royce already knows how we talk."

"Yeah. Still not over the last conversation I overheard."

"And I've been in on some of these conversations," Jon adds from the couch in the living room.

I scoff and roll my eyes. Usually, I wouldn't care about having this conversation in front of people. I don't really give a shit if people know I'm dating or having sex with guys. It's not abnormal for a single woman to do those things. But now Cillian's here, and watching me from the kitchen. I definitely don't want to talk about the last guy I slept with. But London keeps on going.

"So, call him. At least have a fuck buddy. You have needs too! Don't become celibate and cranky. I'll hire you an escort or something."

"An escort? In Gaspar? Good luck," I say with a laugh.

"Oh whatever. Why did you stop talking to him anyway? What was his name again?"

I begrudgingly answer. "Jeff."

"Yeah, Jeff. So what did he do?"

I shrug, glancing up at Cillian who's leaning against the counter in the kitchen, watching me. "Just got boring, I guess."

"Ah. Yeah, that sucks," London murmurs.

"Good thing we don't have that problem, huh?" Royce says, nuzzling into London's neck, turning her into a giggling school girl. Damn drunk, horny people.

"We're gonna turn in," Daniel announces, getting up from the couch and pulling Jon up with him. "We gotta leave early in the morning tomorrow, because I have to be back in town before three."

"Okay, well, good night. I'll see you guys before you take off."

London and Royce decide they can leave because Daniel and Jon did it first, so London spins around and gives me puppy eyes.

"Sorry to leave you so early in the night, but…" She leaves the word hanging in the air between us. She doesn't even have to finish. I know. Because Royce can't keep his hands off of her.

Royce angles his head and throws up two fingers to Cillian. "Night, bro. See ya later."

Cill lifts his chin. "Yeah, see ya."

When all four of them have disappeared upstairs behind their closed doors, me and Cill continue standing where we are, watching each other.

"Come here," he says.

I listen and walk into the kitchen, but I lean against the counter opposite him. "I'm here."

"No, come here," he says, emphasizing *here* as he points to the floor right in front of him.

I place my cup on the counter and take four steps to get to him. My brain feels a little foggy, thanks to the alcohol, my movements seem to be in slo-mo, but my thoughts are rapid fire.

Touch me, kiss me, fuck me.

"Truth or dare?" he questions.

Knowing how this ended last time we played, I answer quickly. "Truth."

"You've been thinking about my cock all night."

I swipe my tongue across my bottom lip. "True." His lips twitch, almost smiling. "Truth or dare?"

"Truth."

"You want to fuck me right now."

"Oh, so very true." He takes a sip of his drink and then places it on the counter behind him. "Truth or dare?"

"Dare."

"I dare you to undo my pants."

"Right here?" I question, looking toward the stairs. If anybody decided to come down, they'd see us right away.

"Right here," he states.

While staring into his eyes, my hands fumble with his button, and then pull the zipper down. My knuckles brush over his growing erection.

"Truth or dare?" I breathe.

"Dare."

"Without actually placing my hands on you, make me touch you."

A cocky smile spreads across his face. He steps forward and nuzzles my neck with his beard before I feel his lips ghost across my skin. He kisses and licks my neck, all the way to my collarbone, and across my shoulder. I almost reach out and touch him, but I slide my hands into my back pockets, hoping I can have some self-control.

When that doesn't work, Cillian takes a step back and then drops to his knees in front of me.

"Oh, God."

The words slip past my lips without even thinking. Cillian's hands move under my shirt, softly grazing my hips as his lips form kisses around my belly button. His hands travel south with his fingers finding the button on my shorts and popping it open.

My hands fly out of my pockets like they have a mind of their own, but right before I touch him, I'm able to stop myself. I place them awkwardly at my side because I want more of what he's doing. The thought of someone coming down doesn't even flicker in my brain. All I want is his mouth on me.

Once he's undone my shorts, he tugs them down just enough to do what he needs to do. He peppers my lower stomach in kisses, his tongue coming out briefly to tease me. Then he kisses me through the material of my bikini bottom, his lips perfectly aligned with my clit. The warmth of his tongue pressing against me rips a gasp from my throat as my hands fly to his shoulders.

He drops a little lower, and through the material, he prods against my entrance. Then, he slowly stands up, and pulls my shorts back up over my hips.

"I win."

I let out a shaky breath. "Not fair." I take a deep breath and try to compose myself.

He grins. "Truth or dare?"

"Dare."

"I dare you to do what you've been thinking about." He reaches through the open zipper of his jeans and grabs his cock through his boxer briefs, bringing my attention to how hard it is.

"And what have I been thinking about?" I ask, even though I already know. I just didn't know he knew. Have I been that obvious?

He cocks his head, his lips turning up on one side. "You tell me. Rather, show me."

Cillian strokes himself slowly through the light gray material. God, I want nothing more than to get my hands and mouth on that substantial cock. Apparently he knows it too.

Again, I ask, "Here?"

"Here. Wouldn't want things to get boring, right?" He raises an eyebrow, challenging me.

My heart flutters and then I reach inside the opening of his underwear and finally wrap my fingers around his erection. It's hot and hard in my hand as I give it a little stroke before releasing it from the confines of the material.

It bobs in front of me as I kneel down and run my fingertips over the veins. The silver, curved bar steals my attention. I grab ahold of his shaft, pulling it down just slightly so I can flick my tongue over the piercing.

I lick around the crown of his cock before opening my mouth wide and taking him inside. Using my hand, I stroke the length of him while tasting some of the arousal that has leaked onto my tongue. Cillian groans above me, and it spurs me on.

I quicken my hand, stroking him faster as I take him deeper into my mouth. The piercing grazes the roof of my mouth, nearly hitting the back of my throat as I try to take all of him.

Cillian grabs a fistful of my hair and starts moving his hips, fucking my mouth like it's the best place his cock has ever been.

"Fuck," he grunts, slowing down and trying to control himself. "Get up."

I hurriedly stand up, ready to do whatever he wants. He reaches into his pocket for his wallet and grabs a condom. I push my shorts to the floor, stepping out of them and kicking them to the side.

Cillian doesn't bother removing his clothes, he just covers his dick with the condom and then pulls me to the counter and bends me over it.

He tugs the teal-colored bottoms down to my thighs, slides his fingers into the wetness that's already accumulated there, and then shoves his thick cock inside me.

"Oh, God!" The words come out louder than I meant them to.

"You're gonna have to keep quiet, sweetheart," Cill says quietly over my shoulder. "Someone may come down and see us."

"Mm," I moan, pushing back on his cock.

Cillian stands back up and grabs my hips and hammers into me. It's hard, fast, and deep. So wonderfully deep.

I bite my lip in an attempt to keep quiet, but I can't. Cillian has to reach around and clasp his hand over my mouth while he pummels into me.

The punishing thrusts, and the fact that we're out in the open, risking being seen, has my orgasm building quickly. Cillian removes his hand from my mouth and places it against my clit, rubbing circles over it while pushing in and out in long, forceful thrusts.

"Oh God, oh God, oh God," I pant, trying to keep my voice low. "Yeah, just like that. Oh shit."

The orgasm hits me like a freight train. I shatter into a million pieces as I ride the wave, my legs shaking beneath me. Cill goes back to covering my mouth as my noises get louder. I bite down into his palm, and then Cillian does his best to keep quiet as he climaxes. He releases a sexy, throaty growl, shuddering over me.

"Holy shit."

As he's pulling out, a door creaks open upstairs. We separate quickly, and I pull up my bikini bottom and reach down for my shorts while Cillian tucks himself into his pants. We start running toward the living room when we hear another door shut.

"They just went to the bathroom," I whisper.

And then we burst into a fit of laughter.

CILLIAN

I wake up early today since everybody will be leaving. We say bye to Jon and Daniel first, but Royce and London stick around to have breakfast.

"Mm. This is so good," London says around a mouthful of French toast that Midge made.

"Mmhmm," Royce agrees, taking a bite of bacon.

I glance across the table at Midge and smile. "Thanks for breakfast."

"You're welcome," she says with a shrug. "I was craving French toast, so really, it was a selfish decision."

"Hey, what time did y'all go to sleep last night?" London asks.

My eyebrows shoot up as I look to Midge. "Uh, I'm not sure. Maybe an hour or so after you all went up."

"Something like that," Midge says.

"Oh okay. I came down after a little while to get some water, and expected y'all to be up."

Well, I'm glad we ended up going to our rooms last night, because it seems like London came down after she went to the bathroom. We were just minutes from being caught, literally with our pants down.

"After I finished my drink I was really tired," Midge says. "So, I just went to bed. Ended up getting up early to clean up and stuff."

"So, you gonna actually enjoy the rest of the day off, or you gonna go into the bar?" I ask Royce, changing the subject.

"Nah, I won't go in today. Me and London have plans, then we're going to Elijah's. You're gonna miss Sunday dinner, and E said he was making steak tonight."

"Ah, damn. Well, I'll be back for next Sunday's dinner. Maybe I'll be able to convince him to make a steak for me."

Royce chuckles, then shoves another bite of eggs in his mouth. "I doubt it."

"Merrick called me last night. Well shit, it was like three in the morning."

"Oh yeah? Where's he at now?"

"Phoenix. They had just got done with a show."

Merrick, our baby brother, is on a US tour with his band, The Unwanted. They recently released their debut album, and it's damn near at the top of the charts.

Royce nods. "I think he's gonna be in Vegas soon. Lucky bastard."

"Aren't they ending their tour in Cleveland?" London questions.

"Yep," I say with a nod. "We'll be driving up to that one."

"Oh, Midge, you can go and reunite with Sky," London says playfully, wiggling her brows.

My brother and his band came home right before their album released and the tour started. While everyone was over at Elijah's house, Midge and Sky seemed to be hitting it off.

However, once the band had left town, I remember asking Midge if she wished Sky was still here. She brushed it off like it wasn't a big deal. She's never been one to be clingy or needy for a relationship, but I have to admit I was a little relieved that she wasn't hung up on him. It would be easy to be since he's the lead singer of a band that's about to take over the world.

Midge rolls her eyes. "Nah. I'm okay. But I'd love to see them in concert."

Once again I breathe a sigh of relief. I don't doubt Sky would love to be with Midge again, but she doesn't seem to be all that interested. However, maybe she's just saying that for my benefit. I mean, we said this was just a friends-with-benefits situation. Maybe she'll still see and hook-up with other guys. We should get some clarification on that.

"Well, it's not till September sometime, but you can come with us when we go," I tell her.

"Cool. Thanks."

Royce and London finish their food, then Royce gets up to take their plates to the kitchen. Since London rode up with Midge, Midge will have to leave when they do, which doesn't leave us with any more alone time.

"I'm gonna grab our bags and put them in the car," London says, pushing away from the table. "Is it unlocked?"

"Yeah," Midge answers. My stuff is already in there. I'll put my dishes away and then be ready to go."

"No rush," London says, before heading upstairs.

When Royce is done washing the dishes, he jogs up the stairs to help London, and Midge gets up to take her plate to the kitchen. I follow her.

"It's gonna be weird as fuck to be here with no noise," I say, taking the plate from her and scraping the food down the garbage disposal.

"Thanks," she says with a grin then leans her hip against

the counter as she watches me clean our plates. "Yeah, but now you can get some work done."

"What's your mom's favorite part of the house?"

"Well, her and Dad spent a lot of time out on the water. They took the canoe out almost every day, and they walked down our private little stretch of land. If you go out to the right, past the maple trees, there's this little clearing. They loved that area."

I nod, taking mental notes to go out and explore the area. I already have an idea of how I want this painting to look, but I need to inspect the property from the lake.

"Cool. I'll check it out."

Royce and London trot down the stairs with a couple of little bags and then go outside to put them in the car.

I dry my hands on the dish towel hanging from the oven door, and then reach out and pull Midge close to me.

"It's gonna suck not having you here."

She grins up at me. "You're gonna have to go back to using your hand for a while."

I laugh. "Don't act like you're not gonna be using your hand, just make sure to think of me when you do it."

She rolls her eyes. "Whatever."

I lean in and plant my lips on hers. What was supposed to be a quick peck turns into a frenzied kiss—a clash of tongues and teeth. She moans into my mouth as she grabs my shirt in her fists, pulling me closer.

When the screen door opens, we pull away from each other, and I turn to put the plates away as Midge opens the fridge, pulling out a bottle of water.

"We're all done," London says, walking into the kitchen.

"Cool. Let me pee, and then I'll be ready to go," Midge replies.

I give Royce a quick hug goodbye. "Let me know when you get back."

"I will," he says with a nod.

Ever since our parents died in an accident, and we couldn't reach Royce right away, we're now very conscious of keeping each other in the loop when we're traveling, even if it isn't that far away.

I give London a hug. "I'll see ya later."

"Yep. Enjoy your peace and quiet, and good luck with finding your mojo."

I laugh. "Thanks."

Midge walks out of the bathroom and into the kitchen to grab her water and keys. I give her a quick hug, too, because that's what I've always done, and not doing it now would be weird.

"Drive safe."

"Always," she says with a smile. "Text me if you need any more info about this place or the area, or whatever."

"Okay."

I walk all three of them to the door and watch them leave. Once I'm alone, I decide not to waste any time. I head to the garage and grab the canoe and haul it to the water.

20

MIDGE

BY THE END OF THE DAY ON WEDNESDAY, I'M ALREADY ready to drive back to the lake and spend some time with Cillian again. Him and his cock have infiltrated my every thought. It's like I'm a sex fiend. But it's not that I just want any kind of sex from anyone. I want him. I want his sex. But I haven't heard from him since I left.

I guess I shouldn't put too much thought into that. He's probably in the middle of creating the painting for my mom. Who knows what goes into an artist's process, but I don't want to ruin it by texting and checking in. Though I have wanted to have a little late night sexting session.

Tonight is the night me and London go down to Royce's bar and have a couple drinks. Sometimes I find a guy to flirt with, maybe get someone to buy me a drink and get a phone number if I'm lucky, but I don't know if I should do that tonight.

Me and Cill are friends who've fucked. Who will probably fuck again once he's back in town. But that's it. We're not in a relationship, but it doesn't feel right to be trying to sleep with anybody else. Plus, I'm sure I wouldn't be able to find someone who could live up to Cillian Kingston and his amazing cock.

London pops her head into my office. "You ready to go?"

"Ugh. Yes! FuckFace John just left. I should've been gone thirty minutes ago."

"I know. I've been waiting in the lobby. Jesus, what did he have to say this time?"

I grab my purse from the bottom drawer of my desk and walk into the hall of the bank. "I had someone in here earlier, and I was just finalizing their loan when he walked in and was acting all high and mighty, asking the guy how things were going. Asking if he had any questions he could answer."

"Wow, what a dick."

"I know! Just because he's older than me doesn't mean I don't know how to do my job. I swear he's a sexist who just thinks I'm incompetent because I'm a woman. Of course the guy was perfectly happy with how I was handling his account, and I think that pissed John off even more. He just wants someone to complain about me so he can try to get me fired."

"Fuck him. Let's go drink and stuff our faces full of fried food from the bar."

"Sounds perfect."

London and I drive to King's Tavern separately, and once inside, we order a basket of mozzarella sticks and chicken strips before we get our drinks.

"Hey, ladies," Royce says, sauntering over to our side of the bar. "Ready for those drinks now?"

"So ready. Let me get a vodka tonic, please."

"Got it."

Royce doesn't bother to ask London what she wants. It's always the same. Johnnie Walker on the rocks. I always switch mine up, because I'm a mood drinker.

Once he serves us our drinks, he travels down to the other end to serve Craig and Jim, another couple of regulars who are always arguing over some sports team.

"I'm still dreaming about the lake."

"Me too." I don't bother saying it's probably for a different reason, because I couldn't care less about the damn water.

"It was so nice getting away for a little while. I bet Cill is just living it up over there."

"Probably," I answer, bringing my glass to my lips.

London swivels in her stool, facing me. "Have you heard from him?"

I shake my head, trying to play it cool. "No, but I didn't think I would."

"Yeah, I just thought maybe he'd check in with you about the painting."

"Oh. Nah, you know how he is with his paintings. He won't talk about them or show them until he's completely satisfied with it."

"True."

Silence hangs between us for a little while. I can tell she wants to say something else, but she's hesitant. Does she know about me and Cill? Maybe we weren't as secretive as we thought.

"So, you're still one hundred percent dead set on just being friends with Cillian and nothing else?"

Her question catches me off guard. "Yes, just friends," I answer with a laugh, hoping she believes me. "Why?"

"Well, for one, those body shots y'all did off each other." Her eyes grow in size as she dramatically fans herself. "Pretty damn steamy."

I laugh again, ninety-eight percent sure it sounds genuine

131

and not at all laced with fear of being caught. "We were drunk."

"Maybe you were a little tipsy, but he wasn't drunk."

I shake my head, a smile on my face. "It wasn't a big deal. We're friends. I'd do a shot off of you and not think twice about it."

Royce pops up right when I say that. "What? You guys are doing body shots? What kind of shot do you want?"

London makes a face at him. "No, Midge is being crazy."

"I'm just saying. I've done body shots off of strangers, it's not a big deal to me."

Which is true. I have done body shots off of people I just met in a bar, and those have never been a big deal. Just some drunken fun. However, the body shots me and Cill did seem to have sparked this little thing we have going on right now.

Royce looks between us, trying to figure out what we're talking about, then his eyebrows shoot up and his green eyes are lit with mischief. "Are you talking about the shot you did off Cill?"

I roll my eyes. "Not a big deal."

He laughs, looking to London then back to me. "It was pretty surprising, though."

"I guess, but you know me, I'm down for whatever."

Royce leans over the bar. "Like, down for my brother?"

"Oh my God, you guys are insane. Me and Cill are friends. Friends!"

"I know, but I'm just asking questions. You know, doin' the brother thing."

"Why? Has Cill said something?" London asks excitedly. "Does he like Midge?"

Royce stands back up. "I'm not getting into this. I gotta get back to work."

"What? You were just in it!"

As much as I want to know what Royce may know, I don't ask. I don't want to let them think I'm interested. But it did seem like he was trying to get some information from me that he could pass onto Cill. Does that mean they've talked?

"Sorry, ladies," he says with a grin, backing away.

"Ugh. Annoying," London pouts. "You think Cill asked him if he thought you'd be interested in him?"

"I doubt it." Which is true. He knows I'm interested. At least in sex.

London huffs. "Well, anyway, I was just making sure you two were just friends, because Royce told me that some girl came into the bar and was asking about Cill. I guess word got out about his breakup with Zoe. Royce said this girl has a history with Cill."

"History?" My interest piques as my head snaps in London's direction.

"I guess they dated in school or something. It was a long time ago."

"Hmm." I take a drink, trying to drown the tiny seed of jealousy growing in my stomach.

"Yeah, so I guess Royce is gonna tell Cill about it. Pass on her number. Girl appears to be desperate, if you ask me, but maybe he'll be into a one-night stand since he's newly single." She finishes with a laugh, completely unaware of how tense my body is.

I can't imagine Cill hooking up with someone else. And now that I know how he gets down in the bed, I don't want some other chick getting what he dishes out.

London excuses herself to the bathroom, and I continue gulping down my drink, investigating why I seem to care so much. I never care about any of the other guys I've hooked up with. Sometimes it's just a one-night stand, and those are easy to get over. You meet a guy, you hook-up, you don't see each other again. Well, in this small ass town, you might, but then you just avoid eye contact and go the other way. However, I've had a couple guys I've hooked up with more than once. But then they got it in their heads that that meant we were together, and that they could start questioning where I was and what I was doing all the time. Uh. No.

After my break-up with Matthew three years ago, I've been a card-carrying member of The Single's Club, and an avid supporter of *doing what the fuck you want*. So why does the thought of Cillian, a friend I'm just going to have a few casual hook-ups with, talking to someone else, piss me off so much?

I should probably re-think this friends-with-benefits thing. We can just say it was something we did at the lake. We don't have to continue it here. It's best to preserve our friendship and avoid any possible blowback.

"Really cute guy two chairs over is totally checking you out," London says as she reappears next to me.

I turn my head to the left and spot a fairly attractive guy with blond hair sneaking peeks at me. When he realizes I've noticed him, he smiles and lifts his glass in my direction. I return the gesture, smiling back at him, but turn back to London.

"Meh. Too pretty."

"Too pretty?"

"Yeah, too put together. He probably takes more time getting ready than I do."

"Wow, when did you get so picky?" she says with a laugh.

"Are you saying I have low standards?"

She gapes at me. "What? No, you crazy. I'm just saying you've always been an equal opportunist. I never thought you had a type."

I shrug. "I guess I don't. I'm just attracted to who I'm attracted to. That guy isn't bad, but meh, not for me."

"Well, all right."

She's right though, I've been with jocks, nerds, older guys, younger guys, gym rats and bean poles. I've never only looked for one specific type of guy. But right now, all I can think about is a six foot two man covered in tattoos with a dark, scruffy beard, and a pierced cock.

21

CILLIAN

I'VE BEEN WORKING IN THE BACKYARD, BECAUSE BEING surrounded by what I'm painting has definitely helped keep me inspired. However, when I went out on the canoe the first day, I took several photos of the house and property so I could recognize what it looks like from the water, since that's where Midge's parents spent a lot of time as well.

I'm also very aware that Midge will see this, and that it'll hang in her parents' house, so I want it to be perfect.

I've decided it's going to be a multi-panel canvas wall piece, because it'll help capture all the parts I want to high-light. It'll be a view from way out on the water, so each piece will have the lake reaching up to the shore, but the first piece will capture the clearing Midge was talking about, as well as the maple trees. The second piece will be the house and trees surrounding it, and the third piece will be a continuation of the trees and the picnic table next to the house, and I'm going to include the canoe, brought up to the rocks of the beach.

With the sun going down, I decide to move all of my supplies to the garage, and then bring a beer outside and watch the sun go down over the water.

It's been three full days of actually painting, and I haven't felt any doubt about it yet. I want to attribute that to being surrounded by nature, but I don't know if that's it or not. Maybe it's the peace and quiet I've had here, and not the usual loud foot traffic I have outside my studio. But maybe it's because I don't have any stress.

The last several months have been annoying, because me and Zoe were constantly fighting and breaking up, just to get back together and fight some more. Since I've been here, I had fun with my friends and brother, had some pretty amazing sex with one of those friends, and now have absolute serenity as I work. Maybe I just needed to get out of that toxic relationship.

As much as I hate that Zoe cheated on me, I know I wasn't the best boyfriend. I did spend a lot of time at the studio, but it was because I was trying to get some space— space I needed from her just so we wouldn't fight. But in doing that, she would get upset and we would fight, and I'd want to escape again. It was like being in a hamster wheel full of bad decisions.

I'm due to go back home on Sunday, and if I keep working like I've been doing the past three days, I feel pretty confident I'll have enough down that I can finish details in my studio. I'll just be sure to take plenty of pictures for reference.

It's nearly nine o'clock when my phone dings from the table next to me. I'm still outside, listening to the water and the rustling of the leaves as the wind blows, lost in my own thoughts.

Midge: *Hey, how's it going?*

I smile when I read Midge's message, and type back a quick reply.

> **Cillian**: *It's going. What're you up to?*
> **Midge**: *Just watching TV in bed. Are you painting now? I don't want to interrupt.*
> **Cillian**: *Not painting. Just sitting outside.*

She doesn't respond right away, so while I wait, I get up and go inside. In the kitchen, I put together a club sandwich, and pour some chips from the bag onto the plate, then take it to the couch.

My phone lights up.

> **Midge**: *Oh okay. Just making sure you were still alive and well.*

I chuckle and wipe my hands off on my jeans before answering.

> **Cillian**: *Glad you're worried about me. I'm fine, though. Just in the zone. Determined to make sure you love it.*
> **Midge**: *Love what?*
> **Midge**: *Oh. The painting. Ha-ha. I'm sure I will.*
> **Cillian**: *What did you think I was talking about? Because I already know you love something else...*
> **Midge**: *Pft. You don't know anything.*

I take a few minutes to scarf down the rest of my food, then place the plate on the table and start typing.

> **Cillian**: *I know you love how I fuck you.*
> **Midge**: *It's all right.*

I laugh out loud.

Cillian: *I know you wouldn't say that to my face.*
Midge: *I would.*
Cillian: *Then I'd prove to you that you were lying.*
Midge: *How so?*
Cillian: *Oh, I have my ways. Many, many ways. And before I would be done, you'd be screaming you love it, and you'd beg for more once it was over.*
Cillian: *So, tell me, do you not want me to fuck you right now?*

She doesn't respond. I keep watching the phone, waiting for those three little dots to appear, hoping I didn't go too far. I've never had a friends with benefits situation before. I've had girlfriends, and I've had hook-ups. Never slept with a friend, so I don't really know the rules.

Midge: *I want it.*

A smile creeps across my face.

Cillian: *Then it's too bad we aren't together.*
Midge: *Yes, especially after teasing me like that, and getting me all worked up.*
Cillian: *That was not teasing. It's not like I sent you a video of me stroking my cock.*

Before she can respond, I call her. She answers before the first ring can finish.

"Hello?"

"It's not like I told you that just thinking about fucking you gets my dick hard."

I hear her suck in a breath. "Oh really?"

"Mm," I groan into the receiver. "And I can't stop thinking about fucking you."

"I can't stop thinking about it either."

"Good."

"I can't wait until you're back in town. I mean, I know you're enjoying it up there, but…"

"I'd prefer being in you. Don't worry, I'll visit you as soon as I get back."

She giggles. "I don't mean to sound so sex-crazed."

"Sex-crazed is fine. I don't mind sex-crazed. If you haven't figured it out yet, I'm the same way."

Another laugh floats across the line. "Yeah, you're very different than I imagined."

"You've imagined having sex with me?" I ask with a laugh. "And how was I in your imagination?"

"That's not what I meant," she replies with a nervous laugh. "I'm not saying I've thought about how you'd fuck me, I just mean, the Cillian I've been friends with all these years is very different from the Cillian that fucks me."

"Well, yeah, that makes sense."

"Yeah, but I'm a pretty vulgar person, even around friends," she says with a laugh. "You kind of know what you're getting with me. I've been vocal about sex in front of all of you, too. You're usually pretty quiet."

I chuckle. "So, what? You thought I'd be a prude?"

"Maybe not a prude, but not as vocal and explicit."

"Ah, and now you know we're cut from the same cloth."

She laughs. "I guess so. I'm just more vocal about things publicly."

"Yeah, I've never been one to talk about my sex life."

"You've also been in a relationship, so it's a bit different.'

"Yeah, I guess so. And you're not a relationship type of person."

"Exactly."

That thought twirls around in my brain for a second. I want to question why that is, but I get the feeling it's a subject she wants to avoid. I vaguely remember her having a boyfriend a while back, but back then she wasn't visiting Royce's bar like she does now, and I only saw her around town from time to time, so I don't know the details.

"Well, I guess I should go to sleep," she says. "Some of us have to go to work in the morning."

"Hey, I'll be working."

"Yeah, but you don't have a boss who will tear into your ass if you're two minutes late."

"Ass tearing, huh? Doesn't sound fun."

She laughs. "It's not. I'll talk to you later. Have a good night."

"Good night, Midge."

22

MIDGE

"TGIF!" I say, throwing my hand in the air as I wave goodbye to everybody in the bank.

"You're leaving earlier than usual," London says, coming around from behind the teller's spot. "You're usually leaving an hour after closing time."

"I know, but I have to go to my parents' house. Mom called last night and said she wanted me to come over to help her with something. She was very vague about it, so now I'm curious."

"Well, all right. See you tomorrow?"

"Yep, you know it."

I fly through the glass doors, trotting out to my little Mini Cooper, and roll my windows down. I drive to my parents with music blaring, and me singing at the top of my lungs. That's usually how I drive when I'm alone, and sometimes London gets to be my one and only guest to my one woman concert.

My parents' four bedroom, ranch style house comes into view at the end of Brighton Boulevard, dead center of the cul-de-sac. It's your perfect little family home. You'd picture the perfect couple living here with their perfect son and daughter, and well-behaved dog. But growing up, it was only me, and I was far from perfect. And we didn't have pets. But since I've been out of the house, they've become those annoying dog parents. They have one shih-tzu, and they make sure he's in their Christmas cards, sometimes the Christmas card is just him wearing a little Christmas sweater. And he's a menace.

When I get to the door, Mom appears, pulling me inside while shushing me. "Shh, come in."

"I didn't say anything," I whisper. "Why are we being quiet?"

Mom looks over her shoulder. "I have to talk to you about your dad."

"What? What's wrong?"

"Follow me," she says, still whispering and pulling me along to the kitchen. "I have a suspicion."

"What?"

I study my mom's face, looking for signs that she's been crying. There's no way my dad would cheat on her. It can't be that.

Her brown eyes look free of the redness that usually accompanies cry fests. She tucks her straight, black hair behind her ear, glances over her shoulder one more time, and then bites down on her bottom lip.

"I think he's planning a surprise party."

I sag in relief. "Oh my God, Mom, you had me thinking it was something crazy!"

"Shh," she says, swiping her hand at me. "I don't want him to hear us."

I relax, leaning against the small, rectangular island in the kitchen. "Why would that be a problem?"

She gives me a pointed look. "Do you remember what your father planned for my fortieth birthday?"

"Remind me."

Mom folds her arms on the island. "That's when he thought I'd like to celebrate my birthday at the bowling alley." She widens her eyes at me. "The bowling alley, Margaret. At forty."

I press my lips together, trying to keep from laughing. She only ever uses my full name when she's serious. She hated that party, but she loves my dad so much, she never said anything. She was grateful that he had remembered, because she has friends whose husbands forget their birthdays, but she hates bowling.

"Oh yeah, didn't you bowl a forty-five that day?"

She narrows her eyes at me. "We can't have another bowling alley birthday for my fiftieth."

"Okay, so what do you want me to do? Ask him what he's up to?"

"Yes! Just try to sneak in some input. Remind him how much I love to dress up. Go somewhere nice. He can plan a dinner with our friends over at the Blue Velvet."

"Oh yeah, Jon had a birthday party there not that long ago. It's really nice."

"Perfect! Just bring that up."

"You sure? Maybe he'll plan this one to be at that putt-putt golf place."

She stands up straight and pins me with another look. "Not funny."

"Well, where is he?"

"I think he's in his office with Kiko." She walks to the fridge and pulls out a pitcher of lemonade. "Want something to drink?"

"Sure. I was wondering why the little demon wasn't in here yapping at me."

"Oh, Kiko is an angel." She pulls out the pitcher and

places it on the counter, then reaches for some glasses. "So, what's been going on with you? Mom told me you went up to the lake house recently."

"Oh yeah. I went up with London and some other friends."

"Mom mentioned Cillian. How's he doing?"

She hands me a glass, and I take a sip before answering. This is my mom we're talking about here. She can read me like a book. "Oh, he's fine. Just broke up with his girlfriend recently. Been struggling with his paintings, so I told him he could go up there and get away for a bit. Maybe it'll help him."

"Well, that's nice," she says, taking a drink. "He's such a good boy."

I laugh. "Hardly a boy, Mom."

"Well, I know, but you're still my baby girl even though you're making your way to thirty."

I raise a hand. "Let's calm down. I'm only twenty-seven. I have a few years before thirty arrives."

Mom laughs, the lines around her eyes becoming more prominent. She looks damn good for fifty. Not that fifty is old, but I can only hope I age like her. Though, I guess that means I should start walking every day like she does. And drink more water. Maybe even eat better.

"So, he's single now?"

It takes me a second to realize she's talking about Cill. "Oh. Yeah."

"Hmm."

"Why? You thinkin' about cheating on Dad?" I joke.

"No, just wondering if you're finally gonna make a move."

"What?" I nearly choke on my lemonade.

"Oh, please, Midge. Don't play dumb with me." She grins. "You've liked that boy since you were a teenager."

"Mom, I liked him when I was a teenager. Not since I was a teenager. But I also liked Brian who lived at the end of the street back then, too."

I wonder if she believes the lie I just told.

"Mm. But you spent the weekend with him at the lake house?"

"Not just him."

"That lake house has magic in it. It's where I fell in love with your father."

I smile at her. I can't wait to show her the painting. She's going to cry, for sure. Even if she is at a putt-putt golf course or bowling alley.

"I know, but I'm not in love with anybody."

"Yet." I tilt my head at her, pursing my lips. "Okay, Okay," she says. "How was it out there? Still beautiful? I need to make some time to go back."

And it's then that I come up with the best idea. Her party should be at the lake house. Now I need to talk to dad and my grandparents. Her birthday isn't for another month and a half, so hopefully we can make it work.

I give her the rundown on our weekend at the lake, minus a few details about sex with Cillian and body shots.

He's due back the day after tomorrow, and I really hope he was being serious about coming to see me, because I have been thinking about it non-stop.

I know I said we should just leave things at the lake to preserve our friendship, but I'm addicted. I wasn't supposed to text him the other day either, but I couldn't control myself.

Cillian Kingston is changing me.

CILLIAN

IT'S ALMOST NOON WHEN I LEAVE THE LAKE HOUSE, WHICH puts me right back in Gaspar around three thirty. My first stop is my house where I drop everything off, including the painting-in-progress.

My second stop is Midge's house. Besides the time I dropped her off after she told me about Zoe, I've only been by a few times. All I remember about her house is that it looks like a little cottage that might be shown in a Disney movie. It's set far away from the road and surrounded by trees.

The last time I was there was almost two years ago, dropping her off after she'd had too much to drink at Royce's bar, and I made a comment about her little cottage. She said she was Snow White, then stumbled into the house and closed the door.

I texted her before I left the lake house and made sure she knew to expect me. I've been thinking about this moment for days now, and wasn't about to show up just for her not to be here.

I rap on the door three times, then I hear her footsteps

approach. She doesn't open the door right away, which makes me wonder what's going on, on the other side. Maybe she's nervous. Maybe she's having second thoughts.

But then the door opens and I'm greeted by her smiling face.

"Hey, Snow White."

She furrows her brow, cocking her head to the side. "What?" She laughs, stepping back to let me in.

"You don't remember?" I take a few steps in and turn around. "A couple years back when I brought you home, you drunkenly said you were Snow White after I said your house looked like a Disney cottage."

She closes the door, laughing. "I don't remember that. Want a drink or something? I have Sprite and grape juice. Or water, of course."

"I'm good. Thanks."

She stands in the small entryway, between the living room and kitchen, seemingly unsure of what to do. In two strides, I'm toe to toe with her. I let my eyes roam over her face before they travel down past the delicate curve of her jaw.

She's wearing a simple black top covered with floral print, and a loose, black skirt that stops several inches above her knees. I reach out and touch the side of her thigh, then let my hand move up, cupping her bare ass cheek.

"No underwear?" I question, bringing my other hand under her skirt and pulling her into me.

"Figured I'd make things a little easier," she replies angling her head up to look me in the eye.

I lean down and cover her mouth with mine. My tongue swipes across her lips before dipping inside when she releases a breathy moan. Midge reaches around and splays her fingers across my back, coming up on her tiptoes to deepen the kiss.

She kisses me with passionate desperation. She's been

thinking about this just as long as I have. The faint taste of peppermint lingers on her tongue as I suck it into my mouth.

Our hands explore each other's bodies as the need for more grows. She slips her hands under the hem of my shirt, touching every inch of skin she can get her hands on. The desire to touch and kiss more of her, to connect our bodies and turn her into a quivering mess of satiated bliss makes me pull away.

"Where do you wanna go?"

"Room," she breathes, her fingertips touching her swollen lips.

I follow her down the hall and into the bedroom at the end of it. Once inside, I make quick work of removing my shoes, jeans, and T-shirt. Midge sits on the edge of the bed and watches like I'm a stripper about to give her a lap dance.

"Are you planning on staying dressed?" I ask, taking a step toward the bed.

She grins. "Maybe."

"Maybe, huh? I don't think so."

I pull the bottom of her shirt up and over her head, revealing a black, lace bra. "This is nice," I say, running a finger over the swell of her breast and then down to the nipple threatening to break free. I gently squeeze the tip between my fingers, and she lets her head drop back with a moan.

My fingers dance softly down her stomach before sliding under her skirt. I palm her pussy, letting my middle finger slide up and down, opening her up for me.

She gasps, letting herself fall to her back. With one knee on the bed, I lean over her and watch her face contort with pleasure as my finger dips inside her pussy.

I penetrate her with my finger for only a minute or so, and

then I yank the skirt down her legs and toss it aside. She parts her thighs, ready for me.

I get off the bed to retrieve the condom from my pants, but as I'm about to get back on the bed, she stops me.

"Wait. Before you put that on, I want to…"

Midge blushes, her eyes flickering down to my cock.

I push the navy blue material down over my thighs and step to the side of the bed. She scrambles across then sits in front of me, taking my shaft in her hand.

She begins slowly, her fist loose around me, and her thumb grazing the underside of my cockhead. I watch as she comes forward, opening her mouth and then closing her lips around the tip.

Her tongue does a sensual dance around the crown while her hand continues to slowly stroke me. She finds the piercing and plays with it, her tongue pushing against the metal. My cock throbs in her hand.

Her pace begins to pick up speed as she strokes me more confidently, and takes more of me into her mouth. She moans and grinds herself on the mattress. Desire spreads through me. She seems to be getting as much out of this as I am.

I reach down between her thighs and find her pussy absolutely soaked.

"Fuck, Midge," I groan.

"Mmm."

I place my hand on her head and gently guide her off. "I have to get inside you."

She wipes her lips and lies back across the bed. I cover my cock with the latex, then kneel down between her legs and press the head into her dripping wet pussy. I don't push all the way in. I continue to watch her stretch around the head of my cock, then I pull out, and repeat.

I lean over her, letting my cock torture her with pleasure

as I only allow a couple inches to go in before I'm pulling back.

"Cillian, please," she begs, reaching around and grabbing my hips, hoping to guide me further in.

"But I love watching you this way," I say, taking my time and kissing her lips, cheek, neck, and chest.

I push in again, just slightly, and pull back.

"I need to feel you. Please."

"Mm," I groan. "Already begging. I fucking love it."

She arches her back, thrusting her hips up and trying to force me inside. "I want it," she pants. "Fuck, I want it so bad."

"I knew you loved the way I fuck you."

"I do. I love it so much. Please," she pleads. I plunge in hard and fast, and she gasps. "Yes!"

"That's my girl."

24

MIDGE

HARD, PUNISHING THRUSTS OVER AND OVER AGAIN. THAT'S what I get. Cillian fucks me like he's in my head reading my every dirty desire. He smacks my ass and squeezes my thighs as he sinks into me.

He plays with my clit while he slowly moves in and out of my throbbing, hot center. He loves hearing me beg, and I find I'm doing that a lot. I need more. I need it all.

"Please, please," I cry. "Please don't stop."

He grunts, pushing my legs back to where they damn near touch my head. He's so fucking deep, and I tell him just that.

"You like it deep?" he asks, though he doesn't have to. I'm calling out his name and God's name in five second intervals.

"I love it, God, I fucking love it."

He drops one of my legs, but I hold it up myself, because this position is too fucking good. He's hitting all the right spots, but with that cock he's wielding, it would be hard not to.

His hand comes down and slaps my pussy, his fingers hitting my engorged clit.

"Oh, my God!" I yell.

I've never had that done to me before, but holy shit, I love it.

"Yeah?" he murmurs, and does it again.

"Ahh!" I squeal. "Yes."

He pulls out, leaving me empty and aching. "Come ride me."

Cillian lays down, and I quickly climb on top of him. I grab the base of his cock and slowly slide down the shaft.

Jesus Christ, it's like it's in my stomach. I take my time at first, leisurely moving up and down, before I place my palms on his chest and start moving my hips back and forth in a quick cadence.

Cillian switches between grabbing my tits and grabbing my ass. I like both just fine, but I really like when he reaches up and grabs my throat and says filthy things.

Yeah, ride that cock, baby girl.

I love being deep in that pussy.

You're so fucking sexy. You have my dick so hard.

I grind myself on him, harder and faster, desperately chasing an orgasm that I know is going turn me to jelly.

My arms and legs are already weak. We've tried out damn near every position, and he's got every single one mastered.

"God, you feel so good," I moan into his neck, my sweat-slicked body gliding over his.

My hips move faster, and my clit finds friction against him as his cock fills me up.

"Fuck yes. Fuck me," he says through breathless grunts. "Come all over my cock, baby girl. Let me feel it."

His words send me over the edge. "Oh fuck," I cry, my hands grabbing fistfuls of the covers underneath him. My whole body tightens up and my pussy throbs around his cock as I'm sky-rocketed into euphoric bliss.

After I've come down from the orgasmic mountain top, he grabs ahold of my waist and thrusts his hips upwards. I have a full-body spasm as he pummels into me. A few minutes later, he squeezes his eyes close and lets out a guttural roar.

I find some energy and move up and down on his cock, clenching my pussy around him. He groans and his dick twitches inside me as he empties his load.

"Fuckin' hell," he breathes.

I delicately climb off of him and drop onto the covers, sweaty and out of breath. My skin is flushed, my hair is sticking to my face and the back of my neck, and I'm sure my makeup is a mess, but I'm almost positive I don't have the energy to stand up. I'd probably crumble onto the floor if I attempted to walk to the bathroom.

"Yeah. I can't walk. I can barely move," I say between breaths.

He chuckles. "The use of your legs will come back soon. Don't worry."

I attempt to roll my eyes, but I'm not sure I have enough energy for even that. "Oh Lord, I've been paralyzed by dick. That's actually a thing."

Cill laughs some more. "You're crazy."

"Whatever, man. You're operating a weapon over there."

"Well, I'll give us some time to rest, but this weapon will be reloaded and ready to fire soon. Just so you know."

I throw my head back and laugh. "You're so stupid."

"Whatever, but I got you to admit you love the way I fuck you, didn't I?"

"That's not fair. That's like a form of torture. I'd admit to a crime I didn't commit if I knew I was gonna get an orgasm afterwards."

154

"Pft. Not just any orgasm, though. A Cillian Kingston orgasm."

I sit up and reach for my skirt on the floor. "You know what…" I laugh and glance over my shoulder at him. "Fine, you're right. I love it. I love everything you do to me in the bed. But you love it too. You love the way I react to you. So, there."

I stand up and pull the skirt over my hips, then find my shirt on the other side of the bed.

"I can agree to that," Cillian replies, sitting up on the edge of the bed. "It's too bad you're opposed to relationships, because I think we just might be perfect for each other," he finishes with a chuckle.

I pause, completely frozen in place. I look toward the bed and find Cillian reaching down for his clothes. The comment was just tossed out there. He probably didn't even think about it, so it's likely not a big deal.

He stands up, clothes draped over his arm, and tied up condom in hand, and walks toward me. "Bathroom?"

I point to the partially open door in the right corner of the room. He grins and plants a quick kiss on my lips before sauntering to the bathroom.

25

CILLIAN

IN THE BATHROOM, I THINK ABOUT WHAT I SAID. *I THINK WE just might be perfect for each other.*

We're friends, and we laugh together, and tease each other. We have amazing chemistry in the bedroom, and we pretty much know everything about the other person's past, so there's no big secrets. So, is it true? Yes.

The only problem is that she's completely against relationships. She's been hurt, I think that's clear. She probably has trust issues, which is understandable.

Having Zoe cheat on me definitely sucked. I was hurt, but not heartbroken, maybe because I wasn't all-in with her. But the fact that she cheated hurts, nonetheless. Why not breakup first? Why not discuss your problems before sleeping with somebody else, like that'll help anything.

Midge may not have realized that I noticed how she tensed up. I saw in her body language that what I said got to her. Hopefully she doesn't want to end things now. The last thing I want to do is scare her off. I need more time. So, I'll watch my tongue from now on and not say anything that she could misconstrue into thinking I want to throw a ring on her finger and lock her down.

"All yours," I say with an easy smile as I exit the bathroom.

I wander around the room and check out some pictures she has on her dresser. One of her and London at King's Tavern. One of her and her parents at some sort of party. And one of her grandparents sitting together on the patio of the lake house.

Midge clearly considers London family. They've only known each other for five years or so, but when you're around them, you'd think they'd grown up together.

I head for a narrow table pushed up against the window and find that she's created a shadow box of sorts out of the table top. Underneath the glass lies dozens of pictures, each cut out in different shapes and put together like an intricate puzzle.

She has pictures ranging from her childhood when she was probably three or four, all through her school years, and important moments in her life. I find her graduation picture, and several birthday pictures. Not just hers, but her family's as well. There's prom pictures, and pool pictures, and pictures of a white and black dog.

I bend down, getting a better look, and find several with me and Royce in them. We're together in the pool with a couple other friends, and Midge has clearly gotten out to snap a photo. I was probably fourteen at the time.

One of me and Midge together makes me laugh. We were in the gym of our high school, and there's people in the background playing basketball. Midge is making a face at the camera, her tongue out and eyes crossed, and I'm standing behind her with my eyes rolled up, and my head dropped back, like I'm completely miserable. I don't even remember what was going on.

As my eyes roam over all the pictures, remembering so much of our childhood through her photos, I find one that makes me come to a stop.

It's me. I'm all by myself in the picture, because it's my senior photo. However, the fact that it's cut into a heart shape interests me. I'm sure it wasn't cut into that shape recently, probably back when we were eighteen, but still.

I scan the collage for more, and the last one I see before Midge steps out of the bathroom is another one of us.

We're not alone in the picture. Royce is in the back with our friend Justin, and two girls are off to the other side. Whoever took this photo took it without telling us, because none of us are looking at the camera. Me and Justin are shirtless, and one of the girls has a bikini top on with cut-off shorts. Maybe we were going to the pool, maybe we were fucking around near Meadow Acres, a small lake in the middle of town. There's not enough in the photo to identify where we were, but all my eyes can focus on is Midge. We're facing each other, but my head is angled over my shoulder, probably talking to Royce. However, her eyes are trained on me. She's gazing up at me with an adoring smile on her lips, like I'm the center of her whole world.

"I'm starving," she says as soon as she enters the room. Her eyes dart between me and the table. She looks nervous for a brief second before she covers it up with a smile. "I'm a nerd, I know. Keeping old photos like that."

I shake my head. "No, I think it's great. I don't have many pictures from when I was younger. It's nice to have these to look back on. Sparks up memories. I forgot how much we did together."

"Yeah, we were always out running the streets like

heathens," she says with a laugh. "Either at the park or going to the playground at our old elementary school. Oh, do you remember going to the skating rink?"

I laugh. "I remember falling at the skating rink, then choosing to spend time in the arcade instead."

"Yeah, you sucked pretty bad."

"Anyway," I start, but the doorbell cuts me off. "Expecting anybody?"

"No," she replies, heading down the hall.

"Well, maybe it's—"

"Shh!" she whispers, her finger flying to her lips as her eyes double in size. "It's London."

"My car is parked out front. She already knows I'm here," I say as quietly as possible.

"Then what's our excuse? Why are you here?"

"Don't worry about that, just open the door, because the longer she waits, the more suspicious it seems."

"Shit! You're right."

She opens the door as I pull my phone out and lean against the back of the couch.

"Hey," Midge greets, a little shrill to be normal. "What's up?"

London looks past her and right at me.

"Hey, Lo," I say.

"Hey, you guys," she responds, smiling and walking past Midge. "Whatcha up to?"

"Oh," Midge looks back at me. "Cillian came by to uh…"

I walk forward and show London my phone. "I wanted to show her these photos."

She takes the phone from my hand. "Oh wow, these look great, Cill."

I don't normally show people my paintings before they're

done, but it was the first excuse that came to mind, and Midge is not very good at playing it cool.

Midge looks at me, confused, but I just wink at her. "Yeah, I'll be workin' on finishing them up in the next few weeks. When's your mom's birthday again?" I ask Midge.

"September fifth."

"Oh, okay. I'll definitely be done in time."

London hands the phone back to me. "Beautiful. Well," she faces Midge. "I was just coming by to drop these off." She hands her two plastic bags. "I'll be heading over to Elijah's in a little, so I figured I'd bring them now."

Midge takes the bags. "Oh, great. Thanks." She lifts them up and looks at me. "Wallets and shoes she was gonna throw out."

"Ah." I lift my head, trying not to smile at how cute she is when she's nervous.

London glances down at her watch. "I gotta swing by Flaky Vicki's to get some dessert. Cill, you comin' tonight? Have any requests?"

"I'll be there, and I'm happy with anything. But some sort of cake would be good."

London laughs. "All right. Cake it is. See ya later." She passes a look to Midge. One of those ones women give to each other to get a message across without saying a single word.

"Bye, Midge. I'll be texting you later."

"Okay, yeah. Bye."

After she closes the door, she leans against it and closes her eyes.

"You're terrible under pressure," I say with a laugh.

"That's because I'm not used to being a liar and having secrets."

"We can tell them."

"No. We can't do that."

I pocket my phone and shrug. "Well, then I guess you're gonna have to become a better liar."

"Ugh. I'm too hungry to think about this."

"Why don't you come to Elijah's with me tonight?"

She spins around, halfway to her kitchen. "What?"

"Dinner. Tonight. At Elijah's."

"Right, but like, go with you?"

I put my hands in my back pockets and smirk. "I'll try not to be offended by the way you asked that question, but no, you don't have to go with me. You can drive yourself there."

She shifts her weight. "Yeah, but that's a family dinner."

"London's not family."

"Yeah, but she's with Royce."

"Okay?"

"So, wouldn't that look like we were together?"

"I think you're overthinking this."

"Well, when London talked about it, she said she was the first one Royce invited over, and that's because he never dated anyone. She also said Elijah hasn't had anyone over since he and Jenn broke up, and I know Zoe used to go when y'all were together. So it seems like a relationship type thing."

"Merrick only invited his friends over, and we're friends, so it's not a big deal."

I watch her chew on her lip while she fidgets with her fingers. She's stressing out. Maybe this is one of those things I shouldn't have said, because now she's thinking this means we're a couple.

"Okay, don't worry about it. You don't have to come. You just said you were hungry, so I was offering a solution."

Her shoulders sag. "I'm sorry. I appreciate it, but I'll just eat here."

"Okay, well, I guess I'll take off then."

"Oh. Okay." She walks to the door. "Thanks for coming over."

I give her a smile, and almost lean in to kiss her, but at this point, maybe I should steer clear of that. She's already been spooked by my *perfect for each other* comment, and now I've invited her to dinner. I guess she's wanting things a little more simple.

Maybe I'm doing it wrong it's just that I've never had a fuck buddy that I've actually cared about.

26

MIDGE

It's nearly ten o'clock when my phone rings. When London's name pops up on the screen, I brace myself for what I know this conversation is going to be about.

"Hello?"

"Hey, whatcha doin'?"

"Nothin'. Just got out of the shower. How was dinner?"

I cringe, regretting the words as soon as they leave my mouth. I should've kept away from any topic involving the Kingston brothers.

"It was good. You should come sometime."

I drop onto the bed. "Yeah, but it's a family thing. And before you say it, I know you're not family, but you're dating Royce, so shush."

She laughs. "It's not like that's a rule. Elijah would love to have you. I don't know why you haven't taken up any of my invitations."

"Just feels weird, I guess."

"Whatever, weirdo. Anyway," she says, dragging the word out. "Cillian was at your place today."

"Yes, I know. I was here, too," I say with a laugh.

"To you show you pictures he had on his phone." She lets the statement hang between us, like she's expecting me to pick up on something.

"Yeah, pictures of his painting." It nearly sounds like a question, because I never saw them. Based on what they had to say, I assume that's what they were, but I'm just now realizing he didn't show them to me.

"Right, but he has your number, so he could've just texted them to you."

Shit. "Well, yeah. I don't know why he came over." God, I'm a terrible liar.

"Mmhmm." I can tell she's smiling. "Maybe he wanted to see you."

"You're crazy," I say with a laugh. "Cillian is not interested in me."

"I think you're the one who's crazy. If you're interested in that man, lock him down now, cause like I said, girls are gonna be lining up for him like it's goddamn Black Friday."

"But you know how I feel about relationships," I say, knowing I'd probably be jealous and annoyed if he was with anybody else. "And we don't even know where he stands on them, considering what he just went through."

"Yeah, but Midge, are you really planning on being single for the rest of your life? Yes, a lot of men suck and don't know how to treat their women, but look at Cillian's case. Zoe was the one who cheated on him! Women suck, too. There will be a man out there who treats you like a queen, but you have to give them more than three dates to prove that."

I breathe down the line. "I know."

"All right, well I'll leave you alone about it for now. You know I love you. I'll see you tomorrow."

"I love you, too. See you later."

After we hang up, I climb under the covers and do a lot of thinking.

Since I broke it off with Matthew, I'm aware of the shift that happened. I used to believe in that fairytale type of love —the love my parents have. I loved to be loved, and I thought Matthew loved me. I loved him more than any other guy in my life. I gave him all of me. Everything I did was for him. And that was wrong. I put him before me. His happiness was more important than my own, but I didn't see it then. Looking back, I know that wasn't real love, but my whole heart was in it and it got destroyed in the demise.

So, I've been enjoying these past few years of being free. Of putting myself first and not having to worry about anybody else. You know the saying, *you have to learn to love yourself before you can love someone else*, well, I've learned to love myself these past few years, so maybe I'm ready. But it's still scary.

It's scary to hand your heart to someone with only the mere hope that they'll take care of it. Knowing it's up to them to protect it and not rip it open with deceit, and that there's nothing you can do about it is absolutely terrifying.

Now the question is, should I really try to have a relationship with Cillian? Is he the best person or the worst person to start something with?

Pros:
He's my friend
He's easy to be around.
He makes me laugh.
I like him.
Great cock.
Smart.

Kind.

Talented.

Cons:

I'm a rebound.

Breaking up would make things awkward for more than
just us.

It could end our friendship completely.

I can't really think of any more cons. Yeah, sure, we won't
have that new couple sensation since we already know each
other, but isn't that better? To not feel shy and uncomfortable? To be able to be yourself completely right from the
beginning? And since we've already been intimate, we won't
have those awkward first kiss and first fuck moments. Luckily, those were both great.

We can still have a first date. There's still a lot of firsts to
have, and that's exciting. The first time we spend a holiday
together. The first time we take a trip together, alone. The
first time we spend the night with each other.

But before I get ahead of myself...is Cillian interested in a
relationship with me? I'm aware of the comment he made
earlier. *We just might be perfect for each other.* But then he
smiled and walked away like it was no big deal. He's so
casual and laid back about everything, I'm sure it was just a
joke. Plus, I'm the first woman he's been with since he got
out of a pretty serious relationship. Is he interested in playing
the field before settling down again?

I mean, I probably made him re-think this whole thing

since I made a huge deal about dinner. And he didn't even kiss me goodbye when he left, so maybe he was upset.

I huff and angrily flop onto my stomach and try to push all the thoughts out of my brain. Maybe I'll just play this by ear. I'm not even sure when I'll see Cill again, but I hope it's soon. And that in itself is new, because I've never been so desperate to be around someone like I am when it comes to him. We were together just hours ago, and yet I'm dying to be around him again.

CILLIAN

I LET TWO DAYS GO BY WITHOUT CONTACTING MIDGE. IT'S now Wednesday night, and since I know her and London are at my brother's bar, I'm trying to decide on whether I should show up or not. It's not like it would be weird. It's my brother's bar. I could be going to visit him. I'm not, but it's not like anybody would know that.

If I play it right, I can pretend I didn't even know Midge would be there. Okay, maybe not. They've been doing this Wednesday bar thing for over a year now. Everybody in that place knows to expect them there on Wednesdays and Saturdays.

I try to re-focus on my painting, dipping my brush into the paint and working on the details of the water. I wondered if my creativity and motivation would fade away once I got back into town, but I've been just as dedicated.

By the time my phone dings with a text alert, I've moved on from the details in the water, and finished the maple trees. I check the phone and find a message from Elijah.

Elijah: *Heading to the Tavern. Want to come?*

Yes! Now I have an excuse besides just wanting to see Midge.

Cillian: *Yeah, sure. Meet you there?*
Elijah: *I'll be there in fifteen.*

It only takes about ten minutes to wash my brushes and palette, then put it all away. Before I shut the lights off in my studio, I take a quick glance around. Midge was right, this place needed a little sprucing up. I've hung a few of my pieces that I'm most proud of. It gives the room a little life. It definitely needs more work, but it's good for now.

The bar is nearly five blocks away, so it doesn't take long for me to get there on my bike. I pull up just a couple minutes before Elijah.

"Hey, man. Were you painting?" Elijah asks, coming around the back of his Audi, twirling the keychain around his finger.

"Yeah, but I had been there since six, so I got plenty done," I say, checking my watch. It's nine-thirty now, so I got a good three and a half hours in.

"That's good."

We walk around the corner and head for the front door. "Yeah, what've you been up to?"

"Not a whole lot, just enjoying the summer break," he replies, opening the door.

When we approach the bar, Royce spots us and gives us a nod, letting us know he'll get our drinks ready.

Five minutes later, Royce walks to the end of the bar and places our drinks on the counter. A pint of Bud Light for me, and a Scotch for Elijah.

"Thanks, man," I say, handing him a ten. "Can you stash this for me?" I hand him my helmet and leather jacket.

"Sure." He takes them and stores them on a shelf under the bar. "Need anything else?"

"We're good," Elijah says.

"Cool. I'll check on you guys later."

Royce travels back down to the other side, leaving us sitting on the end of the bar with a view of the whole place. I scan the crowd, looking for a sign of either Midge or London, but I don't see them at their usual seats along the bar.

"So, I saw Zoe the other day," Elijah says, grabbing my attention.

"What? When?"

"It was while you were at the lake. I ran into her at the golf course."

"The golf course?" I question, making a face. "What the fuck was she doing there?"

"Well, she wasn't alone."

I shake my head. "I see. So the new guy is into golf. Pft."

"I was there, too, you know?"

"Yeah, well, you should really get some new hobbies. You're such an old man."

"I have plenty of hobbies, thanks."

"Anyway, did she say anything to you?"

"She appeared to be nervous at first. I'm sure she knows we all know what happened. She gave me a little smile and wave, but then the guy came up behind her, so she walked the other way."

"And what was he like?"

Elijah shrugs. "The complete opposite of you."

"Whatever. I hope they're happy together."

He turns in his chair. "Really?"

"I don't give a shit, honestly. Haven't really given her a second thought since this all went down. You know how we were."

He nods. "I figured the end was coming soon. Too many break-ups happening in short periods. That can't be good."

"Nah, it wasn't. I was constantly stressed out."

I hear Midge's unmistakable high-pitched cackle, and it draws my head up and my eyes find her immediately. She's back at the bar, only about twelve feet away from me, and she's laughing at something a guy standing next to her must've said. One hand's on the bar, and the other hand touches his arm as she folds over in laughter.

My jaw clenches at the sight.

"Typical Margaret, right?" Elijah says. He's the only one of us that calls her by her given name.

"What do you mean?"

"Life of the party. Loud, happy, grabs everybody's attention."

Well at least it's not just me. "Yeah."

Midge spins around, looking for London, but she finds me instead. She stops laughing, her eyes focused on mine, but gradually, a smile appears on her lips, and she waves at both me and Elijah. We lift our hands in response.

The man standing behind her places his hand on her shoulder, stealing her attention. They have a brief conversation before the man hooks his thumb behind him, followed by Midge nodding. Then he walks in the direction of the bathrooms.

"You okay?" Elijah asks.

"Huh? What?" I peel my eyes away from Midge and look at Elijah.

"You look pretty tense, and if that glass could bruise, it would be, based on how hard you're squeezing it."

I glance down and notice my grip is tighter than usual. "Oh. I'm fine." I let go of the glass and look up just in time to see Midge taking the same path the guy did.

My leg starts bouncing, and I try to keep myself seated and not hauling ass down the hall and toward the bathrooms. It's not my business what she does. Right? I mean, we're fucking, but that's all it is. I guess we're both technically free to do whatever we want. Doesn't mean I like it. Not one fucking bit.

"Are you sure you're okay?" Elijah angles his head over his shoulder, watching me drum my fingers on the bar as my leg continues to bounce.

"Yeah, I just need to piss. I'll be right back."

Once out of my seat, I'm bounding across the room, both wanting to get there before they can do anything, and terrified I'll walk in on them already in an embrace.

I hear someone call my name, but I don't stop to acknowledge it or even try to determine who it was.

I shove open the men's bathroom door and quickly scope out the small room. One of the three stalls is closed, but I don't hear any noise coming from it. Other than that, it's empty.

Back into the darkened hallway, I glance in both directions but don't see either one of them. Maybe they went into the women's bathroom, but I'm not about to go in there to check.

Disappointed, yet somewhat relieved, I start to make my way back to Elijah. Before I can fully leave the hallway, a woman approaches me with a smile.

"Hey, Cillian." Her smile is wide as she pushes her shoulders back and walks with an exaggerated sway to her hips.

"Hey," I respond politely, giving her a quick grin.

"I called out to you earlier, but I guess you didn't hear," she says with a giggle, pulling her red hair over her right shoulder.

As I actually take the time to look at her, and not scan the room for Midge, I realize I went to school with her.

"Jenny, right?"

"You remember. Yeah," she replies with a smile that shows all her teeth.

"Sure. How ya been?"

I remember we dated back when I was fourteen, if you can call it dating at that age. We spent most of our time too shy to speak to each other, and held hands a few times, and maybe kissed twice. I think it lasted a few months.

"I've been good. I spent a year traveling overseas, but I've been back in town for six months now."

"Sounds nice," I say, looking over her head and scanning the bar for Midge.

"Oh, it was so nice! So, how have you been?" She tilts her head to the side, batting her lashes at me.

"Can't complain," I respond with a grin, trying to figure out how to get out of this conversation. I can tell she'll have me here forever if I let her.

"That's good. I had heard, well, I don't want to bring up bad memories, but is it true you and your girlfriend broke up?"

"Yeah." I shrug. "It happens." I take a step to the side, about to excuse myself.

Jenny steps in front of me, placing her hand on my arm. "Oh, well, I was just wondering if you wanted to grab some coffee sometime or something."

"Oh." I'm completely caught off guard by the invitation and unsure how to respond.

Sure, Jenny's cute. She's a natural redhead with freckles sprinkled across her nose and cheeks. She's tall and slender with bright blue eyes, but I'm not really interested.

Before I can say anything else, someone brushes up

against my arm, so I step back to my left and look over my shoulder. It's Midge. She's come up from behind me, so she must've been in the bathroom after all.

She looks at Jenny with venom in her eyes.

"Oh, hey, Midge," Jenny says. Though her tone doesn't sound one hundred percent pleasant. There's an edge in it, almost taunting.

Midge delivers a hate-filled look that should send chills down Jenny's spine, but Jenny only smirks in response. After a few uncomfortable seconds, Midge walks away.

Jenny scoffs, rolling her eyes. "She's such a bitch."

"Midge is a friend of mine, and one of the nicest people I've met." I step around her. "I'll talk to you later."

I rush off, wanting to talk to Midge before she gets back to London, so I take several long strides and grab her arm. She swings around with a look to kill. When she realizes it's me, her face softens a little, but not completely.

"Oh. Done with Jenny?"

"She was just trying to catch up. I guess she's been overseas for a while."

"I don't really give a shit to be honest with you."

"Are you mad that I was talking to her?"

"I heard her ask you out. You going?"

Midge's face stays pinched with anger, but she can barely look at me.

"I wasn't planning on it, no." She doesn't say anything, she just continues to look anywhere but at me. "Hey." I grab her hand and she stiffens slightly. There's several people around us, so I'm sure nobody we know can see, but I let go anyway. "I was looking for you."

She makes a noise in the back of her throat. "Oh yeah?"

"I was, yeah. I saw you walk toward the bathroom with...well, I saw you walk away, so I came to look for you."

Midge finally meets my gaze. "Saw me with who?"

I shake my head. "I don't know. I was just looking for you."

She grins. "You talkin' about the short guy with glasses?"

I shrug. "I don't know what you're talking about."

"That would be Stephen, and he would be one of Jon's friends. One of Jon's very gay friends who is in no way interested in me or anything I have going on."

I try not to breathe an audible sigh of relief, but damn, I'm happy to hear what she just said.

"Cool," I say with another shrug.

She laughs. "Jealous much, Mr. Kingston?"

I twist my mouth up at her. "No, but what about you and Jenny? Looked like you wanted to rip her eyes out."

Her face changes again. "That has nothing to do with you, and everything to do with her."

"Why's that?"

"I don't want to talk about it. Not right now." She glances around, finding her friends at the bar. "I should get back."

"Yeah. Me too," I reply, looking in Elijah's direction.

"I'll be leaving soon. Should I text you when I get home?"

I smile. "Yeah, do that."

"Okay."

She pivots and heads back to London. I just now notice that Jon and Daniel are there, too. And Jon's friend.

When I get back to my stool, Elijah waits for me to sit down and take a drink before saying anything.

"So, how long have you two been messing around?"

"What?" I laugh nervously. "What're you talkin' about? Me and who?" Elijah just keeps looking at me. "Who? Midge?" I laugh some more.

"Are you done trying to bullshit me now?"

I sigh, then take a swig of my beer. I guess it doesn't matter too much if Elijah knows. He doesn't really hang out with us all the time. He'd be unaffected if things ended badly. I know Midge is mostly concerned about Royce and London.

"Since the lake."

"So, not long."

"Nah."

"And nobody knows?"

"You're the first."

"And you're trying to keep this a secret? Why?"

"Well, we're not really together. We're just fucking around. Midge doesn't want it to be weird for everybody else once things die off between us."

"Who says it'll die off?"

"She does. She's sworn off relationships, so I imagine she'll try to push me away soon enough."

He finally shifts in his seat and studies me. "Why do you and Royce play these games?"

My back straightens. "What? What're you talking about? What games?"

Elijah looks at me like I'm stupid. "You know the risk Royce took going after London, but luckily it worked out for them. But now you're getting involved with this woman who's openly against relationships. Now, don't get me wrong, I like Margaret, but you're risking a lot getting involved with her in this way. You could very well fall for her, then she'll be ready to end it because it's getting too deep. Where does that leave you?"

"We're just having fun. Why are you being a downer?"

"I'm not a downer, I'm a realist, and I'm only trying to look out for you."

I release a long breath. "I appreciate it, but you don't have to worry about me."

He takes a sip of drink. "You think I don't remember the first few years after Mom and Dad died? I know you struggled. I remember you struggling to draw or paint anything. You flat out refused to try for a while. And I also remember how you slowly came back to life once you started spending more time with her." He points his glass in Midge's direction. "You started drawing again, and laughing again."

"Where are you going with this?" I ask, frustrated. I don't like to talk about my parents' death for long, or the aftermath.

"You say it's just fun and that there won't be any feelings, but that girl means something to you. She was the bright spot in your darkest days, and she was able to reach you when none of us could. Don't pretend you don't already have feelings. That's all I'm saying."

MIDGE

ON WEDNESDAYS, I TRY TO LEAVE THE BAR BY TEN, BUT CILL came in at nine-thirty and after the run-in with him and Jenny, then our conversation in the middle of the room, and the fact that London's spotted him at the end of the bar and waved both he and Elijah over, it looks like it might be a little past ten by the time I leave.

"Elijah, I can't stop thinking about Sunday's dinner. It was so good," London says.

Elijah chuckles. "I'm glad you liked it."

"What was it?" I ask.

"If you would've joined us, you would know," London teases.

"I asked her to come," Cill chimes in.

I roll my eyes as London turns to face me. "Oh really? I thought she was just ignoring my invites."

Elijah glances at Cill then back at me. "You can join us any time, Margaret. We'd love to have you."

I smile. "Thanks. I'll think about it."

I glance at Cillian who mouths *"told you."*

"Anyway, it was just bacon-wrapped pork tenderloins,"

Elijah says.

"Amazing pork tenderloins," London adds. "And these delicious mashed potatoes and grilled veggies. Mmm."

"All right, you're making me hungry." I check the time on my phone. "I'm gonna head out. See you tomorrow," I aim at London.

"Yep. I'll be leaving soon," she replies.

"Bye everyone," I say with a wave, my eyes lingering on Cill for a couple seconds longer.

A chorus of bye's come from the group as I make my way out of the bar.

"Midge, wait up. I have a question about this painting."

I spin around, my hand still on the door as I step outside. "What's up?"

"Yeah, I just wanted to ask about the clearing," he says, stepping all the way outside.

"What about it?" I ask, letting the door close behind me.

"Nothing."

He steps forward, wrapping his arm around my waist and pulls me into him. His mouth covers mine as his other hand comes up and cradles the back of my head. I moan into his mouth as his tongue darts across mine.

The kiss is quick but full of passion, and I gently bite his bottom lip as I pull away.

"Just needed to do that," he says, wiping his lips. "Did you leave lipstick behind?"

I smile and reach up to wipe away the little bit of maroon color that transferred over. "You're good now."

"Thanks. Text me later. I gotta tell you something."

"Is it bad?"

He shrugs. "I don't think so, but I don't know how you'll feel."

"Just tell me now. It's gonna fucking kill me to wait until later."

"I was only coming out here to ask you about the clearing. Do you want people to become suspicious?" He arches a brow, his lips lifting up on one side.

"Ugh. No, but just text me as soon as you get back in."

"Maybe." He opens the door.

"I hate you."

"We've established that you don't. Or do I need to remind you again?"

I grin, hoping he can't the flush in my cheeks isn't visible. "Maybe."

He chuckles. "See ya later."

"Yeah, bye."

I end up waiting in my car for five minutes, hoping to get a text, but when that doesn't happen, I give up and start my drive home.

Two thoughts fill my brain. The first is what the hell Cill has to tell me. Don't people know to never say things like *we need to talk* or *I have to tell you something* unless they're fully prepared to spill the beans right then and there? It only drives the other person insane.

The second thought is one I've been thinking about for a while. Me trying to get over my fear of relationships and wondering if the right person is Cill. I mean, two days went by without us talking, so I figured I had made him mad. Then again, that's usually the case for fuck buddies. You don't talk every day. And I've never slept with someone more than five times. Me and Cill have had sex four times.

However, I can't imagine the next time being the last time, and I actually want to talk to him every day. But we're friends, so that makes sense, but it also blurs the relationship and fuck buddies line.

I'm still not one hundred percent sure that he's interested in having a relationship with me or totally on board for the friends with benefits thing we have going on. I mean, he was talking to Jenny O'Shea earlier, and I know plenty of guys are interested in her, so why wouldn't Cill be?

I've gotten all the way home, reheated and ate last night's spaghetti, and taken a shower all without getting a text from Cillian. It's not until I'm climbing into bed that my phone rings.

"I've been waiting for you for hours!"

"Mm. You know I love it when you're needy for me."

I can't help the smile that stretches across my lips. "Ugh. Whatever."

"Sorry, I got caught up talking to Elijah. What're you doing?"

"Getting into bed."

"Oh, what're you wearing?"

"Oh, stop," I say with a laugh.

"I'm going to assume nothing but a thong. It'll help me sleep better."

I cackle again. "Whatever floats your boat, but it's nothing sexy at all."

"Come on, you can make anything sexy."

My heart thumps hard in my chest as I find myself at a loss for words. "Uh. Probably not anything," is what eventually comes out.

He chuckles lowly on the other end of the phone. "What are you doing? At home or at the studio?"

"Home. I was at the studio earlier, but I'll probably go back tomorrow before my shift at the shop."

"Everything's coming along okay? No more creative struggles?"

"Nah, no struggles. I think that was related to my struggling relationship. Since that's ended and I went up to the lake, I've had no problems. I guess shit can really weigh you down in ways you don't expect."

"Makes sense. I'm glad things are back to normal."

"Yeah, I'm good." I can hear the smile in his tone.

"Good. So, what did you need to tell me?"

I hear him settling in on the other side, probably getting into bed as well. I try not to think too hard about his naked, tattooed body, and the hard muscles the ink covers.

"One sec. Taking off my clothes."

I internally groan. So much for not thinking about it. Cillian chuckles, so maybe I didn't groan internally after all.

"All right. Don't freak out."

"That's a sure fire way to make me freak out."

"Elijah knows about us."

My jaw drops. "What?"

"Yeah. He saw us at the bar and put it together."

"What? How? We were barely together."

"Elijah's very perceptive. He probably saw the way I was acting when I thought you were meeting up with Stephen in the bathroom and rushed off to go find you."

A small laugh erupts from my throat. "You're crazy."

"No, just...I don't know. Whatever. Yeah, so he watched us and I tried laughing it off, but he knew better. I just don't think we have to worry because it's not like we hang out with him regularly. I figured you were mostly concerned about Royce and London, since that's your best friend and all."

I sigh. "Yeah, I guess so. What did he say?"

"Oh, not much."

"You're lying."

Cill groans. "Older brother shit. Nothing crazy."

I let the vagueness slide. "Well, I definitely won't be going to Sunday dinners now," I say with a short laugh.

"E's not gonna make you feel uncomfortable. He likes you."

"I know he won't do anything, but I'll feel weird just knowing he knows we're sleeping together."

Cill sighs and I wonder if he's getting annoyed with me and my inability to be open about us.

"Hey, so I talked to my mom about you the other day."

"Oh?" His voice perks up.

"Yeah, my gramma told her we went to the lake, so she was asking about it. We talked about you for a little bit. She said you were a nice boy."

Cillian laughs. "If only she knew what this nice boy was doing to her daughter."

"Oh, shush. Anyway, you know she loves you."

"Well, I'm pretty lovable."

"Yeah, yeah. Anyway, I hope this isn't awkward, but she wanted me to invite you over for dinner one day."

"Oh yeah?"

I bite down on my nail. "Yeah. Is it weird?"

"No, I've had plenty of meals at your house."

"When we were teenagers."

"Still."

"Before we were fucking."

"Is it gonna be weird for you? Because I'll be fine. I love your mom, and your dad is cool as hell, too. I haven't seen them in a while, so it'll be nice to catch up."

I almost say it feels like a meeting-the-parents moment, but I don't want to be too annoying. The truth is, my parents have always liked Cillian. He came over quite a bit back in the day. This is just another one of those things I wouldn't have to worry about if he and I decided to get together.

"Yeah, no. It's fine."

"Okay, so when?"

"Mom just said to let her know when you're free."

"I usually work late on Fridays and Saturdays, and since I have dinner at Elijah's on Sunday, I'm only free tomorrow. Unless you want to wait until next week."

"I'll ask her tomorrow morning and let you know."

"Sounds good."

"All right, well, I guess I'll talk to you tomorrow."

"Okay. Goodnight."

"Night."

I curl up with a smile on my face.

CILLIAN

I WAKE UP TO A TEXT FROM MIDGE.

Midge: *Mom says tonight is fine. Six-thirty okay?*

I get off at six, so I'll be sure to take a change of clothes with me to the shop. I typically wear my jeans, black boots, and t-shirt to work, but I don't think I should wear that to dinner. After I get up, I type out a quick response.

Cillian: *Perfect. See you then.*

I toss the phone on the bed and then head to the bathroom to start getting ready. By the time I leave my house, it's a little past eight o'clock, which gives me almost two hours at the studio before I have to be at work.

I'm already really proud of this painting, and it's not even done yet. I still need to add a lot of detail to the house, because I want it to be perfect. The trees are completed, but I need to add some reflection detail in the water. The sky I'll tweak a bit, and I'll add shadows and highlights to certain things to make them more realistic.

Before I know it, it's already almost ten, so I quickly scrub off my brushes in the sink in the small bathroom in the back, then grab my keys and head out.

Just as I lock the door and turn around, I see Zoe walking toward me.

"Hey," she says quietly, a small, cautious grin on her face.

"Hey."

"I figured I'd find you here."

"Yep. What's up?"

She plays with the hem of her light blue sundress, and nibbles her bottom lip with her teeth. She's nervous about whatever she has to say. Luckily, as soon as I found out she was cheating on me, I went to the doctor and got tested for STDs, and everything came back clear. Otherwise, I'd be afraid she was about to tell me she had chlamydia or some shit.

"I'm pregnant, Cill."

My heart plummets straight to my feet. "What?"

She raises her hand. "It's not yours. It's Stacey's."

"Stacey's? What the fuck?"

She has the nerve to roll her eyes. "Stacey's a man."

"Clearly. Nice to know how much of a liar you are. How are you so sure it's his and not mine?"

She plants her hand on her hip and cocks her head. "Really, Cill? You're gonna play dumb? We hadn't slept together in two and a half months."

I knew we hadn't been having sex for a little while before we broke up, but I hadn't realized it was that long.

"Okay, and how far along are you?"

"I went to the doctor yesterday and he said six weeks."

I breathe a little easier. It's not that I don't want kids one day, but I definitely didn't want one with a woman I wasn't with, and who cheated on me.

"Well, congratulations," I tell her.

"I didn't come here for congratulations. I just wanted you to hear it from me first. I'm sorry for how things ended up between us, but we weren't happy for a while, Cill. You know that. Things are better this way."

I nod my head. "You're right. Things have been better these last few weeks."

She gives me a sad smile. "Good."

"And good luck with everything," I say, before straddling my bike. "Really. I hope you're happy."

She smiles again. "Thanks. See ya around."

I slide the helmet over my head and start up the bike as I watch her walk back down the street where a guy waits for her in a car. The infamous Stacey, I'm sure.

When I drive to work, I'm surprised at my lack of animosity toward her. And Stacey for that matter. Maybe they're meant to be together. All I know is that me and Zoe weren't, and that's fine.

I still have Midge to look forward to seeing tonight, and thinking about her keeps a smile on my face, so my day hasn't been ruined.

MIDGE

"MOM, YOU SURE YOU DON'T NEED ME TO BRING ANYTHING?" I ask as I cradle the phone between my shoulder and ear and change my pants for the second time.

"I have it covered, don't worry. He's not all of a sudden a vegetarian or anything, is he?"

I laugh and then the phone plummets to the floor. "Shit. Sorry, I dropped the phone."

"Where did you learn language like that?" Mom jokes.

"Pft. You. Anyway, no, he's not a vegetarian."

"Then we're all good. Why are you all huffy and out of breath? What the hell are you doing over there?"

"I'm changing pants. The other ones made my ass look weird."

"Honey, nobody cares about your ass."

Cill might, but I don't say that. "I do!"

"Well, good luck with that. I'll see you soon."

"'Kay. Love you."

"Love you. Bye."

After I get the second pair of pants on—a pair of white slacks with thin, black stripes, I turn around to get a look at my ass in the mirror. Definitely better. I grab a black blouse out of my closet and pair it with some black wedges, and I'm good to go.

A glance at the clock on the wall lets me know I need to leave now. I only have fifteen minutes before it's six-thirty, and I really want to be there before Cill gets there. My parents live about ten to twelve minutes away, so as long as he isn't early, I should be good, but I'm cutting it close.

I rush through my front door and down to my car in the driveway. I hit every fucking red light. It's a small town, but to get from my house to my parents' house, I have to cross four traffic lights, and two of them hold for an ungodly amount of time.

"Jesus McChrist! There's nobody there!" I yell to the light, gestures and all.

By the time I turn down my parents' street, the clock in my car reads six thirty-three. Not too bad. However, Cillian's Jeep is parked in the driveway.

"Great," I mutter to myself, hurriedly shutting off the car and then throwing the keys into my purse.

The first thing I hear when I walk through the front door is, "She didn't!" My mom gasps. "My little Midge?" She and my dad start laughing.

Oh Lord.

"Yep," Cill replies with his own laugh.

"Good for her," my dad chimes in.

I burst into the kitchen and slam my purse on the counter. "All right, why are you guys already talking about me?"

Cill smirks from behind the island in the kitchen, and I almost start salivating when I lay eyes on him.

He's changed it up just a bit by wearing a white, button up shirt. Nothing too fancy, but more dressed up than the usual T-shirt. His hair is slicked back, and his beard is trimmed nicely. As I study him, his tongue swipes across his bottom lip and all I can think about is sitting on his face.

The top button of his shirt is undone, revealing the tattoos snaking up his neck. His hands are decorated as well, and I eye them as he drums his fingers across the counter. Fuck, he's hot.

"Oh, Cillian was just telling us a story," Mom says, touching his shoulder.

I give him another once over, noticing the dark jeans and nice shoes. My eyes travel back up to his gorgeously sculpted face to find him still grinning at me.

"What story was that?" I ask my mom, finally looking away from him.

"Well, when he came in, I made a comment about how big he is, and how he'd definitely be able to protect you." Mom glances at Cillian again with a smile. Lord have mercy. "And then he told us you didn't need protecting, and mentioned this story about some guy at the bar trying to touch you, so you kneed him in the...well, you know."

"Balls, honey," my dad chimes in.

"I'm not gonna say that," my mom says, swiping her hand through the air.

Mom likes to act like she's really classy when other people are around, but when it's just us she's telling jokes about masturbation and whatnot.

"Oh yeah. That's not the only time I've done that either. Men need to know," I say with a shrug.

"Atta girl," Dad says.

"How long have you been here? I wasn't that late," I say, walking around to the fridge to grab the pitcher of lemonade I know is there.

"Maybe ten minutes. I got here a little early. I was just

gonna wait outside, but your mom heard me drive up and came out and waved me in."

Of course she did.

"Any other stories you guys shared in my absence?" I question, looking around the room.

"We're saving those for later," Mom teases. "Anyway, dinner's about ready, so if you all want to head to the table, I'll bring everything out."

"I'll help you, Mrs. Halcomb," Cill states.

"Aww, well, that's very nice. Thank you. You can take those dishes right there," Mom says, pointing at a dish full of rolls and one full of salad.

"Yes, ma'am," Cill replies, continuing to charm the pants off my mom.

Once his back is turned and he's walking to the connected dining room, Mom looks at me with huge eyes and gives me the OK symbol. I grin and shake my head at her.

"Midge," she whispers harshly.

"What?" I reply in the same tone.

"Go help him."

"Help him put dishes on the table?"

Before she can say anything else, Cill is back. "Anything else?"

"These are done," she says, handing him two plates of chicken piccata and buttery noodles. "Midge can take the rest."

"Yeah, can't just be sittin' pretty, Midge," Cill teases, walking away.

Mom laughs.

"I think you like him more than you like me," I say with a faux pout, waiting for the plates.

"Nonsense. I like you both the same." She gives me a wink as she hands me two more plates. "I'll take this one."

When we get to the dining room table, Mom looks around the table. "Drinks? What does everyone want?"

"Oh, I have a lemonade in there," I say, turning toward the kitchen.

"I'll take a lemonade, too, but I'll get it," Cill says, standing up. "You guys want the same?" he asks, looking at both my parents.

"Fine with me," Dad replies.

"Yes, thank you," is Mom's response.

In the kitchen, I pour three more glasses of lemonade.

Cillian comes to stand next to me, our bottom halves hidden behind the island. His hand brushes against my thigh as he leans back to check out my ass.

"Glad you changed your pants. Your ass looks great in these."

I put down the pitcher and glare up at him and he chuckles.

"Mom!" I whine.

"What?" her voice floats through the open doorway.

"Nothing, never mind." I lower my voice again. "Is nothing private around here?"

"Really, though. You look great."

I try to hide my smile and spin back to the fridge to put the pitcher away. "Thanks. You clean up pretty good yourself."

"Yeah, I noticed you noticing me."

I shake my head and laugh, grabbing two of the glasses. "Whatever."

Back in the dining room, we place the glasses on the table and sit down. It's a square table, so we're all on opposite ends, with Mom and Dad to my left and right, and Cill right smack dab in front of me. Dinner with a view.

"So, Cillian, it's been a while since we've seen you,"

Mom starts. "I mean, I've seen you out and about a few times at the store or a restaurant, but we haven't said more than a few pleasantries. How have you been? Catch us up."

Cill piles some salad onto his plate, then starts talking. "I can't complain too much. I have my own tattoo shop now. We've been in business for nearly three years. Uh, I'm still painting."

"Oh, good!" Mom clasps her hands together, genuinely happy to hear that.

After Cill's parents died, he went nearly a year without drawing anything. My parents witnessed the moment he picked it up again. We were here when he decided he wanted to try to sketch me. I think I had said he wouldn't be able to. I challenged him in some way, because that's who I am, and he came through. It was on a piece of printer paper I stole from my dad's office, and it was only in pencil, but it was amazing. Mom and Dad came in when he was nearly done, and Mom almost burst into tears.

Cillian's mom bought him his first sketchpad. He told me the story about how she was tired of him drawing on the walls, so she bought him a leather-bound sketchpad that he could refill with paper whenever he ran out. When they died, he hid it away for a long time. It probably hurt too much to look at.

"Yeah, I've been to a few art expos and I've sold some pieces. Everything's been good."

"I'm so happy to hear that," Mom says.

"That's good, son. You've got some real talent," Dad states.

Cill smiles. "Thank you."

"And your brothers? How are they?" Mom asks.

"They're great. Royce loves his job over at King's Tavern, and Elijah's still teaching at the college. And I'm sure you've heard about Merrick. He's on tour right now, living it up."

"Yes," Mom exclaims. "How exciting. Your parents would be so proud of you four."

Cillian stiffens a little, then smiles. "I think so, too. Thank you."

Dad clears his throat. "Yeah, You kids have really done well for yourselves."

"And I'm pretty damn amazing myself," I say, lightening the mood.

Mom and Dad laugh. "Yes, we're very proud of you, Midge," Mom says.

"My favorite kid," Dad says, making the same joke he always does as he reaches over and squeezes my arm.

I respond the way I always do. "That would still be the truth if you had more than me." I glance up at Cillian. "Though it seems like Cill's giving me a run for my money."

Everybody laughs, and my mom brings a napkin up to her mouth. "Now we just need to get you married off."

I nearly choke on a piece of chicken. "Okay, Mom. Now's not the time."

"Why not?"

"Oh, Barbara, give it a rest," Dad mutters.

"You were a toddler when I was your age," Mom says, and not for the first time.

"I know, Mom. Don't worry, I still have child-bearing years left."

"She's a good catch, don't you think, Cillian?"

Cillian finishes chewing his food, nodding his head. "Oh, yes. A great catch."

I want to slide under the table and die. "I'm not a fish."

Dad laughs, and Mom scoffs. "I'm just saying."

"Yeah, yeah. You're always just saying."

"Cillian, is Elijah single? He's a good man, right?"

"Oh, Elijah is the best," Cillian says, looking at me with a grin. "Probably the best choice for Midge."

I slap my hand on my forehead. "You guys are really annoying."

"I'm not saying anything," Dad mutters, digging into his chicken.

"Maybe you should get Elijah's number." Mom keeps on talking, and I continue to want to die.

"Mom, no. I'm kind of seeing someone anyway."

Everybody stops moving.

"What? Who?" Mom questions, her hands frozen in midair.

I glance up and notice Cillian watching me. He seems just as curious as they do. I look to my mom and shrug. "Just a guy. I don't want to talk about it yet."

"Is it serious?"

Another quick glance at Cill's face while I pretend to just be looking around the room. He gives nothing away. His expression is neutral, and he slowly goes back to eating.

"Uh, I don't know. Which is why I don't want to talk about it. I just don't need anybody's phone number. That's all."

"Well, I only care that he treats you right. Does he treat you okay?" Dad asks.

I nod, giving him a smile. "Yes, Dad. He's great."

Dad gives me a single nod. "Good."

Cillian smiles at me from across the table and my cheeks start feeling hot. Fucking Christ I hope my mom isn't looking at me right now. She'll know. I know she'll know.

I take a few seconds to focus on my plate before I let my eyes travel in her direction. She's watching me carefully, then her eyes slowly slide over to Cillian before landing back on me.

"Well, I'm sure he's a fine young man if you've chosen to spend time with him.'"

And thankfully, that's the end of the conversation. For now.

CILLIAN

"Dinner was great, Mrs. Halcomb. I really appreciate it."

She waves me off. "Oh, please. I've done it a million times before, and you're always welcome to come over. Please don't let too much time pass before we see you again."

"I won't," I say with a smile. "Want me to help you with the dishes?"

"No, no. You and Midge go out back. John can help me with these."

John mumbles something from his chair, but Barbara just rolls her eyes and shoos me and Midge out of the room.

We exit out the glass doors in the kitchen and emerge onto their stone pathway with a view of their in-ground, kidney shaped pool.

"Ah, this pool holds some memories," I say, following Midge to a couple of chairs nearby.

She laughs. "Yeah, you and Royce torturing me, Christina, and Laura. Little heathens."

"Oh, please. You and Christina threw mine and Royce's towels into the pool."

She glances at me. "That was only after you two kept doing cannonballs when we were trying to sunbathe."

"Oh yeah."

She shakes her head with a smile on her face. "It was a lot of fun back then."

"Growing up sucks."

"Yeah. Laura got married to a guy in the military and moved away like three years ago. I'm not even sure what happened to Christina. After high school, she seemed to disappear."

"She was desperate to get away from this town," I say, remembering her always complaining.

"Yeah, I used to hate it, too. It's grown on me now, though."

"I couldn't imagine leaving," I say. "Too many memories here."

Midge exhales softly, staring out at the water. "Your parents?"

"Yeah. It's weird, because they're gone, but if I moved away, I'd feel like I was leaving them."

She nods her head quietly, then reaches over and squeezes my hand. "I'm glad you don't want to move."

My eyes roam over our connected hands before looking into her eyes. "I'm glad you've stuck around."

For several moments, we stay connected—both by our hands and our eyes. She eventually pulls away and looks back at the water, lit up by lights both inside and out.

"Do you still have that picture you drew of me?" she asks. "The one on a piece of printer paper?"

I let my mind travel back to that day, remembering the determination to get it right, to have my first drawing since my parents' died be something they'd be proud of. "I don't think so."

"Yeah, it's been like ten years. I was just thinking about it earlier."

"Want me to draw another one?"

Her head swivels over her shoulder, a flirty grin playing on her lips. "You want to draw me like one of your French girls?"

"Funny," I say with a low chuckle. "I wasn't thinking that way, but hey, I'm down if you are."

She throws her head back and laughs. "I can't imagine lying naked across a couch for hours. It'd end up being a hideous picture of me sleeping with drool coming out of my mouth or something. No thanks."

"You could never be hideous."

Her fingers briefly touch her cheeks, like she's trying to hide the blush. "You're either being sweet or a liar, but thanks, I'll take it."

The glass door slides open, and we both turn back to see Mrs. H coming outside.

"I'm not staying," she says immediately, her hands up. "I convinced your father to take me out for ice cream," she tells Midge. "I just wanted to say bye to Cillian in case you're gone before we get back."

I stand up from the chair and wrap her up in a hug. "Bye, Mrs. H. Thanks for dinner. Hopefully I'll see you around soon."

Her arms go around me and pat me on the back. "I hope so, too. You take care of my girl, okay?"

"Yes, ma'am," I say with a smile.

She kisses Midge on the cheek and walks back into the house.

"God, I love your mom."

Midge laughs. "She's a good one. Oh, and I'm trying to help my dad plan her birthday party. Long story, but Mom doesn't want to end up at a bowling alley again." My eyebrows shoot up, but Midge raises her hand and shakes her head. "Dad thought she'd love it. She did not. So, I'm talking with my grandparents, and we're gonna try to have it at the lake house. You think you'll be able to come?"

"September fifth?" I ask.

"Yep."

"I'll be there."

She smiles. "Good."

Midge starts taking off her shoes, then I watch her walk to the water and dip her foot in. "Pretty warm. Wanna play Truth or Dare?" she asks, a mischievous smile on her lips when she glances back at me.

"I don't know, that game seems to only end one way," I reply, lifting a brow.

"You scared?"

"Never. Do you have self-control?" I ask with a smug smile.

"Nope."

I get up from the chair and join her near the water. "Then we probably shouldn't play, otherwise you might end up on your knees out here, and this concrete doesn't look soft."

She flushes, taken by surprise by the look of her parted lips and wide eyes. "Who says I'd be on my knees?"

"Are you saying you wouldn't want to be?" I challenge.

Her tongue wets her bottom lip in one slow swipe. "I'm not saying that."

"Hmm." I step closer. "Then what are you saying?"

She moves into me, her hands undoing the buttons on my shirt, before her fingers dance across my chest. "Maybe I just want to touch you."

"You can touch me whenever you want."

"Yeah?" she muses, opening the shirt wider. "What about kissing you?"

Her hands move lower, coming to rest on the waist of my pants as her lips plant soft kisses along my torso.

"You can do that, too."

"Whenever I want?" she whispers.

"Whenever you want."

"Mmm."

It's taking everything in me to not rip the rest of my clothes off, throw her to the ground and take her right here and now. I don't think her parents would appreciate that very much, and it wouldn't be the most comfortable situation for us either. If rug burn is bad, I'm sure concrete burn is quite the bitch.

"Midge," I warn as her fingers dip into my pants and her tongue slides across my stomach.

"You said whenever I want," she replies.

"Yeah, but I really want to fuck you right now, and I'm going to assume you don't want that to happen in your parents' backyard."

She giggles softly, then brings her head up and looks me in the eye. "Remember when we were seventeen and came out here to hide from my dad after he caught us speeding down the road."

"You were speeding. I was the innocent passenger, but yes, I remember."

"We hid behind that tree over there." She tilts her head just barely, but neither of us look in the direction of the tree.

"I remember."

That was the day I wanted to kiss her. Well, I wanted to kiss her plenty of other days, but that was the day I almost did. I've regretted not doing it since. We were crouched behind the massive tree and several bushes that surrounded it.

Midge was cracking up, and I had put my hand over her mouth while her dad had stormed into the backyard looking for us.

"I wanted you to kiss you then," she says in a tone so soft I'm not sure if I heard her right. "I debated with myself the whole time we were hiding. It was maybe only five minutes, but I envisioned it happening, and right before I got the nerve to do it, you stood up."

I told her that her dad had gone back inside. I remember because I had been right on the verge of kissing her, too. It's not like we were locked in a moment, staring at each other. We were peeking out from behind bushes, trying to stay low and undetected. When I put my hand over her mouth, it was while both of us were laughing and looking behind us, and it wasn't for very long.

It wasn't a typical near-kiss moment, but while we kneeled on the grass next to each other, watching for her dad, the thoughts were running through my mind. I had no idea she was going through the same thing.

"You liked me back then." Not a question. A realization.

She nods then takes a step back, her hands falling to her sides. "Yep. And do you remember what you did after we came from around the tree?"

My eyes widen moments before she changes her stance and her hands shove me backwards into the deep end of the pool.

When I emerge, Midge is bent over, laughing her ass off. Serves me right, I guess. Though revenge was served ten years later.

Yes, I pushed her into the water after I nearly kissed her. Why? Who knows? To remind myself we were just friends? To take my mind off of wanting to taste her when I was sure she wasn't interested in me that way? Because I was a stupid, immature teenager? Probably a combination of the three.

"Someone holds onto a grudge."

She laughs some more. "I'm sorry, I couldn't help myself. That was for back then, and for dipping me in the water at the lake."

A thought hits me. "Was that whole story just so you could push me into the water?"

She sobers up. "No, that was all true."

"You wanted to kiss me?"

She nods in response, and I start walking toward the edge. I bring my hands out of the water and push the long strands of my hair out of my face.

"And you liked me?" She nods again. "You want to kiss me now?"

She bites down on her bottom lip, then gives me another nod. I continue to get closer, then I ascend the few stairs and come to a dripping halt in front of her.

"So, kiss me."

And she does. The wet shirt doesn't deter her as she pushes herself against me and presses her lips against mine.

I plant my hand on her ass and bring her even closer. Water drips from my hair down both of our faces, but we don't stop. Our tongues continue their dance until we hear her parents car doors slam.

When we separate, she looks down at herself and laughs. "I'm almost as wet as you."

"No, you're not, but I can get you that way."

She grins. "Oh yeah?"

I nod, then wrap my arms around her, lifting her up, and nuzzle my head into her neck.

"No! Cillian, no!" she screeches, pushing away from me.

I put her down on the ground and she takes off. Her

parents step outside as I'm chasing her down. I catch up to her, lifting her off her feet from behind, and she lets out a high-pitched squeak.

"I see some things haven't changed," Mrs. H says right before a laugh. "Come on, John. Let's leave the kids alone."

MIDGE

BECAUSE WE DON'T WANT TO DRIP WATER ALL OVER THE house, we exit through the side gate and walk to the driveway to get to our cars.

Cillian immediately rips off his shirt and tosses it in the back of his Jeep, then he starts looking under the seats.

"What're you looking for?"

"I thought I left some gym shoes in here. Ah, here they are," he says, grabbing the white tennis shoes. "Now I don't have to drive home in wet socks and shoes."

I grin. "But you will drive home shirtless?"

He shrugs. "It's dark, people won't notice."

"Not like they'd care," I murmur.

He glances up and smirks, then finishes changing his shoes. "So, I have news."

I lean back against my car and cross my arms over my chest. "Oh yeah? Good or bad?"

He tilts his head back and forth. "Just news, I guess."

"Okay, spill it."

"I saw Zoe today."

My stomach drops. "Oh?"

He stands back up and pushes his hair out of his face again. "Yeah, she stopped by the studio as I was leaving."

All I can think is that she wants to get back together. That he might actually go back to her, because that's what they've always done. But if that were true, why would he come here? Why all the flirting and kissing? No, Cillian wouldn't do that. My emotions are just getting the better of me, and I'll stop and think about why that is later.

"What'd she have to say?" I ask, trying to keep the bitterness out of my voice.

"She's pregnant."

"What?" I exclaim, my arms dropping to my sides as I lean forward with wide eyes.

"It's not mine," he says. "Apparently, it's the new guy's."

"Are you sure?" I ask, because while I'm just now trying to get on board with trying a relationship, I am one thousand percent sure I'm not ready to start one with potential baby mama drama, and Zoe reeks of it.

"Yeah, we hadn't really been sleeping together for a while toward the end of the relationship. It couldn't be mine."

I breathe a sigh of relief. "Well, that's good. I mean, not, you know. I don't know. Is it good?" I ask, stuttering through my sentences.

Cill laughs. "It's fine. I definitely didn't want to have a baby with her. We're not compatible, but I'm also not mad that she's pregnant by someone else. I hope it works for them," he says with a shrug.

"Are you like the coolest guy in town?"

He smiles. "Probably."

"Wow, well, that's quite the news to have dropped on you."

"Yeah, I guess, but it's whatever. No big deal, you know?"

I nod, relaxing back into the car, and we fall into a comfortable silence, both lost in our own thoughts as we look down the street.

After a while, Cill speaks up. "Earlier, you told your parents you were kind of seeing someone and didn't need anybody's number."

My go-to strategy is to make a joke and play it off, but I'm interested in what he's about to say. "Yeah," I respond tentatively, almost like a question.

"Is it safe to assume then that you aren't planning on hanging out with anyone else?"

I crack a grin. "And by hanging out you mean sleeping with?"

"I'm new to this friends-with-benefits thing, so I'm not sure how it works. Just looking for clarification."

"No, I'm not sleeping with anybody else."

He nods, but a hint of relief sparks in his eyes. "Me either."

I mimic his nod and try to hide my glee. "So, we're monogamous friends with benefits?"

He chuckles. "Kind of contradicting, no?"

"I guess, but how else would you describe it?"

His eyes bore into mine intently, like he's contemplating if he wants to say whatever's running through his head. "A relationship?" I stare back at him after the words leave his mouth, unsure of what to say. "But since you're anti that, then we can call it whatever you want," he says with a shrug.

I open my mouth to say something. Anything. But I don't know what I want to say. It does feel a little bit like a relationship, except nobody knows. We're being secretive, and what if that's the only thing that's keeping this exciting?

Before I can finish my thoughts, he cuts me off. "Don't worry about it. It is what it is," he says, casually lifting up his shoulder. "We don't have to slap a label on it. Let's just have fun and see what happens, yeah?"

He closes the gap between us in two strides and wraps me in his arms. I nod against his chest. "Okay, sounds good."

"Good."

"Cill?"

"Hmm?" he murmurs, resting his head on mine.

"You're still fucking wet."

He chuckles. "I know."

CILLIAN

I GET SLAMMED ON FRIDAY AND SATURDAY AT THE SHOP. I forgot Friday was Friday the thirteenth, so we had a flash sale going on all day, and anybody who came could choose pre-drawn tattoos for a lower price.

That seemed to grab a lot of attention, so Saturday was also busy. I didn't get to see Midge at all on those days, but we were able to text late at night when I was finally home.

I spent most of Sunday morning and afternoon at my studio working on the painting for Mrs. H, knowing I would be at Elijah's for dinner.

Before I leave the studio, I take out my phone and send a text to Midge to find out what her plans are. She may say no to dinner with me again, but I have to ask, just in case she changes her mind.

When I'm in my Jeep, she replies back and says she's going to her grandparents' house, so we make plans to meet up later tonight.

At Elijah's, Royce and London are already there, and dinner is nearly done.

"Mm, smells good in here. What is that?" I ask, walking to the stove.

"Chicken piccata," Elijah answers.

"Oh, I just had that at," I stop myself. "This restaurant I went to the other day."

London looks at me funny, but nobody says anything.

"Merrick said he's gonna try to call later," E states.

"Oh, good. Then I can give him shit for not responding to my text from a couple days ago. I only know he's alive because I can read reports about him and the guys on the internet."

Elijah shakes his head and Royce laughs as we take our food to the formal dining room. The house is old, but Elijah's been updating it over the years. New floors throughout the house, and new appliances in the kitchen. The dining room has a new coat of paint from when we were kids. I actually think it used to be wallpaper, so I'm glad he got rid of that.

Midway through the meal, London mentions Midge's idea of having her mom's party at the lake house.

"So, we'll get to go back!" she says excitedly.

"It's probably just for the day, babe," Royce says with a grin.

"Maybe we can make a little trip of it," she says with a nudge.

"Yeah, it'll be nice," I chime in. "I loved it there."

"How's the painting coming?" Elijah asks, cutting into his chicken.

"Really good. I'm happy with it."

"Based on what I saw, it's gonna be gorgeous," London says.

"You saw it already?" Royce questions, looking between me and her. "You never show us your shit before you're done."

London mouths *sorry* to me before pressing her lips together and shuffling vegetables around her plate.

"I happened to be at Midge's when she showed up, so I showed her."

"Wait, you were at Midge's?" Royce asks, forgetting about the painting.

I glance around at their eager eyes. "Yeah, it was right when I came back into town. I was just showing her the progress." Before they can question why I didn't text them to her, or ask any other questions, I change the subject to something that'll capture their attention. "So, Zoe's pregnant."

"What?" they all ask simultaneously with unblinking eyes and parted lips.

"Yep. She came to the studio today to tell me."

"Wait, what?" Royce asks again.

I tell them the short story and they listen with rapt attention. When the story's done and we're in the middle of putting our dishes away, Elijah's phone rings.

"It's Merrick," he says, pressing the button that brings Merrick's face onto the screen.

"Hey!" Merrick says excitedly, a huge grin on his face.

"Hey, man," Elijah greets.

Me and Royce run up behind him and shove our faces into the screen. "Hey, dude," Royce says.

"What the fuck is up?" I ask, a smile on my face.

"We're in…" He looks over his shoulder and yells out, "Where are we again? Oh yeah, Seattle."

"Don't even know what city you're in?" I ask.

He rubs his forehead, pushing his light brown hair out of his face. "Man, it's all running together at this point. We sleep, wake up, do a show, party, eat, sleep while we travel, wake up, do a show, party. I don't even know, but it's been a fucking blast."

"Have fun, but make sure you're being smart," Elijah lectures.

Merrick shakes his head, smiling and rolling his eyes. "I know, I know."

"You got my VIP tickets yet or what?" I ask.

"Yeah, of course. I have six. Is that good?"

"That's probably good," Royce says. "Us three, and I'll bring my girl, and..." Royce looks around. "I think Midge might come?"

London nods, so I don't have to. But I do hope she comes with us.

"Cool. That'll be my late birthday present to you. Sucks I won't be there."

"Yeah, man, but it's okay. We probably won't be doing much."

"What're you talking about? We're having a party at the bar, hiring you a stripper, and having a good fucking time," Royce says.

"That right?"

Royce nods with a grin curving his lips.

"Well, I'm sure you can have plenty of that whenever you want, huh?"

Merrick grins. "Drinking? Yes. Strippers? Only occasionally."

"Yeah right," Royce says with a laugh.

"When you get done with this tour, you'll be able to come home for a while, right?" Elijah asks him.

"Yeah, for little bit. Then we'll probably be back in the studio to record another album.

Elijah nods. "Makes sense."

Somebody in the background yells something to Merrick, grabbing his attention. When he turns back to the camera, he says, "I gotta go. I'll try to call again next weekend."

"Sounds good, bro."

"Take it easy."

"Take care of yourself."

We all say our goodbyes, then the screen goes black. We help clean everything up, then I glance at my watch and discover it's already nine o'clock.

"Well, I'm gonna head out," I say. "See y'all later."

"Take it easy," Royce says. London smiles from her position next to him.

"Talk to you later," Elijah states.

In my Jeep, I text Midge to see if she's home. When she says she is, I back out of the driveway and make my way to her house.

MIDGE

AFTER I GOT HOME FROM MY GRANDPARENTS, I JUMPED IN the shower and pulled out a sexy little lingerie set I bought a while back when I was walking through the mall. I've never had a reason to wear it until now. Tonight, I want to blow Cillian's socks off.

The black, lace bra, panties, and garter belt combo leave little to the imagination. I connect some fishnet thigh highs to the garter belt and throw on a black, satin mini robe, but don't bother closing it.

When Cillian says he's on his way, I slip my feet into a pair of black pumps that give me four more inches in height. I keep my makeup light, opting for a nude lip and moisturizing Chapstick rather than a bright color or gloss. It's all going to come off anyway. My hair's cut into a medium bob, allowing the longer strands to barely touch my shoulders.

From the kitchen, with a wine glass in hand, I watch as Cillian pulls into my driveway and saunters up to my house. When he knocks, I take a deep breath and strut toward the door. When I pull it open, he slowly lifts his head, tracing my legs, hips, breasts, and eventually my face with his eyes.

"Jesus Christ," he mutters.

"Come in," I reply, taking a step back.

Cillian doesn't take his eyes off me as he walks past. When I close the door and turn around, he's still gawking.

"What did I do to deserve this?" he asks.

"What're you talking about?" I play dumb, sashaying around him and heading toward the couch.

He chuckles and rubs his hand over his face like he's in disbelief. "Fuck, Midge. You're killing me."

I take a seat on the couch and cross my legs, then take a sip of wine. "I'm just lounging, Cillian."

"Oh yeah? This is how you lounge around the house all the time?"

I grin. "Maybe." He inches closer, trying to touch me, but I stop him. "I have to finish my wine." He growls, low and deep. "So, how was your night?" I ask, angling my body in his direction.

His eyes find my tits, pushed up and together in this amazing bra. "I'm not even gonna pretend I can talk to you about anything normal right now."

I smile, then finish the wine and place the glass on the table. He starts leaning forward, so I uncross my legs, shift in the couch like I'm about to lay down, then bring my foot up and push him back with the toe of my shoe.

With my legs spread in front of him, his gaze finds my pussy, barely covered by the panties. His large hand grabs my calf and his eyes flicker up to mine. "You're driving me crazy."

With a gentle shove, I push him back with my foot and then lay back, resting my legs in his lap. "That's the point."

"It's already been a week," he says, massaging my calves and slowly inching his way higher and higher. "I don't know how much longer I can wait to be inside you." He puts my

215

right leg over the back of the couch and crawls in between them. "And then you come to the door dressed like a wet dream and think I'll be able to keep my hands off of you?" His mouth skims over the swell of my breast, his beard scratching my skin as he moves to kiss my neck. "Not possible. I need you too much."

Warmth travels to every part of my body. "Then take me."

And like he was waiting for my permission, he attacks. His hands touch and squeeze my breasts as he rocks into me, letting me feel his erection through his jeans. He sucks on my neck, then pulls my chin down with his thumb before plunging his tongue into my mouth.

My hands fly to the back of his head, bringing him closer. I fight for control over the kiss, my tongue sliding across his before I suck on the tip. He grunts and pulls away, moving down my body with a mission.

He'll never figure out the garter straps. I'm about to tell him how to unfasten the hooks, but then he just yanks the material to the side and slides two fingers inside me.

"Oh fuck," I moan.

"God, I love how wet you are for me already."

He removes his fingers and hurriedly gets up to remove his clothing. While he's pulling the condom out of his wallet, I quickly unsnap the garter straps, so he can remove my panties without a problem.

"Stand up," he commands, giving me his hand.

He pulls me up and walks me around the back of the couch, making me stand in front of him. He removes the robe and throws it onto the couch, then steps up and presses his chest into my back.

"You are a fucking masterpiece," he growls, his hand cupping my ass.

I moan in response, then he slips the panties down my

thighs, and lets them drop to the floor where I can step out of them.

"Spread your legs wider."

I obey, and I'm rewarded when he slips his fingers inside me again.

Bracing myself on the back of the couch, I bend over slightly while he penetrates me with his long fingers.

"Oh God."

He moans, working me over with just his hand, and then he grunts. "Fuck, I need to taste you." He drops to the floor behind me, spreads me open, and goes to fucking town.

"Jesus," I breathe, bending all the way over and spreading my legs a little further.

Cillian's hands stay on the sides of my ass as he buries his face into me, eating me like I'm his favorite dessert.

My fingers dig into the brown cushions as desire burns passionately in my veins. Every time his tongue runs over my clit, my legs shake. When he fucks me with his tongue, I push back into him, wishing he could go deeper.

After several minutes, Cillian stands up and I hear the condom wrapper tear open. Thank fuck, because I need to feel him inside me.

The crown of his cock prods at my entrance, but only for a second, because then he's pushing all the way in. Cillian grips my waist and pummels into me with hard, deep thrusts.

He leans over my back as his arm snakes around my waist and his fingers find my engorged clit.

"Oh yes," I moan.

My body responds to him like he's the owner. He plays me like an instrument, and his fingers always hit the right keys. He already got me worked up with his fingers and mouth, and now with his cock filling me up while his fingers rub circles on my clit, I'm about to explode.

"God, Cillian."

Pleasure prickles up my spine, currents of electricity fire through my body, hitting every pleasure point there is, and the orgasm sets me on ablaze.

"Oh yes. Fuck!" I scream.

Cillian doesn't stop touching me or fucking me, and as I come down from that blissful peak, I can tell he's about to reach his.

He grabs my thigh and lifts my leg up, resting my knee on the back of the couch. His thrusts become faster, his grip tighter, and then he releases a loud grunt.

"Oh fuck."

He keeps going at the same pace before he slows down as his muscles tense, and then he comes deep inside me with a husky growl.

After we separate, I turn around and say, "God, I needed that."

He chuckles, taking off the condom and walking around to the other side of the couch to get his clothes. "Well, I'm willing to give it to you whenever you want. Don't forget that."

I kick off my heels before I start trotting down the hall. "I'm gonna use that bathroom in my room, you can use the one in the hall."

"All right."

After I'm done freshening up and passing back through my room, I take a second to check my phone that was left plugged in on my nightstand. I have a text from London.

London: *Call me when you're free. We need to talk.*

Uh-oh.

CILLIAN

I THINK I'M STARTING TO FALL FOR MIDGE.

Sure, I crushed on her in the past, and I've liked her for many years as a friend, but things are changing. At least on my end. And as much as I hate to admit that Elijah was right, he may be.

I want more with Midge. I want to be open about us. I want to take her out and not care if anybody sees us kissing or flirting or holding hands. But she doesn't want that, and unless we're on the same page, this isn't going to work.

I'll give it some more time with the hope that she'll come around and realize it doesn't matter if our friends and family know. Shit happens all the time, and if this ends badly, then we're just going to have to be adults about it and figure shit out, but why hold ourselves back for other people?

"London texted me," she announces, entering the living room. "She said we need to talk."

"Uh-oh."

"My thoughts exactly. Do you think she knows? How could she?"

I lean against the back of the couch and cross my arms. "I don't know. It's not like you and I are always all over each other."

She chews on her nail, something she does when she's nervous. "I don't know what to tell her. She's gonna be pissed and things will become awkward as fuck, because she'll probably tell Royce, and then both of them will be staring at us when we're together. And we're not even in a relationship!"

I sigh, pushing away from the couch. "Why are you freaking out about this? Maybe she doesn't know. She could want to talk to you about something else. But even if she does know, maybe that's good. Now you won't have to lie anymore."

"I'm not freaking out," she says, in the middle of her freak out. "How are you not worried about this? You don't care that this can become weird for people?"

"Why do I give a shit about other people?" I say, my tone a little sharper than I intended. "Honestly, Midge, nobody should think about other people when it comes to their own intimate relationships." She levels a look at me. "Or fuck buddies or whatever the hell you wanna call it."

Midge takes a deep breath and runs her fingers through her hair, tugging at the roots and looking one thousand percent stressed out.

"I just don't want people to know."

I want people to know, but I don't tell her that. She's too fragile about this whole situation, and I'm trying to remind myself that this isn't personal. She'd be this way about anybody. Then again, I'm not just anybody. I'm not one of her random hook-ups. I'm her friend. She's known me for years, and maybe that's why it sucks so much.

I release a long breath. "Maybe we should cool it, then." I say the words I never wanted to say. I came into this hoping I'd be able to prove to her that we're meant to be together. We have a bond most people don't have. She was there during my darkest time, and it meant everything to me to have her in my life. Perhaps my feelings are deeper than hers for that reason alone.

"What?" she asks softly, her hands falling to her side as she watches me with wide eyes. "This is over?"

I give her a sad smile. "No, Midge. I don't want this to be over, but I don't want you to be on the verge of having a breakdown over the fact that your best friend might know that there's something going on between us."

"It's not that, it's just…" she stops talking, unable to find any words.

"Let's just call it a breather, huh? If nobody sees us together, then they can't think anything's going on, right?"

"Cill, it's not that I'm embarrassed or anything."

I gently grab ahold of her shoulders and look into her eyes. "It's okay. I'm gonna go, though, and I guess I'll see ya around?"

She sniffs. "Yeah."

"Okay."

And then I walk away from one of my best friends, and someone I'm pretty sure I'm falling in love with.

People always want to talk about how love is beautiful. How love is this wonderful emotion, and you're constantly happy and in a state of bliss.

Bullshit.

Love is a force of nature not to be fucked with. It hits hard and has the ability to destroy you. Love makes you vulnerable. It cuts you open and leaves your heart exposed. Love is beautiful, sure, but sometimes to get there you have to overcome a few hardships. Like Midge said, what love story doesn't have complications?

I'm walking away now, but not forever. I'm giving her what she may need to realize we're meant to be together instead of apart. Here's to hoping.

MIDGE

I CALL IN SICK TO WORK THIS MORNING, FEIGNING FLU-LIKE symptoms. Nobody wants to be around someone who supposedly has a fever and is coughing up phlegm all over the place.

Truth of the matter is, I'm sad. I'm also trying to avoid London, because I'm still unsure what she wants to talk about, though I have a strong suspicion it involves Cillian. But now that me and Cillian are over, if London asked if we were together, I wouldn't be lying if I said no.

Okay, I know. Semantics. She deserves to know what's been going on, but now I'm too fucking sad to talk about it. I'm aware that when we started this, I, myself, said this would die off. But to be honest, I've been having fun. I love my time with Cillian, and I wasn't ready for it to end.

I decide to send London a quick message, just so she knows I'm alive.

Midge: *Taking a sick day. I'll talk to you later.*

I don't expect to hear back from her until lunch, so I spend the morning in bed before eventually dragging myself to the kitchen and becoming a cliché character in a romantic comedy movie. I grab a pint of ice cream and a spoon, and plop on the couch to watch rom-com movies.

The day moves surprisingly fast considering I'm doing absolutely nothing. But as time goes on, karma sneaks in and bitch slaps me. My head begins to ache and my nose becomes stuffy. Hours later, I'm curled up on the couch clutching toilet paper and drinking a cup of hot tea.

I told my work I was sick, and now it appears I'm getting sick. Just fucking great.

My medicine cabinet holds only Tylenol and Advil, but nothing for colds. I take what I have and hope it helps combat the headache, send an email to my boss regarding my sickness and tell him I'll need the week, then I crawl into bed and hope to wake up slightly better.

I wake up in the middle of the night feeling like death. It takes me hours to go to sleep again, and by the time I wake up, everybody I know is at work. I texted my mom and she said she'd bring some stuff by when she got off. London sends well-wishes, but she's stuck at work, too. So, until my mom comes over, I stay in bed.

"Oh, honey," she says as soon as she sees me. "Go get back in bed. I'll put some stuff in your kitchen and bring you some medicine."

I drag my sock-covered feet along the wooden floor and wrap my robe around me a little tighter. My skin burns like the surface of the sun while my body shivers like it's been dumped in a frozen lake.

My nose is already raw from all the blowing I've had to do, and my chest is sore from all the coughing. I'm miserable.

"Here you go," Mom says, dropping a couple pills in my hand and offering me some water. "You need to try to stay hydrated. I'm gonna leave this Gatorade on the nightstand too. These pills may make you sleepy, but it's probably best to sleep through as much as possible."

"Thanks, Mom," I croak.

She places the back of her hand on my forehead. "Watch that temperature. If it gets too high, you need to go to the hospital, so let me know."

"Okay." I pull the covers up to my chin and curl into a ball.

"I put some soup in the pantry and some orange juice in the fridge. There's also more medicine and cough drops in the cabinet."

"Thanks for bringing everything." I sniff then start hacking up a lung. "I don't want you to get sick. You should go."

Mom comes closer and kisses my forehead anyway, brushing back my hair. "Call me if you need anything else, okay?"

"I will. Love you."

Mom leaves and I eventually fall back asleep. On Wednesday morning, I'm still sick, but manage to get in the shower because I feel like germs are just stuck all over my body. I Lysol the shit out of my bed and anything else I've touched, then wrap myself in my fluffy, purple robe, and put on my thick, fuzzy socks, and make my way to the kitchen.

I don't have much of an appetite, but I figure I should try to eat some soup just to put something in my body. Hopefully it helps with the lethargy.

Before I get to the kitchen, someone knocks on my door. I shuffle my feet and peek through the peephole, jolting upright when my gaze falls on Cillian.

I stand there, thinking I should just wait until he goes away, because I don't really want him to see me like this. My nose is constantly red, and the skin around it is peeling.

Thanks, toilet paper. I have no makeup on to help cover the dark circles under my eyes or my sickly pallor.

But then I start coughing. I cough so hard, I plant my hand on the door and bend over, thinking I'm about to puke all over the floor. My brain pounds against my skull as I suck in a wheezy breath.

"I'm pretty sure you're in there," Cill says from the other side. "Open up."

I pull open the door, looking as awful as I feel, I'm sure. "What's up?"

He shows me the two plastic bags in his hands. "I brought some stuff."

"Why?"

He tilts his head like he doesn't understand the question. "Because you're sick. Can I come in?"

"You might get sick."

He shrugs. "I'll be fine."

I step back and let him in, and he instantly goes to the kitchen and starts pulling things out of the bags. I drop into one of the chairs at my dining room table and watch him.

"To help keep me from getting sick, we have these," he says, showing me a couple of surgical masks.

I try to laugh, but it turns into am embarrassing, phlegmy cough. "Probably a good idea," I say as soon as I'm done coughing.

Cill hands it to me and I put it on. "I brought some choco-late chip ice cream for whenever you're feeling better."

"You remember?"

He cracks a grin. "How could I forget when you nearly bit my head off for bringing you cookie dough that one time?"

"That was in high school, and I was on my period and feeling pretty hostile. Sorry."

Cill laughs. "You went on a ten minute rant about chocolate chip ice cream. I'm still scarred."

He turns and puts the ice cream in the freezer, then shows me everything else. More medicine, a jar of Vicks, vitamin c tablets, and a couple of coloring books and colored pencils.

"Coloring books?"

"Yeah, well, I wasn't sure if you still read those stupid tabloid magazines or not, and I know you hate crossword puzzles, and I know you read books on your phone rather than buy paperbacks, so, coloring books."

"I have TV."

He gives me a look. "You don't remember?"

"What?"

"I think we were twelve or thirteen, but you were so mad that I could draw and you could barely make a decent stick figure, so you would challenge me to coloring contests because you swore you were the best colorer in the world."

I start laughing before it turns into another coughing fit. "God, don't make me laugh." I rub my chest. "But yeah, I do remember. I'm pretty sure I won those."

"Yeah, I don't think so."

I move to stand up, but Cillian points a finger at me. "Sit down, what're you doing?"

"I need some tea. My mom brought over some special tea that's supposed to help with coughs."

"I'll make it. Where is it?"

I explain where everything is and Cillian makes me a cup of tea and then a bowl of soup, and takes them to the living room.

He comes back for me, taking my arm and escorting me to the couch like I'm an eighty-nine year old lady.

"I can walk, you know?"

"Yeah, but you're probably weak, and if you slip because

of these ridiculous socks on this wooden floor, you'll hurt yourself."

"My socks aren't ridiculous," I whine.

He shakes his head and deposits me onto the couch with my soup and tea waiting for me on the end table.

I watch him take his shoes off and sit down on the other end of the couch and put on his own surgical mask as I remove mine to eat.

"What're we watching?"

"You're staying?"

"Yep."

I bite down on a smile. "You don't have to do that, Cill. I appreciate everything, but I don't expect you to stay."

He looks over at me, most of his face hidden behind the mask, but his eyes are serious. "I'm staying and making sure you're okay. Deal with it."

"Yes, sir," I reply, cracking a grin.

His eyes twinkle. "Good girl."

CILLIAN

"How did you know I was sick?" Midge asks from her end of the couch.

"London. I saw her and Royce last night."

"Oh."

"Yeah, she mentioned she hadn't been able to get in touch with you. Said you sent out a couple texts and told her to stay away from your diseased house."

"Yet, you come to my diseased house. Don't blame me when you're dying in a couple days."

I chuckle. "Okay."

We spend the next couple hours watching TV, and only talk about the show's storyline or characters. We're clearly both staying away from any topic that could relate back to us. I know she's wondering why I chose to come here after we just agreed to take a break, but I couldn't stay away. I heard she was sick and needed to make sure she was taking care of herself.

I know her parents work during the day, and since her grandparents are older, I'm sure they don't want to risk getting sick. So, here I am, making sure she's eating, hydrating, and not dying.

"Cill," she says, looking over her shoulder at me. "I'm feeling a little hot again. I think I'm gonna go lay down."

I jump up. "Yeah, sure. Here." I grab her hand and pull her up, then walk her down the hall to her room.

"I'm gonna pee first," she says, disappearing into the bathroom.

When she comes back out, I pull the covers back and wait for her to climb in, then I cover her up. "I see you have your own little pharmacy over here," I say, looking at the variety of medicines on her nightstand. "What do you need? Tylenol? Or DayQuil?"

She has a coughing fit then rips off her mask. "Ugh. DayQuil is fine. Thanks."

I hand her the pills and some water, and as soon as she's done, I go into the bathroom and wet a washcloth to drape over her head.

"I hope you feel better."

"Thanks."

Midge wakes up about an hour and a half later and stops in her tracks when she walks into the living room. "Hey."

"Hey," I reply, looking over the back of the couch.

"You're still here."

"I am."

"Why? Haven't you been bored?"

I gesture to the TV with the remote. "I have stuff to watch."

She shakes her head and walks into the kitchen. "So, how long are you planning on staying?"

I get up from the couch and meet her by the fridge. "Until I know you're gonna survive."

She coughs out a laugh. "I'm pretty sure I'm not gonna die."

"They always say rest is important when you're sick. So, go sit down and tell me what you want. More tea? Food? Water?"

She leans against the counter. "I was gonna get some juice. I'll try to eat later. Everything tastes like crap, anyway."

"Okay, I'll get the juice. You wanna sit on the couch or go back to your bed?"

"Bed. It's more comfortable."

After I pour a glass of apple juice, we make our way back to her room. Midge gets under the covers, but sits up with her back leaning against the headboard of her queen-sized bed.

"You good?" I question.

She shakes her head, putting the glass of juice on the nightstand. "Stay in here with me? I'm not going back to sleep, and we'd just be up watching TV in two different rooms."

I pull my mask out of my pocket. "Good thing I'm prepared."

Midge laughs and finds the remote under her pillow. "Really don't wanna get sick, huh?"

"Would you come over and take care of me if I was?" I ask.

She flips through a couple channels before answering. "Yeah, I would. If you wanted me there."

Her eyes flicker to mine for the briefest of moments, a simple statement, left hanging between us as a question. Would I want her at my house taking care of me if I was sick? Yes. Fuck yes. But would we be just friends or something more? Back to the benefits? Or an actual relationship? Because, obviously we're still not quite on the same page.

"I'll be right back," I say, heading to the living room.

Once I'm back in the room, I toss the coloring books and colored pencils in the middle of the bed.

"Really?"

"Yes," I reply, getting on the bed and leaning against the headboard with her. "We have to have our contest."

She grabs a book and pours the pencils out of the box. "Who's gonna decide? Because, obviously, if I'm choosing, I'm gonna win."

I flip through the pages looking for a picture. "Oh, so you're gonna lie to yourself? I guess, I'll decide since I can be impartial."

She snorts. "Right."

Midge rips out a page about five minutes in and crushes it in her palm. "I messed up."

"Let me see." I laugh, reaching for the wrinkled paper.

"I'll cough on you. Get away."

"How did you mess up?"

"I don't really wanna talk about it."

I shake my head and go back to my picture while Midge chooses a new one. We focus on our pictures while half paying attention to reruns of an old TV show.

"How ya doin' over there?"

"Pretty good. You should definitely be scared. Though, I don't know why you couldn't get a regular child's coloring book and not one of these adult coloring books. This is gonna take forever."

"We have plenty of time. You'll still be sick for the rest of the day, and probably tomorrow."

She stops coloring, and I see her head turn in my direction through my peripheral vision. "Are you staying over?"

I don't look over, I just continue to color. "Do you want me to?"

She hesitates for several seconds. "You probably don't need to. I'm sure I'll be fine. I've been sick before."

"I'm sure you're right."

She keeps watching me. "But, you could stay if you want. Or just stay late and then come back tomorrow. Or, you know, whatever you wanna do."

I grin, staring down at my page. "Okay." When she keeps watching me, I say, "You better get back to coloring."

The hours fly by as we switch between coloring, watching TV, eating, and playing card games. It isn't until almost ten o'clock when we finally stop pretending their isn't an elephant in the room.

"Cill?"

"Yeah?" I ask, looking up from my phone.

"I really appreciate you spending the day with me, especially considering we aren't, you know, whatever we were before," she says, focusing on her coloring page.

"We were friends before and we're still friends," I tell her.

"I know, but you know."

"Look, I only said we should take a break because you seemed to be really concerned about people finding out about us. Not because it's what I wanted to do. Midge, we're clearly not on the same page right now, but I'm hoping all you need is a little more time."

She puts her book and pencil down, angling her head up to look at me. "I have trust issues."

"Okay."

She looks at me like that should be enough of an explanation. "So, relationships are hard for me."

"I get it," I answer with a nod.

She shakes her head and opens her mouth to say something else, but instead, she has another coughing fit.

I go to the kitchen to make her some tea and grab some cough drops. When I get back to the room, she's taking a couple pills and climbing under the covers. "Sorry."

"It's okay." I put the tea and cough drops next to her. "I'll let you get some rest. Text me if you need anything, otherwise, I'll be back in the morning."

"Okay," she says with a nod. "Thanks again."

"Anytime."

I make sure to lock the door behind me, and then I make my way home.

MIDGE

By Thursday evening, I'm rested and almost completely rejuvenated. Cillian's already been by to check on me, and even brought some food that wasn't soup. I didn't eat a whole lot, but at least food is starting to taste a little better.

I shooed him away once I learned he called out of work yesterday just to hang out with me. He stayed for a couple hours earlier, but I didn't want him missing any more work because I was sick.

Unfortunately, we didn't really talk about where we stand, but I'm assuming we're still taking a break, and I'm starting to wonder how long that's going to last. What determines when we can start things back up? When I decide I'm ready to go public?

My phone goes off, and I find a text from London.

> **London**: *You still alive over there?*
> **Midge**: *Alive. Feeling better.*
> **London:** *Good.*

Her brief response makes me wonder if she's upset with me,

but thirty minutes later, London's at my door.

"I know you got my text." London confronts me the minute I open the door.

"Yeah, I know. I responded."

She narrows her eyes at me from the doorway, then proceeds to march inside and sit on the couch. "I meant my other text. The one I sent before you were sick."

I close the door as slowly as possible, buying time, then unhurriedly make my way to the living room. "Oh yeah. Well, I've been sort of dying."

"And making sure I kept away."

"I didn't want you to get sick."

She crosses her arms and studies me. "You and Cillian are hooking up."

She flings the statement out there and lets it sit between us. She studies my face intently, waiting for me to either deny or confirm it. The fact that she said it with so much confidence makes me wonder what she heard or saw. It's been killing me to keep this from her. She's my best friend. A sister I never had. And she's about to be incredibly pissed.

I let loose a sigh and plop onto the couch cushion. "Yes."

She gasps dramatically, flying back like someone gave her a violent shove. "Are you kidding me?"

"You said it like you already knew!"

"I was assuming, but for real?"

"I know, I'm sorry. It's been killing me. I've been dying to talk to you about this, but..."

"But what? Midge, I'm your best friend! Why wouldn't you tell me this?"

The hurt on her face breaks my heart. "I didn't want things to be weird for you. Or Royce. Or all of us." I take a deep breath and blow it out. "Truth is, I think things have already ended."

"What are you talking about?"

"If we had told everybody, it would be really fucking awkward right now. We all hang out around each other. I'm at the bar with you and Royce twice a week, and Cillian pops in from time to time. We have parties and barbeques, and I wouldn't want it to mess up my friendship with Royce or have it to where we all can't hang out anymore. Cillian said we should take a breather, but I think it's because I was having a minor panic attack about you maybe having found out."

London shakes her head. "I'm confused."

"Your initial text. The *we need to talk* text. I was freaking out about you knowing. I think it upset him. I mean, clearly it did. He hasn't outright said it, but I think he's ready for more. To go public. And I'm over here having a panic attack over you finding out." I roll my eyes at myself and huff. "Pretty sure I messed this up. I knew we wouldn't last, and this is why I didn't want anyone to know."

London rests her hand on my knee and gives it a gentle squeeze. "You're crazy. You're an insane person, you know that?"

"What?"

She huffs, looking around the room before zeroing in on me again. "I don't know that me and Royce are gonna last. I just hope. I hope beyond everything that what we have keeps working. That we continue to love each other more than anything. That's it. That's all anybody has. Hope.

"Have you ever thought about what would happen if me and Royce broke up? Would our nights at the bar have to stop? Would you feel inclined to choose me over him, even though you've been friends with him longer? Would you stop going to the bar? Would I have to stop talking to his brothers?"

My brows draw together as I chew on the corner of my lip. "I hadn't thought of that."

She exhales. "I have, but you know what? What me and Royce have is worth the risk. Isn't that what love is all about? Taking a risk? Being vulnerable?"

Who knew all I needed was my best friend to tell me how dumb I was being? I needed London from the start. Every girl needs a best friend to tell you like it is. No bullshit. If I'm being dumb, someone needs to tell me. I hadn't thought about her and Royce breaking up. They're so perfect together it doesn't make sense for them to be with anyone else. Maybe that's how I should start thinking. I get so caught up on the *what ifs*. I worry about the past way too much to even allow myself a peek at the future.

"You're so wise," I say with a grin.

She tries to suppress a smile. "And you're so stupid. I can't believe you didn't tell me this! Now I need all the details!"

"What does it matter now? We're done."

London frowns. "You said he was upset because you were freaking out about me knowing, right?"

"Yeah."

"But now I know. And everything's okay."

"True."

"And I've graced you with my wisdom, and now you know that it shouldn't matter who knows."

"Right, but—"

"Ah!" She raises her hand and cuts me off. "No buts."

I make a face at her. "I hate you."

"Sure, now give me details!"

"First, tell me how you figured it out."

She snorts. "I hadn't. Not completely, but I had my suspicions. And then at Elijah's on Sunday, he made chicken piccata, and Cillian said 'Oh, I just had that at...' and trailed off and ended up saying some restaurant or something. But you had just told me you had chicken piccata at your parents' house. So, what the fuck? Y'all are having family dinners together?"

"Damn chicken piccata," I say with a laugh. "No, my mom wanted to invite him over because she hadn't seen him in a while. It was a family dinner in the sense that my mom acts like he's her long lost son, but not like I'm bringing home my future husband."

London looks at her phone, replies to a text, then places it on the cushion and meets my gaze. "I need the quickest rundown ever. Go."

I sit up straight, take a deep breath, and finally tell my best friend everything I've wanted to tell her since this started.

"It started at the lake house after the body shots."

"I knew it!"

I ignore her and keep going. "We kept drinking, everybody left, we got close and played a game of Truth or Dare, then ended up having sex."

"Oh, my God."

"When y'all went to the beach, we had sex then too. And the night before y'all left."

"Horny bastards."

"Oh, whatever, like you and Royce weren't doing the same thing."

She grins. "Okay, keep going."

"Oh. He's pierced."

"What?"

"Pierced. His dick. And it's huge."

Her mouth forms an O, and her hand covers it. "Wow, that's...wow. Okay."

"Yes, and he's fucking phenomenal. Like, the best. Anyway, we've hooked up a few more times since he's been back in town. Like the day you came over and he was here."

"I knew it!" she repeats, pointing at me.

I playfully roll my eyes. "And Sunday."

"That's why he left all early."

"Yeah, but that's also when he said we should stop." I look down and pull at fibers in my robe. "But before that, we agreed we'd be monogamous friends-with-benefits."

London cocks her head to the side. "So y'all are, or were, only sleeping with each other?"

"Yes."

"But it wasn't going to be a relationship?"

"No."

"Why?"

I sigh. "I've been thinking about trying, but I was afraid of going public because I didn't want things to be weird."

"But again, now that I know, and you've heard all of my sage advice, none of that matters."

I shrug. "Maybe."

"Look, I know you have trust issues. I get it, I do, but you can't put every man into the same category as Matthew. Especially not Cill. He's great. You've been saying that forever. If anybody defies the stereotypical man who doesn't give a shit about a woman's feelings and cares only about himself, it's Cill."

"I know, and I do really like him. I admitted how I felt about him back in high school. Well, I didn't say that I was head-over-heels in love with him back then, but no need for all those details."

London laughs. "I don't see the problem then."

Excitement blooms in my chest as a smile grows on my lips. "Maybe there isn't one. Maybe I'll tell him we can take this public and see what happens."

"Yes!" London says, grabbing my hand and squeezing.

"I'm still afraid it's bad timing on his end. Maybe I should let him sleep around for a little bit first."

London rolls her eyes. "Ugh. You're terrible! Maybe he doesn't want to sleep with half the town."

"He's single, though. And half the town would drop their panties for him. Why wouldn't he take advantage?"

London strokes my hand. "Honey, you have got to stop thinking all men are the same. And he's so obviously into you."

I run my hands through my hair. "Ugh, I know. See, I have problems."

"Tell him your issues. Be up front about all of that."

"I mean, he knows, but he doesn't know all the details about what happened between me and Matthew."

She glances at the time again. "I gotta go. I'm meeting Royce in a few." Pointing a finger at me, she says, "You figure your shit out and talk to Cill about it. His birthday is this weekend, you could surprise him by kissing him in front of everybody!" Her eyes are full of glee.

I give her a level look. "I don't know about all that, but I do like the idea of telling him on his birthday. I'll think about it."

Once she's gone, I breathe a sigh of relief. A weight has been lifted from my shoulders, and the thought of going forward in an actual relationship with Cill makes my stomach do a somersault and my heart skip a beat. Let's hope I'm not too late.

CILLIAN

IT'S SATURDAY NIGHT, AND I'M OFFICIALLY TWENTY-SEVEN. For the past three days, Royce has been talking about the party non-stop. He's not closing the bar down to the public, so we'll just be partying amongst the customers, but I still look forward to it.

I look forward to seeing Midge tonight, even if we're back to only being friends for the time being. I've checked in on her via text a few times, and she says she's back to normal. She also seems pretty excited about giving me my present. I tried to pry it out of her, but she wouldn't tell me what it was, and then I tried to tell her I didn't need anything, but she didn't want to hear that either.

Before me and Elijah head to King's Tavern, he presents me with a gift.

"Figured I'd give this to you now," he says, handing over a gift bag. "You may be wasted before the night's over."

"Hopefully," I say with a grin. "Thanks, man."

I take the bag from his hand and reach inside, pulling out sketch paper, charcoal pencils, oil paints, brushes, and everything else an artist could need.

"I know you use the sketchpad Mom bought you, but I noticed the last time you were at the house with it that it was running low on paper. Bought everything else I could think of. I'm sure you'll put it to use."

I smile and give him a hug. "You know I will. Thanks, E. I appreciate it."

"No problem. You ready to go?"

I place the gift bag on the kitchen counter, and grab my keys, wallet, and phone. "Yep. Let's go."

We hop into his Audi and start the drive to the bar.

"So, how are things going?" E asks, and I don't even have to ask for clarification, because based on his tone, I know he's talking about me and Midge.

"Well, I don't know." He's silent, waiting for me to say more. "Okay, I like her. That's what you want to hear, right?"

He doesn't grin or laugh or say I told you so, he just keeps looking out at the road. "That was never a question. We all like her."

"Right. But yeah, I like her more than you should like a friend. I tucked those feelings away for many years, but now that we're doing what we're doing, it's been hard to keep them from bubbling to the surface."

"She likes you, too."

"I mean, yeah, sure. You're not gonna sleep with someone you don't like."

"Maybe you should tell her how you feel. How you always felt. It might make her change her mind about it being a short-term thing."

"She scares easy," I say, looking out the passenger window. "She thought London might have found out and looked terrified. I told her we should stop for a little while, but then she got sick and I went over to make sure she was okay. We didn't really get to talk about what's happening with us, but we're definitely not on the same page."

"I'm sorry, man. I really hope it works out for you. Give her some time. It hasn't been too long."

"Yeah, I know. Thanks, bro."

When we pull up to the bar, I can tell it's going to be packed, because both the parking lot and street side parking is full.

"What the hell did Royce say to get all these people to come here?"

Elijah shrugs. "Who knows?"

As soon as we walk through the doors, nearly everyone yells out happy birthday. I spot Royce behind the bar with his arms in the air and a huge smile on his face. He's clearly proud of himself.

As we maneuver through the crowd, I see a lot of familiar faces and get plenty of birthday wishes, handshakes, and hugs. My eyes instantly find the stage area, because Royce has a white backdrop hanging over the red brick wall, and black balloons spelling out happy birthday, surrounded by LED lights. A variety of white, black, and silver balloons float throughout the room, and I can't imagine Royce going through all this trouble. London must've helped him.

"Happy birthday, bro," he says, handing me a shot and a beer. "No time to waste."

"Thanks, man. Place looks good."

London pops up next to me, giving me a hug. "Happy birthday. Like the balloons?"

"Your doing?"

She grins. "Mostly, but Royce did help."

"I love it. Thanks."

Royce pours two more shots and hands one to Elijah. "Come on, guys."

The three of us take our first shots of the night, then I chase it down with a gulp of beer. I try not to make it too obvious that I'm looking for Midge, but my eyes definitely roam around the room a few times.

Jon and Daniel push their way to the bar. "Happy birthday! Feelin' old yet?" Jon asks.

"Not yet," I reply with a chuckle. "Maybe in a few more years."

Daniel nods. "Yep. It'll happen before you know it. One day you're fine, the next day you wake up to aches and pains in your knees and back."

Jon laughs. "Oh, please. You're not old."

Daniel levels a look at me, and I laugh. "Well, then I'll live up these next few years, I guess."

Me, London, Elijah, Jon, and Daniel all hang out near the bar, talking and drinking, with Royce coming by every chance he can.

"Dude, are you really gonna be working this whole night?" I ask.

"Nah, I'm just helping out. I'll be drinking soon, and then when I'm too drunk to work, I'll be on the other side of the bar with you guys," he says with a laugh.

London playfully rolls her eyes, shaking her head. "I'm surprised he doesn't have a bar in his house. It's where he's most comfortable."

"Good idea, babe," Royce says.

"Look what you did," I joke. "Giving him ideas."

London makes a face. "Anyway, Midge will be here soon."

"Okay," I say, pretending like I haven't been wondering where she's at this whole time.

A tiny smile plays on her lips. "Yeah, she texted me a little bit ago."

"Cool," I reply, nodding my head.

Two more drinks later, I'm approached by Jenny again. London is up at the bar with Royce. Jon and Daniel are dancing, and Elijah left me at the booth to go to the bathroom.

"Hey, birthday boy," Jenny flirts, giving me a wide smile. "Twenty-seven looks good on you."

I chuckle. "But twenty-six didn't?"

She takes a seat next to me. "You've always looked good. What about me?" she questions with another smile.

She's wearing a black, deep-cut top, showcasing her cleavage, and I'm pretty sure a pair of skin-tight blue jeans, but I honestly wasn't paying that much attention when she walked up. Her red hair is pulled up into a high ponytail, and a pair of long, dangling black earrings swing from her ears.

"You look great," I tell her. "Who you here with?"

She doesn't look anywhere but at me. "Just me. I heard about your party, so I figured I'd stop by and say hello."

"Well, I appreciate it."

She scoots closer and trails her red-painted fingernail over the ink on my forearm. "I've always loved your tattoos. What's the story behind them?"

I try to move away without being too obvious about it. The fact that I'm almost up against the wall as it is, doesn't give me much space. She's being very direct and coming onto me hard, and if I wasn't into Midge, I'd probably be all for this, but unease coils in my stomach. I haven't seen Midge yet, but she could very well come in at any time. And where the fuck is Elijah?

"Well," I reply, gazing down at my arm. "Each one means something different. Some don't mean anything," I say with a short chuckle.

She giggles, placing her hand on my thigh as she leans forward. My head snaps up like someone called my name.

Except nobody said anything, I just knew she was here. I could feel it. And sure enough, Midge stands just a few feet away, looking drop-dead gorgeous. Only, she's fuming.

To make matters worse, as my gaze is stuck on Midge, Jenny leans into me, her hand gently resting on my chest, and whispers into my ear, "Why don't you come home with me tonight?"

40

MIDGE

WHEN I SEE CILLIAN SITTING WITH JENNY, MY FEET FALTER, leaving me standing nearby, unable to pull my gaze away from them. My face flushes with anger, and my jaw clenches tightly.

I'm late to the party because I changed my goddamn outfit six thousand times in an effort to make Cillian's jaw drop. I wanted to drive him crazy all night long until he couldn't take it any longer, and needed to steal me away to a private spot.

Yet, here he is, cozied up in a booth with Jenny. At least he has it in him to look scared. More like busted.

Before I fly over there in a rage and make a scene, I rein in my emotions and turn away, telling myself this is why I don't do relationships. This is why I don't allow myself to get close to people. Everyone will disappoint you.

"Midge!"

I turn my head to the right, seeking out the female voice who called my name. It's London.

I give her a forced grin, and as soon as she meets my gaze, recognition flares in her eyes and she rushes over.

"What's wrong?"

It takes me a few seconds, because I'm afraid my stupid emotions are going to make me cry as soon as I open my mouth and explain what I just saw.

This! This is another reason why I don't fuck with relationships. Crying? I don't cry. I'm not a weepy, little girl. Yet, here I am, on the verge of tears, because the night I was going to tell a man I was ready for more, I catch him cuddling with another woman. I guess he didn't need much time to move on.

Instead of speaking, I turn around and look in the direction of the booth they're sharing. London's eyes find the table, only now, Cillian is fighting to get past Jenny, his gaze trained on me.

"Cillian and Jenny," I state simply.

London gasps softly, and I take off toward the bathroom, not wanting to talk to Cill right now.

As soon as I'm in the comfort and silence of the room, I lock the main door so he can't get in, because I know he'll try.

A woman exits one of the stalls and washes her hands before heading to the door. I quickly unlock it and give her a lopsided grin.

"Men."

She smiles like she's been there before. "Gotcha. Good luck."

Once she's gone, I lock it again and lean my back against the door. Sure enough, less than a minute later, Cillian's at the door.

He jiggles the doorknob, but when he realizes it's locked, he slaps his hand against the wood.

"Midge, let me in."

I ignore him.

ISABEL LUCERO

"I get that what you walked in on looked bad, but you have to believe me, nothing happened."

I roll my eyes. Typical.

"Midge!" He hits the door again. "Jenny came to me. Flirting and trying to touch me, but I haven't laid a finger on her. I swear."

I squeeze my eyes closed. Cill's always been honest, and I'd have no reason to doubt that he's telling the truth now, plus, it is Jenny, and I know how she is.

I sigh, then turn around and open the door.

Growth. That's what this is.

Cillian's hands are braced against the door jam, his back hunched over, and gaze trained on the floor.

He lifts his head when the door opens, then straightens up, breathing a sigh of relief.

I keep my stance on the other side of the threshold, watching him.

"I am not messing around with Jenny," he states simply.

I sigh, trying my best to not let my past issues come into play now. "It looked like you two were pretty friendly."

"I know. I'm sorry. She's very pushy, and I didn't want to be an asshole. I was hoping Elijah would be back soon, and she'd leave."

"Jenny's the one who my boyfriend cheated on me with," I admit.

He tilts his head and frowns. "I'm sorry, Midge."

I wave my hand through the air like it doesn't bother me, but I guess I'm still holding a grudge. "She's always hated me. We worked together, and my boyfriend at the time, Matthew, would come to the bank to get me for lunch or just stop in, so she knew we were together. She's always been a flirt, and she would flirt with him, but he would always pay it no mind. At least at first. He convinced me he wasn't interested in her, but then they started sleeping together. I'm not even sure how long it lasted. I got two different answers from them, and I'm not inclined to believe either one, so I'm assuming it was a few months." I take a breath. "Anyway, I guess I just figured maybe she got to you, too."

Cillian steps forward and gently grabs my arms. "I'm not interested in Jenny. I'm not interested in anyone but you."

I peer up at him with a small grin. "I'm sorry I over-reacted."

"I don't think you did. Maybe if you didn't take the time to hear me out, but you did. I get it. I'd be pissed if I saw you with some guy like that."

"We're not together, though. Maybe I don't have any right to be mad."

Cillian runs his hands from my shoulders down to my wrists. "Whether you know it or not, whether you admit it to people or keep it to yourself, I'm yours. You can be mad if you want to be."

My lips curl into a smile. I'm surprised he said he was mine and not I was his. Most alpha males are all about claiming you, but he's presenting himself to me.

"If you're mine, then what am I to you?"

"I'm waiting on you to tell me."

We stay locked in on each other for several seconds, his fingers threading through mine. My lips part as I suck in a breath, ready to tell him that I'm his. That I'm willing to give him my heart and trust, and hope for the best.

"Excuse me, I have to pee. Are y'all gonna be here a while or what?" a woman asks, shifting back and forth on her feet.

"Oh, sorry," Cillian says, pulling me out of the doorway. "All yours."

The woman blows by us with a quick, "Thanks."

"Guess we should head out here and have some fun, huh?" Cill asks.

"Sounds good." I grab his hand and tug him back before he leaves the hallway. "Happy birthday."

He grins. "Thank you."

Once at the bar, he gets Royce's attention. "Hey, let's get another round of shots."

Royce nods and grabs a bottle from the glass shelf behind him, and then lines up seven shot glasses.

Me, Cill, Royce, London, Jon, Daniel, and Elijah clink our glasses together and offer cheers to Cillian's birthday. After that, Royce makes me a margarita on the rocks, and we all cluster around the bar to drink and talk.

London gives me a questioning look, so I make sure to give her a smile and whisper that everything's okay. We'll definitely talk more about it later, but for now, I'm going to enjoy myself.

Cill casually rests his arm on my shoulder. "Hey, you're not so short tonight."

I lift up my foot, showing him my six inch heels. "Now I'm only half a foot shorter than you."

He eyes the heels then whispers, "I'd like to see you in nothing but those."

A smile stretches across my face as my stomach clenches. "Oh really?"

"Mm." His gaze moves from my lips to my eyes, like he wants to say so much more, but is restraining himself.

After I went through my six thousand outfit changes, I settled on a form-fitting white skirt that hugs every curve I have and comes to a stop just above my knee. It has red flowers on green stems with black accents, and my snug, red shirt is tucked into it.

"I'll drop your present off tomorrow," Royce tells Cillian. "I have to load it into the truck."

Cillian raises his brows. "Big, huh?"

"Yeah, and you better fucking appreciate it," he says with a laugh.

London told me Royce handmade Cillian a custom cabinet for his art supplies and canvases. He most definitely will appreciate it.

After a while, London pulls Royce from behind the bar, and we all go over to the backdrop they had set up for the party and take a few group shots. Me and London, of course, take several selfies, and then Cillian pops up behind us to get in the picture. When the rest of the group is preoccupied, London offers to take one of me and Cill. Nothing out of the ordinary, but my heart picks up speed anyway.

Cillian wraps his arm around my lower back, his hand coming to a rest on my hip, so I wrap my arm around his waist and smile a cheesy smile for the picture.

"That better make it to your collage in that table," Cill says.

"What do you mean? I'm blowing it up and framing it for my living room," I joke.

"Even better."

I playfully roll my eyes and turn to look for London. Her and the rest of the group have moved a little farther away, talking to some other people. When I spin back to look at Cill, I spot Jenny making her way over.

"Jesus Christ," I mutter under my breath.

"What's that?" Cill asks, but then he notices her, too. "Oh."

"Hey, Cill. I see there's a photo session going on over here. What do you say you and me take one together? Midge, you wouldn't mind taking a picture of us, would you?"

I want to take the phone from her outstretched hand and slam it over her fucking head to wipe that smug smile off her face. The bitch has balls. Granted, she doesn't know me and Cill have been fucking around, but good God, she knows me and her are not friends.

Cillian drapes his arm over my shoulders, bringing me closer to him. "Sorry, Jenny. Midge is my girl, and I've been made aware of y'all's history. I'm not about to do anything to piss her off. Thanks for coming out, though."

Then he guides us around her body, seemingly frozen in place, shocked expression on her face, and toward the bar. My lips stretch into a wide smile as my stomach flip-flops and my heart skips a beat. God, he's the best.

I peek up at him, smile still plastered in place, and he glances down at me. "What?"

"You didn't have to do that."

"I wasn't about to have you take a picture of us together. She was clearly just trying to piss you off."

"Yeah, probably."

"Plus, what she did to you before, that's not cool. I'm on your side, Midge."

My cheeks hurt from smiling so much. "You also said I was your girl."

At the bar, we wait for Chad, another bartender, to head our way. Cillian stares into my eyes before responding. "Well, you are."

"Yeah?"

"Doesn't matter if we're not sleeping together right now. You're the only one I want, and maybe I'm just being an optimist, but I think things might work out between us." He nudges me and gives me a wink.

Now's the perfect time to tell him. "Cill."

"Yeah?"

"All right, sorry about that. Busy night," Chad says, coming to a stop in front of us.

"No worries, man," Cill answers. "You still having a margarita on the rocks?" I nod. "Okay, margarita on the rocks for the lady, and I'll have another Bud Light."

"What were you saying?" he asks, leaning over to hear me.

"Oh, I was just gonna say…"

"There you guys are!" London says, flinging herself against the bar. "There's so many damn people here. Cill, you're loved."

He smiles. "I think Royce offered everybody a free drink or some shit. Who knows why so many people are here."

London orders a drink, and then the rest of the crew joins us, so I decide I'll just tell him tomorrow. There's way too much going on right now. Tonight's not the night for serious conversations. Tonight's the night for drunken shenanigans.

"Let's go to the special, reserved booth," I say. "Time to play drink while you think."

"Oh no," a couple people grumble.

"Oh yes," I say.

"And here's where we get drunk," Cill says, following me to the table.

"Isn't that the point? To get the birthday boy drunk?"

While we scoot into the booth, Cill whispers, "The birthday boy has other plans."

I grin, glancing around to make sure nobody's paying attention. "You gonna tell me what they are?"

He squeezes my thigh under the table but leaves it at that.

41

CILLIAN

EVERYONE'S DRUNK. I'M HORNY. I WANT TO LEAVE.

Two in the morning came fast. We've been here drinking since nine, and though we paused the drinking to eat some food and have some of the cake London brought in from Flaky Vicki's, drinking has been the predominant activity.

Yes, some of us got up to dance. Not me.

Yes, we played more drinking games. Elijah bailed out of the games early, because he's responsible and didn't want to get too drunk to where he couldn't drive home.

Yes, I struggled to keep my hands to myself when it came to Midge. I managed a few under-the-table touches because nobody's looking down there.

But it's fucking late, and I can't stop thinking about getting Midge naked and underneath me. Tonight, without too many words, and with plenty of touching, I think we've decided to start things back up again.

"All right, people. Thanks for everything. I'm heading out," I announce, slightly running my words together.

"You're not driving, are you?" London questions.

"Yeah, didn't Elijah drive you?" Royce adds.

Elijah left an hour ago because I told him I'd be getting a ride home with Midge. Nobody else knows that was the plan. Well, Midge does, but Midge is drunk, too.

"Oh shit."

"You could stay upstairs with me and London," Royce suggests, though I know they'll want their own alone time.

"I'll grab a Lyft."

"Me too," Midge says, grabbing her phone. "I have the app. Wanna share?"

"Sure."

London chokes back a laugh. It definitely seems like she suspects something. I've seen her watching us a little more closely than usual.

Jon and Daniel left a little bit ago, I'm assuming via Lyft as well, because they both had a lot to drink.

I say goodbye to Royce and London, giving them both hugs before they disappear to the apartment upstairs.

Only a few people remain, but Royce has two bartenders and his manager here to close things down for him.

Me and Midge stumble outside, enjoying the cool air and the fact that we're now out from under watchful eyes. She takes off her shoes and checks her phone.

"Five minutes."

"Your house or mine?" I ask, because we both know that wherever we're going, we're going together.

"Yours is closer."

I give her a drunken, happy smile. "I like your thinking."

We crash into each other, our mouths connecting in a frenzied kiss. A car drive's up next to us and honks, so we pull away to get into the Lyft.

The drive to my house isn't long, but when I close my eyes, I find it hard to open them again. My blinking slows way down, and I know the alcohol and late hour are getting to me. I shake my head, trying to snap myself out of it.

Once we pull into my driveway, I take the keys from my pocket and head up the walkway to unlock the door.

Inside, I don't bother turning on any lights, I only head straight to my room.

"Want anything?" I ask, after we've already passed the kitchen.

"Just a bathroom."

Once in the bedroom, I point toward the attached bathroom, and Midge disappears behind the door. When she flicks the light on, she says, "Oh God, bright lights are no good." She gasps. "I look like shit."

I chuckle, removing my shoes and jeans, then flop onto the bed to wait. I close my eyes, and the room tilts. Oh man.

I hear Midge knock something over, followed by a drunken laugh, and then I don't remember anything else.

Lights out.

~

When I finally wake up, it's because my phone is vibrating and dinging on the table next to me.

I reach out and grab for it, squinting at the screen to read the message from Royce.

Royce: *I'll be there later. Hungover as fuck.*

Well, at least I'm not alone. Now that I'm awake, I push back the covers and sit up, scratching my head. I don't even remember falling asleep last night.

I get up and make my way to the bathroom, because my bladder feels like it's going to explode. After I piss, I stand at the sink and read a message written across my mirror in lipstick. Well, not a long message. All it says is *You're cute* and a little heart underneath.

Midge. She must've done this when she was in here last night. I don't doubt she came out and was disappointed to find me asleep. God, that's embarrassing. I spent most of the night whispering promises of sexual adventures just to pass the fuck out.

As I brush my teeth, I realize I didn't see a text from her on my phone. Did she leave and go home last night? I didn't notice her in the bed, but then again, I didn't really look around. My back was to the rest of the bed, and I just sat up and came straight to the bathroom.

I quickly finish up, then walk back to the bed. The covers are all bunched up, and initially, I don't think she's here, but then I hear a slight snore. My feet carry me to the other side of the mattress, where I find Midge curled up, almost completely hidden under the blankets. I only spot some of her hair splayed out on the pillow.

She stayed.

My lips curve up as I listen to her soft snore. I decide to let her sleep as I head into the kitchen to put on a pot of coffee and scrounge up some food.

As the coffee's brewing, I trot over to the laundry room and pull a pair of clean lounge pants and a white T-shirt out of the dryer. I'll shower later, but for now, I have to get out of last night's button up shirt.

The coffee pot beeps, letting me know it's done, and I find eggs and bread. Well, it's not much, but it's something.

I drink a full cup of coffee before I start making the food, just to give Midge some extra time to sleep. As the eggs are cooking, I hear the toilet flush in the master bath, and as I'm putting the bread in the toaster, Midge turns the corner.

"Smells good in here."

I smile at her. Not because of what she said, but because of what she's wearing. She's no longer in her skirt, instead she's in one of my T-shirts.

"Looks good on you. Not sure if I prefer this or the lingerie."

She looks down at the shirt and grins. "Well, this does nothing for my figure," she jokes. "Hope you don't mind. I found it folded up on your dresser. I didn't want to sleep in that damn skirt."

The toast pops up. "Perfectly fine with me. I thought maybe you left. I didn't know you were in the bed until I came out of the bathroom and heard you snore."

She gasps. "I don't snore!"

"You do," I say with a laugh. "Not like a bear. It was a cute, light snore. Like a baby bear."

"Oh, that's better," she says, rolling her eyes. "A baby bear is still a bear."

"You sleep all the way under the covers, too. Like, you're hibernating."

She steps forward, heading toward the coffee pot. "Can I get some?"

"Of course."

"I wasn't hibernating," she says. "It was fucking cold in your room last night. I was freezing."

I laugh. "Sorry, I like it to be cold when I sleep."

"Yeah, me too, but that was like sleeping outside in Alaska."

I put the toast and eggs on the plates, then take them to the small, round table that's in the kitchen nook, near the windows.

"You could've cuddled up next to me. I would've kept you warm."

She turns around with coffee cup in hand. "Yeah, wasn't sure if you were the cuddly sleeper type." Her eyes dart around the kitchen counter. "Sugar?"

I point to a black dish in the corner. "There's creamer in the fridge."

"Cool, thanks."

"I'm not sure if I'm a cuddly sleeper," I say, using her words. She makes a face at me and I laugh. "I'm serious. But you could've tried."

She walks toward the table. "You were pretty out of it. When I saw you were asleep, I pulled the covers out from under you, which wasn't easy. You're like a tree. But with all the jostling and shoving I did to get you under the covers, you didn't wake up," she says with a laugh. "And sleepiness crashed into me like a wave, so I stole your shirt, climbed into the bed, and was probably asleep ten seconds later."

"Well, I'm glad you stayed."

She smiles at me from across the table. "Me too." Before she digs into her food, she says, "Oh, I also stole some of your mouthwash."

"You're just a thief, aren't you?"

She shrugs. "Maybe. I'm also gonna need to steal some Tylenol or something."

I laugh. "You can take whatever you want."

"I'll remember that," she says, her gaze roaming over me.

42

MIDGE

ONCE WE'VE FINISHED OUR FOOD, CILL TAKES OUR PLATES TO the kitchen and comes back with water and Tylenol for both of us.

"Thanks." I grab the pills and pop them both in my mouth, swallowing them down with a gulp of ice-cold water. "And for breakfast."

"No problem."

Cill starts talking about something that happened last night at the bar, and though I'm listening and nodding, my head is elsewhere. Now is the time to tell him. Maybe this conversation isn't a big deal to most. Maybe other people would have no problem telling someone that want to have a committed relationship, but I'm not those people.

He stops talking and studies me. "What's going on? You seem zoned out."

"Yeah, sorry," I reply, giving him a small smile. "I uh...well, I've been thinking about some stuff, and wanted to talk to you about it."

Cill straightens up, his face tensing up. "Okay," he says hesitantly.

"Let me give you some history first. So, I told you about Jenny sleeping with my boyfriend, right?" He nods. "Okay, so Matthew was the last boyfriend I had. It was three years ago, and we were together for two and a half years. I met him when I was twenty-one, and fell for him hard and fast. He was a few years older than me, and I thought the sun rose and set with him. I was young and stupid, yes, but he never gave me a reason to think he wasn't perfect.

"Anyway," I say, waving my hand through the air. "Everything I did was for him. I never wanted to disappoint him or anger him. I was the perfect girlfriend. I let him have guys' nights or guys' weekends without complaining or nagging him. I didn't go out with my friends almost at all, because he didn't like that. He said he wanted me to be safe and that he was worried about me when I went out, so I thought he was just being a caring boyfriend." I roll my eyes, realizing how stupid it all was.

"To sum up, he was a jerk. He was very controlling. Things had to go his way or he'd be angry, and I never wanted him to be angry with me. When he was happy, everything was fine. We laughed, we went out to dinner, we were normal. I mean, I thought so, anyway. Blah, blah, blah, fast forward and he meets Jenny. She's a huge flirt, and doesn't give a shit about people's relationship status. We worked together at the bank, and she would flirt with Matthew whenever he would come in. He was polite, but when I asked him if he thought she as attractive, he said she wasn't his type.

"Fast forward some more, and I start becoming suspicious. He's out more, he's not responding to my texts or calls. He visits me late at night, then he's gone early in the morning. So, one day, I get into his phone while he's in the shower, and I come across tons of messages between him and Jenny. It went back a few weeks, but I don't know if there had been a previous thread he deleted or what. I found out everything I needed to know in a matter of minutes.

"He didn't care about me at all, he told her he didn't love me, though he told me he did every time we were together. They exchanged explicit messages and photos, and she talked shit about me, and he would laugh about it. It was awful. And it's because of that situation that I've been happy being single for these past few years. Well, for almost a year I was still beaten down and insecure. I replayed every message they sent to each other, recalling every negative thing they had to say about me. I believed it.

"But one day, I woke up and decided to hell with all that. I began to love me, flaws and all. I went out, I met people, and I did whatever I wanted to do. I no longer had someone holding the reigns of my life. I was free, and I never wanted to give that up."

Cillian leans forward and clasps my hands in his. "Midge, you should always be able to have your freedom, even in a relationship. It's not healthy to only spend your time with one person. Having friends and a social life is good, and you can do that in a relationship. You were just with some selfish fucking asshole who got off on manipulating you."

I give him a small, crooked grin. "I know. Because of him, I've thought all men would be the same way. He led me to believe that was the case. He used my inexperience against me, and told me I just didn't know how serious relationships worked. Looking back, I see the bullshit, but I was blinded by what I thought was love."

"Well, I can see why you're anti-relationships if that's the only one you were in."

"I had boyfriends in school, but it was school, so nothing was too serious back then," I say with a shrug. "One cheated on me, one broke it off because I wouldn't sleep with him after a week." I roll my eyes.

"Guys suck," Cillian says.

I laugh and look him in the eye. "Not all of them." He grins. "I think I'm ready to try again. With you."

His eyes widen in surprise. "Yeah?"

I nod and look down at his thumb caressing my hand. "I've liked you for a long time, Cill. Back when we were just kids, and even more now. We never took a step to be anything more, so I figured you didn't see me as anything other than a friend. But I loved our friendship so much, I didn't mind as long as you kept coming around. I know we went a few years without talking much once we left high school. We were busy with college and work, then got into relationships, so we went from talking and hanging out every day to just saying hi to each other when we were out and about. But man, I'm glad we became closer these past couple years."

Cillian smiles at me from across the table. "God, Midge, we really should've learned to communicate better when we were teens."

"Why do you say that?"

"Because I had the biggest crush on you back then."

"What?" I screech.

43

CILLIAN

I LAUGH, RELEASING HER HANDS AND SITTING BACK IN THE chair. "Yeah, I thought you were the coolest chick in school. You had your no-nonsense attitude, and you were always speaking your mind, whether it was to a student or a teacher. You wore those plaid skirts with black tights and combat boots."

Midge covers her face with her hands. "Oh God, I thought I was so punk rock back then."

"It worked for you."

"So, you liked me the whole time you were coming to my house?"

"Yep. Before then, too. But I really realized it after my parents' died, and you were there for me. People don't know how to act around a kid who lost his parents, you know? People at school stared and kept a distance, like I had some sort of disease. You didn't though. You took me in like I was a lost puppy. You brought me home to your parents and y'all fed me and let me have some semblance of a family. Not to say my brothers didn't act like family, but we were all struggling. Things were rough at home, and it wasn't a happy place for a while."

She tilts her head slightly to the left. "I get it. I'm glad I was able to help you in some small way during that time."

"Small? You brought me back to life. I hadn't really thought about it like that until Elijah mentioned it to me the other day. You kept me going when I just wanted to curl into a ball and stay in bed. You invited me and Royce out, and had me over to your house all the time. If I didn't have you, I would've been depressed for a lot longer. I can't imagine what it would've been like without you."

Midge presses her lips together like she's trying to keep her emotions in check. Her eyes become glassy with unshed tears. I don't want to see her cry, so I change the topic.

"And I feel like shit for letting any amount of time go by where we weren't talking."

She waves me off. "It wasn't just you. It happens to a lot of people. Once we leave high school, we start our path to adulthood, and sometimes things and people get left behind. At least we made it back to each other."

"We did," I say with a smile. "And now you're my girl. Like I've always wanted you to be."

She chokes out a laugh. "I can't believe we both liked each other, but never said anything. We could've had years together."

"Maybe it was better this way," I say. "We had our time to be friends, and we had time to be without each other and try out other relationships."

Midge moans and rolls her eyes. "Eck."

"Even if they were bad," I say with a laugh. "And now we're here."

"We're here," she repeats.

"And we like each other a little more than friends," I say with a grin.

She brings her thumb and forefinger together. "Just a little."

"And we're going to tell people...when?"

She ducks her head and chews on her thumb nail. "Well, London knows."

"What? Since when?"

"Last week, and you know what gave it away?"

"What?"

"You and that damn chicken piccata!"

I rear back, confused. "What?"

Midge laughs. "You went over to Elijah's and mentioned having had chicken piccata recently, but I had already told her I had it at my parents' house. She got suspicious and questioned me about it."

"Wow. Chicken piccata givin' us up."

"But she didn't tell Royce. She said she'd wait until me and you had a talk about taking us public."

"Well, that's two people down. Really, only Royce is left."

"And Jon and Daniel," she adds.

"I don't think they'll care."

"Maybe not. I also have to tell my parents, but I'm pretty sure my mom knows."

"Probably," I snort. "Moms are perceptive."

"Well, at least she already adores you."

"Easy to do," I say with a grin.

Midge rolls her eyes. "Pft."

I stand up and reach for her hand. "I have a confession. Come with me."

She takes my hand and stands up. "Confession scares me."

"Well, it was a tiny fib. I didn't want to scare you off by thinking I was a psycho."

She trails behind me as we march down the hall and toward my room. "Even more scared."

In the room, I make my way to a vintage wooden secretary desk. It was a piece my parents' had for years, and I'd always pull open the door, which served as the desk once open, and sit down to draw. I stored my pencils and papers in the little compartments inside, and basically took it over from my mom. She didn't seem to mind.

Inside, I pull out a folded and wrinkled piece of paper and hand it to Midge.

She eyes me with nervous curiosity before taking the paper and slowly opening it. She flips the paper around and then brings her shaky fingers to her lips as she studies the drawing.

"You do have it," she whispers.

"Of course I have it."

She glances up. "Why?"

"Two reasons. One: It's the first picture I drew after my parents' died. It took a while to want to do it again. I felt like if they couldn't see what I was creating, it didn't deserve to be created. They both played integral parts in me becoming the artist I am, and it felt wrong to do it without them. Elijah helped push me through that type of thinking. He told me they wouldn't want my talents to go to waste. And then that day you challenged me to do it. Granted, in your own, teasing, shit-talking way, but you were there pushing me to create art again, and I would've done anything for you. Two: It's you, Midge. Why would I throw you away?"

Her lip quivers and then she throws her arms around me, lifting up as high on her tip-toes as she can. I bend down and hold her in my arms.

"You're so perfect," she whispers into my neck.

I chuckle. "I'm really not."

She backs away and takes another look at the paper before handing it to me. "You did a really good job. I'm glad you kept it. Why did you say you didn't?"

I fold the paper back up and place it back in its' compartment. "You seemed to be freaking out a little. I said we might be meant for each other, and you froze. I invited you to dinner at my brother's house, and you almost had a panic attack. I wasn't about to tell you I'd been keeping a photo of you from ten years ago. It's the same reason why, when we were at your parents' house, I didn't tell you that I liked you when we were kids. I didn't want you to know just how much you meant to me, and for how long, because you may have packed your bags and skipped town."

She twists her mouth at me. "I wasn't having a panic attack."

"Sure," I reply with a smirk.

"I hate you."

I step forward and place my hands on her waist. "Do you?"

She fights her grin. "Yep."

I lift her up off her feet and she wraps her legs around me. "I think I should prove to you that you don't."

"I might take a lot of convincing."

"I have time, baby girl."

She squeals when I drop her onto the bed, covering her body with my own.

MIDGE

"OKAY, OKAY," I PANT, TURNING TO THE SIDE. "I DON'T HATE you."

He smacks me on the ass as he gets out of the bed. "I know."

I watch as he pulls the condom off, my eyes zoning in on that beautiful piercing. Which reminds me.

"By the way, I went and got some tests done. You know, to make sure I'm not carrying any infectious diseases."

He snorts. "Sexy."

"Well, I should have word back this week. Though, I've always been careful, and doubt I have anything."

He throws the condom in the bathroom trash, then wanders back to the bed, crawling toward me with a grin in place. "Someone wants to feel everything, huh?"

I bite my lip. "Yep."

"Good. Well, I got tested after I found out Zoe cheated on me. No infectious diseases here either."

"That's good."

He kisses my lips then backs up off the bed, standing in

front of me, stark naked. "So, I'm about to jump in the shower. Wanna join?"

"How could I say no?"

"I was hoping that'd be the case."

He gets the water started as I detangle myself from the sheets. A few minutes later, we're both under the warm spray of the shower.

"You're big body is blocking most of the water," I complain.

"It's not my fault you're small."

I smack him in the stomach. "Move."

He laughs and switches places with me, then grabs his loofa sponge and squeezes some soap on it.

"Do you have separate shampoos and conditioners, or a two-in-one kind of thing?"

"Two-in-one."

"Ugh. Men. Better than nothing, I suppose."

He hands it to me, and I wash my hair with this bottle of crap that won't leave my hair soft and silky, but whatever.

After he's washed himself up, and I've rinsed out my hair, he moves in, rubbing his palms over my hips and cupping my ass. He brings me closer, dipping his head under the stream as he leans down and kisses my neck.

Before we can even get started, the doorbell rings, pulling both of us apart.

"Oh shit. I forgot Royce was coming by." He does another quick rinse before stepping out of the shower. "Meet me out there?"

"Guess he has to find out somehow. Why not right after we were showering together?" I say with a smirk.

"He'll be fine."

I finish up my shower while Cillian rushes to the door. As I'm drying off, I can hear their voices traveling down the hall.

Cill must've left the bedroom door open. Which sucks, because I don't have any clothes in here. I wrap the plush, white towel around my body, use Cillian's comb to tame my hair, then I slowly emerge from the bathroom.

As soon as I step into the bedroom, I spot Royce through the open bedroom door, standing at the end of the hall. He does a double take when he sees me.

"Uh, what?" he says, looking back at Cill before glancing in my direction again.

I lift my hand and give him a small smile. "Hey."

His confused face makes both me and Cill laugh. I keep moving across the room and out of his line of sight, searching for my discarded clothes.

I hear him asking Cill more questions as I get dressed in last night's garments. I don't really hear what Cill says, but I hear them chuckling about something.

I appear in the doorway when Cill says, "We'll see you tonight at E's." They both look back at me. "She's definitely coming this time."

"Yeah, well, I look forward to hearing this story," Royce says. "Bye, Midge," he adds with a stupid grin and small wave.

"Bye, Royce." I mimic his wave and smile.

Royce punches Cillian in the shoulder before opening the front door.

"Thanks for the gift, man. It's fucking awesome."

"No problem, bro. See ya later."

Once Royce is gone, me and Cill meet in the middle of the hallway. I get on my tip-toes, wrapping my arms around his neck as he leans down and encircles me with his arms.

"Well, one more person down," he says.

"You know once I tell my parents, you're gonna have to come over to dinner more often, right?"

He laughs. "That's fine. It'll be like the old days."

"Except now they'll know we're fucking."

"Let's hope they don't spend too much time thinking about that," he replies with a deep laugh.

"So, what time is dinner?"

"Six-thirtyish."

"What time is it now?"

We walk back down the hall, into his bedroom. "Three-forty."

"Okay, well, can you take me home so I can change? I'll probably call my parents, too."

"Yes, ma'am," he says, smacking my ass as he goes to his closet to find a shirt. "I'll pick you up around six."

"I can meet you there," I offer.

"Nope. I'm picking you up."

I roll my eyes, but my smile reveals my happiness. "Okay."

CILLIAN

AT FIVE FIFTY-FIVE, I'M AT MIDGE'S DOOR WITH A SMILE ON my face and flowers in hand. She makes a face at me when she sees the flowers.

"What?" I ask behind a laugh.

"You being romantic now, Mr. Kingston?"

"It's kind of like our first date, right?"

She takes the flowers, and I follow her inside while she finds a vase in her kitchen. "First date with two of your brothers and my best friend?"

I shrug. "Well, okay, maybe not a traditional first date. But we are having dinner, and there most likely will be sex at the end of the night."

"Hopefully not with the aforementioned people," she jokes, filling the vase with water.

"Ha-ha. No, not into orgies with my family."

Once she gets the bouquet settled into the vase, she leans in and inhales their scent. "These are beautiful. Thank you."

"Not a problem. You ready to go?"

"Yep."

Twenty minutes later, we pull into Elijah's driveway.

"We're first?" she questions.

"Looks like it. Nervous?"

She grins. "A little. Is that weird?"

"I guess I understand. There's been a shift in our relationship, but Elijah and Royce won't treat you any differently."

She takes a breath. "Okay, let's go."

On the short walk to the door, I take her hand in mine and look over and smile. We walk right in, because Elijah knows to expect us, so the door is always unlocked around this time.

Elijah's dog, Sugarfoot, comes trotting around the corner to see who's here. Sugarfoot is the calmest dog I've ever known. He hardly barks, so he's not the best guard dog, but he loves attention, so he'll definitely jump up on you and wait for you to pet him.

Midge reaches down and runs her hand over his long, golden fur. Sugarfoot rubs his body against her black jeans, because he loves to leave his fur on everybody's clothes.

"He sheds a lot," I say, giving him a couple pats on the side.

"But he's so cute!" she replies, unbothered.

"This is Sugarfoot. Elijah's best friend. Probably only friend," I say with a laugh.

"I heard that," Elijah calls out.

"Sugarfoot is the cutest name," Midge squeaks.

Elijah joins us in the foyer, wiping his hands on a towel. "I can't take credit for that, but it is fitting," he says, nodding toward the dog's front left paw. "Looks like he dipped that paw in a bowl of sugar and it just never came off."

Midge straightens up and faces Elijah. "Thanks for having me tonight."

E grins. "It's not a problem. So, you two making things official now, huh?"

I glance at Midge and her red cheeks. "Yeah," she answers, glancing over at me. "He wore me down."

"Only took a decade," Elijah jokes, turning and walking to the kitchen. "Come on, Sugarfoot." He pats his leg and the dog follows him.

"I wasn't trying consistently for a decade," I say, rolling my eyes as we follow him into the kitchen. "Jeez, you're making me sound like I have no game."

Midge angles her head in my direction, smirking. "Well…"

"Oh, shut it."

Elijah chuckles. "Cill, grab the plates, will you?"

"What's cookin'?" Cill asks, sniffing the air as he reaches for the plates.

"Chicken teriyaki casserole."

"Ooh, that sounds good," Midge says. "You always been the chef around here?"

Elijah shakes his head with a laugh. "I was forced to learn. For a while, we all ordered takeout or went to fast food places. If it wasn't that, it was sandwiches and frozen meals. Easy stuff. But, after a while I started looking into cookbooks and trying to come up with meal ideas."

"I was good with pizza," I say with a shrug.

Elijah shakes his head. "And Merrick only wanted macaroni and cheese, and Royce was obsessed with Hot Pockets."

I remember those early days after Mom and Dad died. We had meals that people brought over for the first two weeks. After that, we ate what we found in the pantry, or like Elijah said, went out to get unhealthy crap from McDonalds or Taco Bell. Not that we complained. Me and Royce were teenagers, and Merrick was only eleven, so we were fine with junk food. Elijah did his best to remain stoic and strong. We barely saw him cry. I can remember one time that he broke down. He suffered in silence. Then one day, he was cooking meals, and making sure we were doing our homework, and really took on the role of guardian.

The front door opens and Royce's heavy steps mixed with London's click-clacking heels make their way to the kitchen.

"Hey, family," Royce greets.

London's face cracks with a wide grin as she rushes over to Midge, giving her a hug. A few quiet whispers are exchanged between them before both sets of eyes meet mine. Well, no need to wonder who they're talking about.

Royce leans back against the counter. "So, who's telling me the story, because apparently, I'm the only one who didn't know about this," he says, gesturing between me and Midge.

"Not much to tell," I say. "We, uhh, got together at the lake house. It continued here. We just made things official. That's it."

Royce's eyes bounce back to Midge. "That was boring. Midge, come on, tell me the good stuff."

Midge laughs. "But what he said is true."

"Does nobody have a storytelling gene in their body around here? We got together. It continued," he mocks. "Really?"

I roll my eyes and cross my arms over my chest. "And how would you tell the story of you and London getting together?"

Lo smiles, leaning against the island next to Midge. "Yes, how would you describe that?"

Royce rubs his hands together, his smile growing. "Well, one day, a woman with sun-kissed hair and sky-blue eyes blew into the bar with an infectious laugh that could cure even the saddest sap. I was frozen in place, watching her saunter toward me. She was the most beautiful woman I had ever seen, but as soon as she sat down, she got a call from her boyfriend. Not one to back away, I flirted relentlessly. I asked her to break up with him at least once a month. We had a chemistry you couldn't deny. She was mine the minute she walked into my bar. It took some time, but she finally realized it."

London watches him with adoration, her smile so wide her cheeks must hurt.

I scoff. "Okay, we get it."

"Hater."

"Please," I say, making my way to Midge. "Me and Midge have history. We have a story that spans a decade."

"Oh, you're finally admitting to those old feelings, huh?" Royce teases. "You had been denying those even leading up to our trip to the lake."

Midge peers up at me through her dark, thick lashes, and I drape my arm over her shoulders. "I didn't need you giving me shit for what I thought was unrequited...feelings."

Royce cocks a brow at my hesitation. "So this whole time you've both been lusting after each other and never said anything."

"I said some stuff," Midge chirps. "To London."

Midge and London laugh. "It's true. She did."

I squeeze her into me. "Like what?"

"Just that you're gorgeous and amazing and stuff like that," London answers, waving her hand in the air like it's no big deal.

"Oh yeah?"

Midge rolls her eyes. "Okay, it's not a big deal. Everybody knows the Kingston Brothers are the cream of the crop around here."

"So, you think we're all attractive?" I tease.

She slaps her hand on her forehead. "Oh God."

We all laugh, and I pull her into a hug. "It's okay. As long as you think I'm the hottest."

Royce scoffs and Elijah laughs. Midge gives me a little squeeze and looks up at me. "I do."

Elijah starts taking things to the dining room, but Royce keeps talking.

"So, y'all were like fuck buddies?"

"Royce," Elijah warns.

Royce laughs. "What? I'm serious. I just wanna know why the secrecy."

Midge huffs. "You're annoying. Look, it's no secret that I haven't been in a relationship for a while. Just like you hadn't been before you met London, so shut up. I have my own issues, and before feelings came into play, I thought this would be a short-lived fling. No need for you and London to be caught up in the awkwardness when it was over. But then shit changed." She shrugs. "Cillian's the best man I've ever known, I've adored him since I was fifteen, and I'd be foolish to not give a relationship with him a try."

I smile, then the rest of the room smiles. Midge blushes.

"Well, okay, then," Royce says, finally satisfied.

Using my forefinger and thumb, I tilt her chin up and plant a kiss on her lips. "I adore *you*," I say softly.

She rolls her eyes, blush tinting her cheeks once again, but her smile lets me know she's anything but annoyed.

"All right, love birds, dinner is ready," Elijah announces.

As we're walking into the dining room I say, "So, E, when are you gonna get a girl?"

"Don't start, Cillian."

46

MIDGE

"FOR REAL, THOUGH," CILLIAN CONTINUES. "YOU AND Sugarfoot need a lady around."

"Why?" Elijah asks, grabbing his fork.

Cillian looks around the table, hoping someone jumps in to help him. "Uh, you know, so you're not lonely."

"But I'm not lonely."

"Right, I know, because you have a Rolodex of women's numbers."

"Rolodex?" Royce questions. "What year is this?"

"Well, you know, Elijah's like an old man. I'm sure he has a rolodex in his office."

Elijah bites down on a smile, shaking his head. "The Rolodex in my office isn't for women's numbers."

"I knew it!" Cillian shouts, pointing at Elijah.

"I have a cell phone with women's phone numbers. And just because you two have started to settle down, doesn't mean I have to."

"You're the oldest."

"I'm only thirty-five. That's not old."

"Leave him alone," I say, feeling bad for Elijah.

Elijah gives me a warm smile. "Don't worry about it, Margaret. They're always giving me shit about something or other."

Cillian picks up his fork. "All right, I'm sorry. I just worry about you here. You're alone, and you weren't dealt the easiest hand in life."

"None of us were," Elijah adds, picking up his water glass.

"I'm not just talking about losing Mom and Dad. You had to drop everything to finish raising us. You were already out of the house and doing what you wanted. Then you came back and took care of us three. You've never talked about it, but I'm sure that sucked for you. That had to be hard, and yet, you did it. Then what happened with you and Jenn..." Cillian trails off. "Anyway, I just want you to have some happiness in your life."

The table goes quiet, everybody unsure of what to say. I shove some food in my mouth and discreetly glance around at everyone.

"I appreciate that," Elijah says, breaking the silence. "Yes, it was hard, but it didn't suck. Y'all are my brothers, and I'd do anything for any of you."

Royce and Cillian nod, accepting his response, but me and London share a look across the table. Elijah didn't say he was happy.

After everyone takes a bite or two of food or a sip of their drink, I speak up. "So, my mom's birthday is on the fifth, and me and my dad are planning on having her party at the lake house, so is everyone gonna be available?"

"You know I'll be there," Cill says with a grin.

London claps her hands together. "Yes, of course."

"Elijah, you'll come, right?" I ask, wanting him to be included this time.

"That's a weekend?" he questions.

"It's Sunday. Monday is Labor Day, so most people will have that day off. Mom and Dad aren't coming up until Sunday morning, and I plan on getting up there Friday or Saturday to set everything up."

Elijah nods. "I can make it then. School starts up next week, but as long as it's on a weekend, I'll be free."

"Awesome."

The rest of the dinner continues without any heavy topics, and conversation runs smoothly. Cill was right. There's no awkwardness at all. After all, we're still friends. Nothing's changed except me and Cillian have seen each other naked now. Okay, and maybe a little more, but still. Our friendship remains the same.

After dinner, everybody makes their way to the den to hang out. London rushes over to the wall lined with pictures and gestures for me to come over.

"Midge, you have to see this photo of Royce and Cill."

"Oh, God," Royce murmurs.

"Which one?" Cill asks, coming to join us.

"Look how cute!" London squeals, pointing to the picture of Royce and Cillian in the bathtub together.

I put my hand over my mouth and laugh. Cillian's hair is all wet and spiked up in every direction. Royce's hair is plastered to his forehead, and he's gripping what looks like two different colored dinosaurs. Cillian has bubbles on his face like he was trying to give himself a beard.

"I'm not sure why Elijah keeps these up," Cill grumbles.

"Mom loved those pictures," Elijah says from the nearby armchair. "Of course they're staying up."

"Yeah, but where are your embarrassing photos?"

He points to a picture across the room. "Have you seen

that photo of me with braces? And what was I wearing? Corduroy overalls?"

"Until you have a picture of you in the bath, not the same."

Elijah's phone rings, stopping the conversation.

"It's Merrick," he says before answering.

"Oh, our own little rock star, huh?" I say to Cillian.

"I know. I still can't believe it. He'll be back next month."

"Are all the guys coming back home?" Royce asks Cillian.

Cill shrugs. "Probably. All of their families are here."

"So, after their concert in Cleveland, they get a break?" I ask.

"Yeah. I don't know for how long, because he said they'll have to start working on the second album."

"First album sold like crazy, right?" I ask.

"Oh yeah. Big time. Still selling like crazy."

"That's awesome."

"Everybody's here," Elijah says, turning the phone to the room, so we can see Merrick's face on the screen.

"Hey, guys," Merrick says with a big smile.

We all wave and say hello, then Merrick leans forward, squinting his eyes.

"Is that Midge?"

I take a few steps forward and give him another wave. "Hey, Merrick. Long time, no see. You doing anything worthy of a True Hollywood Story episode on E! yet?"

Merrick laughs, his baby face looking less like a baby with the dirty blonde scruff he's growing out. He runs his hand through his hair, a shy smile on his face. "Maybe, maybe not."

"Oooh," I tease.

"Is that Midge?" another voice questions in the background.

I instantly tense up. It's Sky, their lead singer, and someone I hooked up with before they released their album and went on tour.

Sky's face barges into the screen. He's good-looking, no doubt, like he was born to be a rock star. He has vivid blue eyes, black hair, and a permanent cocky smile to go with his attitude. But he still pales in comparison to Cillian.

"Hey," I say stiffly.

"There's my girl. Been a while, yeah? You miss me yet or what?" He smiles like he knows I'm going to say yes.

"Not really, no," I reply.

He laughs. "Sure. You comin' up to the show in Cleveland?"

Cillian steps up and wraps his arm around my shoulders. "Yeah, we'll be there."

Sky turns his gaze to Cill. "Oh, are y'all...is this..." He never finishes his question.

"Yeah, we're together now, bro. So whatever happened in the past is gonna stay there."

Sky chuckles. "All right, man. I gotcha. No disrespect." His eyes glance around. "See y'all later."

Merrick comes back in, shaking his head. "Well, that's Sky for you."

"He's a mess. Probably sleeping with a new chick in every city, yeah?" Royce asks.

"Sometimes two or three."

"Jesus," Royce mutters under his breath.

Merrick and Elijah continue talking while the four of us have our own conversations. London and Royce start talking about hosting a game night, and Cill sits down in another armchair, pulling me into his lap.

"I'm almost done with the painting," he says softly against my neck.

I turn around. "I still haven't seen them. And you showed London." I cross my arms and pout.

He chuckles. "I wanted you to be surprised. And I look forward to seeing your face when you see it for the first time, one hundred percent complete."

"When will that be? Tomorrow?"

"Middle of the week, probably."

"Fine. I guess I can wait."

"In the meantime, you can let me paint you," he whispers quietly.

"I told you I am not laying around naked for hours."

"No. Paint *you*," he emphasizes, dragging his fingertip across my arm.

I stare into his eyes and bite down on my lip. "Mm, that might be interesting."

47

CILLIAN

INSTEAD OF GOING TO EITHER ONE OF OUR HOUSES, WE END UP at my studio. I run in first and turn the easels around so she can't see the paintings.

When Midge steps in, she takes in the changes. "Looking better in here."

"Yeah, I took someone's advice."

"Must be a really smart someone." She throws me a grin over her shoulder as she saunters to the new couch. "Looks comfy." She drops down, wiggling her ass in the center cushion. "Super comfy," she moans, leaning back.

"And no more flickering light."

"I noticed. Now I won't have any seizures or migraines."

She gets up and moves to inspect some of the art on the walls.

She focuses on the one I painted several years ago. A deserted path surrounded by trees in the middle of fall. Their leaves are a mixture of bright oranges and vivid reds and yellows. The path is the middle of the woods, curving across the ground and littered with fallen foliage.

I watch her as she studies my work, a smile curving her

lips upwards as she admires them. The next photo is of a couple of wild horses galloping across an open field. She carefully runs her finger over the horse, as if she were petting it.

"These are amazing, Cill." Her voice is full of astonishment. "You'd think this was just a picture you took one day."

"I loved working outdoors up at the lake, so I figured I'd surround myself with some outdoor work."

"Makes sense," she says, walking toward me.

I keep an eye on her as I add paint to my pallet. If she thought I was kidding about painting her, she's about to find out I wasn't.

"Strip."

She stops. "You're really gonna paint me?"

"Yep. And it would look much better without your clothes on."

She tugs on the hem of her shirt. "Only if you take your clothes off, too."

I put the paint down and rip my shirt over my head. "Done."

She slowly pulls her shirt over her head, then drops it on the floor.

I eye her pants. "I think the pants need to go, too."

"Then so do yours," she counters.

"Fair," I say with a smile.

She watches as I undress, leaving me in only a pair of white boxer briefs.

"Your turn."

She follows suit, removing her shoes and pants. After a brief pause, she unhooks her bra and drops that too.

I arch my brow and she shrugs. "Only fair. But I'm not taking off the bottoms. No paint needs to end up anywhere down there."

A loud laugh erupts from my throat. "Okay. Let's get started then."

For the next hour, I try not to let my perfectionism get to me. Otherwise, we might be here forever.

Her neck and chest are covered by a collar I created with a mixture of gold, black, teal, and blue. Intricate shapes and designs make it look pretty similar to what Egyptian goddesses would wear.

I paint her breasts and the space between them, creating jewelry and gems with the paint.

She watches me intently as I work.

"You're so focused," she says softly.

"I can't mess up my new favorite canvas."

She snorts. "I'm afraid to look down and mess up the paint. Are you turning me into a flower? A clown?"

"Definitely clown," I say with a smirk.

I continue painting gold bands around her arms, a thin belt around her waist that connects up to the piece the falls between her breasts.

Once I force myself to finish, I take my phone from my previously discarded pants, and take a picture.

As she's about to protest the photo, I turn it around and show her.

"Oh my God," she gasps, taking the phone in her hands. "I look good." She giggles, then zooms in on the picture, checking out the detail. "Wow, Cill. You've turned me into a model. I may have found my new profession."

"Yeah, I'm glad I took this picture, because it's a real shame."

She gazes up at me. "What's a shame?"

"That I'm about to mess all this up."

I advance, taking my phone from her hand and putting it on the floor, then swiping a condom from my pants' pocket.

My hands find their place on her hips as I back her up until we hit the couch.

She wiggles her panties down and steps out of them. I remove mine and take a seat on the middle cushion while I rip open the condom wrapper with my teeth. Midge turns around and watches me as I roll the latex over my length.

"Come ride me, baby."

Midge doesn't hesitate. She straddles me, then lifts up and grabs my cock in her hand before sliding me inside of her.

Her head falls back as her eyes squeeze shut. "Ohhh," she moans.

I grab ahold of her hips, but let her take control. At least for now.

She rocks back and forth, taking me deep.

"Fuck, Midge," I grunt.

"Mmm," she purrs, her eyes still closed.

I grab her throat. "Look at me."

She listens, gazing into my eyes as she continues to move.

"So agreeable when I'm fucking you," I say with a smirk. "I love it."

I slide my hand up, ruining the paint, and put my thumb on her chin as my fingers curl around the back of her neck. I pull her forward and capture her mouth with mine. My tongue swirls around hers softly and gently. She shudders, and her fingers twist in my hair as the kiss becomes feverish.

She continues to grind herself on me, tortuously slow. Her pussy teases my cock, so I tease her mouth. I pull away and swipe my tongue across her lower lip. Midge attempts to pull me closer, but I back up.

I kiss her chin and the corner of her mouth, and press my hand to her lower back, stopping her movements.

Midge whimpers. "Cillian."

I kiss the other corner of her mouth, then suck on her bottom lip before sinking my teeth into the soft flesh.

My thumb grazes her cheekbone as I plant a chaste kiss on her lips. She pushes forward, wanting more, so I finally give in to her and plunge my tongue into her mouth.

She releases a grateful moan, then begins rocking her hips back and forth again. This time, it's fast and needy. Midge breaks the kiss, her arms going around my neck as she molds us together. Her painted chest pushes up against mine, her heavy breaths brush against my neck, and her explicit chants find my ear.

"I'm gonna come," she breathes.

"Yeah," I grunt, needing that tight pussy pulsating around my cock.

"Oh, God."

Her hips move as if they're set on fast forward, and then her whole body tenses up and she freezes, her fingernails digging into my shoulders. "Fuck!" Her pussy clamps around me, then she's moving again, and her voice fills the studio as she cries out.

She leans to the side, resting her head on my shoulder as she attempts to catch her breath. "Jesus Christ," she pants.

After a minute, Midge slowly climbs off of me, careful to not get any paint on the furniture, and then I stand up next to her and bring her to the side of the couch.

"Brace yourself on the arm, okay?"

She nods and I move behind her, using my knee to spread her legs out a little farther. I grab the base of my cock and slide into her wet center, then hold onto her waist as I thrust in and out.

I move faster and deeper, then shove my hand in her hair, twisting the strands around my fingers as I pull her head back.

"Yes," Midge hisses.

I don't slow down. I fuck her deep and hard and watch her ass jiggle as our skin slaps together.

When I climax, I release her hair and dig my fingers into her hips, shoving deep inside her.

"Fuck!"

I hunch over her back, my arm coming around her stomach, holding her up as I rest on top of her. My cock twitches, still releasing my load, and she tightens her pussy around me.

"Oh, God," I groan.

As soon as I'm able, I pull out and get rid of the condom.

Midge looks down at herself. "I'm a mess."

"Me too," I say, looking down at my chest and stomach. "And my handprints are on your ass and back. I think you should keep them."

She rolls her eyes. "I don't think so."

"Fine. Maybe I'll just tattoo my name across your ass cheek."

"Pft. I'm not about to be branded like a cow."

"You don't have any tattoos," I state.

She pulls on her underwear and pants since she doesn't have any paint on her lower body. "Nope."

I toss her my shirt. "Wear that so you don't ruin yours. Why haven't you gotten any ink? Not your thing?"

She ogles my tattoos. "Oh, it's most definitely my thing."

I smirk at her. "Good."

"Maybe one day," she says with a shrug before pulling my shirt over her head. "I happen to have an in with a pretty good tattoo artist."

"Oh yeah? Just pretty good?"

"Yep."

"You love giving me shit, don't you?"

She smiles, showing her teeth. "I really do."

"I'll allow it, but only because you're so cute and small."

Her smile is replaced with a scowl. "Dick."

"Again? So soon?"

She fights a smile. "I hate you."

"Nah. I don't think so."

"It's true, I do," she says, turning her back on me and slipping her feet in her shoes.

"Truth or dare?" I question with an arched brow, knowing she'd be forced to tell me the truth.

She bites down on her lip. "No, thanks."

"I thought so."

48

MIDGE

On Wednesday, I saw the painting Cillian created for my mom and it took my breath away. His work is so lifelike, I could almost feel the breeze and hear the water hitting the rocks. My mom is going to love it.

It's now Friday, and since I couldn't take off from work, I'm driving up to the lake house tonight. I won't get there until almost eleven, but that's okay, because Cillian's coming up with me.

I haven't had the chance to tell my mom about me and him yet, so I'm going to give her a call now, so she isn't surprised to see us together at her party on Sunday. Me and Cill saw Jon and Daniel at King's Tavern on Wednesday, and neither of them seemed too surprised about us being together.

My mom answers on the second ring.

"Hello?"

"Hey, Mom."

"Hey, baby. How you doing, huh?"

I walk in circles around my coffee table. "I'm doing pretty good. I just wanted to call and tell you something."

"Oh no. Should I sit down? Is it bad? What did you do?"

I laugh. "Calm down. It's nothing crazy."

She sighs. "Okay, good."

"So, you know me and Cillian have been friends for a long time."

"Uh-huh."

"Yeah, well, uh, we're sort of together now." I turn around and circle the table the other way. "Actually, not sort of. We are. We're dating."

"Honey, that's great."

"Yeah?" I ask, a huge smile on my face.

"Of course. How new is this? Because I thought you two were together when you were over for dinner."

"What?" I screech. "Why did you think that?"

"He couldn't take his eyes off you, for one. You both seemed extra smiley around each other, and when you talked about being with someone, you gave him a look. Never mind what we came home to. You guys running around, flirting and laughing."

"We weren't flirting."

"Okay, sure." I can tell she's smiling when she says that.

"Ugh. Anyway, it's fairly new."

"I'm happy for you, sweetie. You two have always had a special connection. Let me ask you this, did it start at the lake?"

I hesitate. "Maybe."

Mom laughs. "I told you there was magic there."

No need to tell her how it started. I'm sure she doesn't want to hear about his magical dick giving abilities.

"I guess so."

"Well, you two need to come back for dinner. As an official couple this time. Let me know when works best for you."

"Okay, Mom. Love you."

"Love you, too, baby."

"Bye."

She hangs up, and I'm left with a giddy smile on my face. A few minutes later, Cill knocks on my door.

"Hey," I say when I pull it open. "Almost ready. I got caught up talking to my Mom for a minute."

He steps inside and places his hand on my waist as he leans in and gives me a kiss. "Oh yeah? You tell her?"

I kiss him again. "Yep. But apparently, she knew." I roll my eyes. "She says we were flirting."

Cill laughs. "I thought I was doing pretty good."

"And I guess you kept staring at me," I say with a flirty smile.

"Oh really?" He grins. "Can you blame me?"

I look down at myself and toss my hair back. "No, no I can't."

He shakes his head, laughing, then grabs my bag. "I'll take this to the car."

"Okay. Be out in a second."

I do a quick run-through, making sure lights are off, hair appliances unplugged, and sinks aren't dripping, and then I head outside and climb into Cillian's Jeep.

"Our first road trip," he says with a grin when I climb into the passenger seat.

I'm not sure why I ever thought it would be weird to be in a relationship with someone you were friends with. I'm still having plenty of firsts. He still makes my heart race and my stomach clench with a single look.

"Let's do it right, then," I say, blasting the music and singing along as he pulls onto the street.

"Oh, no," he groans.

"Oh, yes." I hand him the invisible mic in my hand, waiting for him to sing.

He quickly glances over at me and shakes his head. "I'll be the audience. Merrick's got the voice. Not me."

I roll my eyes and continue my concert, making Cill laugh the whole time.

We pull up to the house nearly four hours later.

"Ah, where the magic happens," I say.

Cillian angles his head at me with a curious look, and chokes out a laugh. "What?"

I chuckle. "Mom said this house has magic in it. It's where she fell in love with my dad, and where we started."

His lips turn up in an amused smile. "I see. Well, I guess she's right."

"Was it the house or the alcohol that got us together, though?" I ask, arching a brow.

"Maybe a little of both, but I'll be honest with you, Midge. I came here hoping we'd get some alone time, so alcohol or no, I had an agenda."

I stare at him bug-eyed and slack-jawed. "I'm sorry. What?"

His chuckle is low. "Let's go inside."

Once he's taken both of our bags to the room he stayed in last time, he comes back and joins me on the couch.

"Okay, so you were saying…"

"I know I had just broken it off with Zoe a week before, but in that week all I could think about was how we'd be up here together, and we'd both be single. I've liked you for years, and prior to my relationship with Zoe, I had a short-lived relationship with someone else, and before then, you were with Matthew. And honestly, I was starting to get the idea that maybe you liked me more than a friend. I was determined to find out for sure when we were here."

I gape at him. "What do you mean you had an idea I liked you? I never gave anything away." I think about it for a minute. Did I?

He shakes his head. "It was just little glances here and there. Maybe I was making it into something it wasn't because I wanted you to be into me. But I started thinking about you in ways I shouldn't have before I had even broken up with Zoe."

"Whaaaat?" I can't keep the huge smile off my face.

Cillian grins. "I just found myself watching you. Not in a creepy way," he adds with a laugh. "You entranced me. If you were around, I couldn't keep my eyes off of you."

"Probably because I'm so loud," I joke.

"You've always captured my attention. But when I saw you with Sky that night at Elijah's, I found myself getting jealous when I had no right to. When I asked you about him the night of the bonfire, and you didn't seem too bothered about him leaving, I felt relieved."

I can't stop grinning. I straddle his lap and wrap my arms around his neck. "If we're being honest, I always hated Zoe. I never thought she was good enough for you."

Cill throws his head back and laughs. "Is that why you always found a reason to disappear when she was around?" He cups my ass through my jeans.

"Maybe."

"You're probably too good for me," he says, his hands crawling up my back and bringing me closer. He kisses my neck. "But I'm just selfish enough to not care. I'm not letting you go. I wasn't lying before. I really think we were made for each other."

I run my fingers over the muscles in his shoulders and

then push them through the strands of his hair. "I think you're right."

He backs up. "You're actually agreeing with me?"

With a shove to his chest, I say, "Yeah, but don't get used to it."

Cill laughs. "I won't."

"Bedroom?" I ask, lifting a brow and biting on my lip.

He stands up, holding my ass in his hands as I wrap myself around him. Cill strides across the room, dropping me to the bed, and instantly stripping himself of his clothes.

I quickly do the same, throwing every article of clothing I have on the floor. Tonight we finally get to have sex without a condom. My blood test results came in yesterday. Clean.

Cillian stands at the side of the bed, his chiseled and art-covered body making heat swirl in my stomach. I make my way to the edge of the mattress, and hold his thick cock in my hand. As I stroke his length, he runs his fingers through my hair, twisting the strands in his fist to keep them from getting in the way.

My lips part and my tongue swipes across the underside of his crown. I take my time teasing him with soft licks and firm strokes before taking him as far into my mouth and throat as he could go.

After about ten minutes, Cillian takes a step backwards and instructs me to lie on my back. Of course, I happily oblige.

I spread my legs for him and he crawls between them, hovering over me. He reaches down between us, his fingers sliding into me.

"I love that you get this wet from just sucking my cock," he says, penetrating me with one and then two fingers.

"Well, I love your cock," I reply, arching my back.

"Mm. Well, I won't keep you waiting."

He withdraws his fingers and quickly replaces it with his dick. When he pushes in, I gasp and he grunts.

Cillian teases me with long, slow thrusts, making my desire for more grow. The piercing without the protection of the condom makes a difference, especially when his cock drives in deep.

"Oh, yes!"

He thrusts his hips harder and faster, giving me everything I could ever want. His cock reaches my g-spot, sparking fireworks behind my eyelids as I slam my hands into the bed and fist the covers. Then he pulls out. Before I can protest, his face is between my legs and his tongue swipes across my clit.

"Oh, God," I moan, covering my eyes with my palms.

Cillian tastes every drop of arousal between my legs, lapping me up like it's his only job. My clit throbs and my pussy clenches as soon as he slides his finger inside.

Once again, he brings me to the precipice of bliss, then stops.

"Cillian!" It's a half plea, half scolding.

He chuckles, getting up and guiding himself inside my needy, wet center. "I got you, baby girl."

Cill buries himself deep, hitting my g-spot with his perfect cock, and that piercing is the fucking cherry on top. He hits that spot over and over again, and my orgasm builds every time his hips pound against mine. My need to come makes me delirious, and I yell out words that probably don't make complete sentences. I beg and plead for more as my body feels like it's on fire.

My body tightens as I reach my climax. "Oh, yes," I cry out, turning the word into a hiss as I drag it out.

I squeeze his biceps, my nails creating crescent-shaped moons in his skin, as my pussy contracts and clenches his cock.

Cillian grunts, his own frenzied need to come making him drive into me with passionate force. He curses under his breath, and I cling to him, riding out the aftershocks of my orgasm, my soaked pussy still contracting around him.

"Oh, shit." He nearly fucks me through the mattress as he finds his release, coming with a deep growl.

"Oh, yes," I purr, my hands on his back and my thighs squeezing his hips.

He shudders above me, his whole body reacting to his orgasm. He stays inside me for another minute, taking his time to get his bearings.

I suck in air like I've just completed a marathon, and a couple drops of sweat fall from Cillian's head as he shifts, and land on my skin.

"Holy shit," he breathes, slowly pulling out.

"I agree." I stretch my aching legs out, my thighs spasming.

"So glad I don't have to wear those damn condoms anymore," he says, rolling onto his back.

"You and me both."

His head flops over, his eyes finding mine. "Guess I should've asked before, but...birth control?"

I grin. "Oh, for sure. Since I was sixteen."

"Okay, cool."

Cillian rolls to his side and wraps his heavy, sweat-slicked arm around me.

"Ugh. It's too hot."

"Shh." He throws his leg over mine and pushes his head into my neck.

"You're lucky that I…"

"I'm lucky that you're so small you can't overpower me?"

I give him a shove and he doesn't move. "Oh, whatever."

He laughs and detangles himself from me. "Fine. I'll go get clean."

"No, me first!"

He jumps up from the bed and darts to the bathroom. "Gotta be quicker than that."

I run after him, completely naked and sore, but determined to get in the shower first. "I'll hurt you."

That makes him laugh. "Right."

I grab his semi-hard cock, hoping to threaten him. "I won't?"

He makes it twitch, grinning down at me. "You love it too much."

He's not wrong. I let go and lunge for the shower, turning the water on and climbing over the side of the tub. "I'm first." The cold water hits me like tiny shards of ice penetrating my skin. I gasp, sucking my stomach in and taking a step back.

Cillian holds his stomach, cracking up at me, so I cup my hands under the stream and throw it at him.

"Oh, that's it," he says, climbing into the back of the shower.

"No!" I squeal, but then I dissolve into a fit of laughter.

Luckily, it doesn't take long for the water to heat up and for us to get clean. Before I know it, we're in bed, curled up together and falling asleep.

Cillian nuzzles the back of my head with his nose. "Mm. Guess we are cuddly sleepers."

I giggle and push my ass into his crotch. "I like it."

49

CILLIAN

WHEN MIDGE AND I WAKE UP SATURDAY MORNING, WE GO straight to the store to grab everything we need for the party.

"Remember when we went shopping together for Royce's first bonfire?" Midge asks.

"Yeah, I remember you thinking I wouldn't know what to get if I went alone."

"And I was right, because you didn't even want to go down the bread aisle, when we obviously needed hot dog buns."

"You went down every single aisle!"

"You never know what you need until you see it."

"Is that how you shop?" I ask with a laugh.

"Yep. Isn't that how everyone shops?"

I shake my head, laughing. "Okay, let's go down every aisle and see what we need."

And we do just that. We go down every aisle the store has and Midge finds at least one thing from each one. I think she just picked out random things to try to prove a point, because there's no way she needed some of the stuff she got. Toilet bowl cleaner tablets? Probably not necessary.

Back at the house, we put everything away, and then start putting up some of the decorations.

"Mom would die if it was *too gaudy*," she says, making a face.

"I'm guessing she's said this before."

"Only about a million times. She should plan her own parties, because she's way too picky."

"Does your dad know that she knows?"

"Nah, he's clueless. Mom doesn't know it'll be up here, and that in itself is the surprise." Midge grabs the multi-colored Happy Birthday sign, and hands it to me on the ladder. "She's been giving me all these instructions and rules on how to decorate, what the cake should look like, and how it shouldn't have candles on it."

"No candles?"

"She says she doesn't want to blow out all those candles."

"What if you just got the two giant numbers?"

She shakes her head. "Said she doesn't want her age to be out there for everyone to see."

I tack up one side of the banner, then move the ladder to get the other side up. "Um. You know this banner has her age on the side, right? And all these colors and glitter are probably considered gaudy."

Mischief twinkles in her eyes as she looks up at the brightly colored banner that not only says Happy Birthday in the center, but says, *You're fifty*, on each end.

"She can't get everything she wants."

Midge grabs the bags of balloons and sits in front of the mini helium tank she bought and starts filling them up.

The balloons and banner are the only decorations, and the cake she picked up from a local bakery is free of candles and doesn't have any flowers made from icing as per her mother's request.

"She doesn't like flowers?"

Midge laughs. "Not on her cake. She finds them—"

"Gaudy?"

"Yep. And overdone."

"I see."

"Don't worry, if for my birthday you want to buy me a cake that's shaped as an actual fucking flower, I won't complain. Just never get me carrot cake or cheesecake."

I laugh. "Duly noted."

"Okay, so the place is clean, the decorations are up, and the caterers will be dropping off the food right before they get here, which should be about half an hour after all the guests are supposed to arrive."

"So, we're done?"

"Yep, we're done."

"Good, because I have plans. Grab your shoes and meet me out back."

While Midge is in the room, I run to the fridge and grab the sandwiches I pre-made earlier, a couple bottles of water, and then head out back and shove them into the duffel bag I've already prepared.

When she comes through the doors, I stretch my hand out to her and sling the strap of the bag over my other shoulder.

"Come on. Magic awaits."

She rolls her eyes but takes my hand anyway. "What're you up to?"

"Not much."

We walk across the yard and toward the old maple trees, cutting through them and getting to the clearing she told me about.

I drop my bag and pull out a blanket to protect her legs from the sharp blades of grass.

"A picnic?" she says, her voice going up an octave with her excitement.

"Nothing fancy. I have some sandwiches, chips, water, and…" I stop, reaching into the bag. "What's this?"

She gasps, reaching for the box like a child reaching for his favorite toy. "My donuts!"

"Well, save one for me, okay?"

She clutches it to her chest. "Can't make any promises."

We enjoy our picnic with the view of the water, and Midge allows me to have two of the six donuts, as we stretch out on the blanket and look up at the sky. She says she's saving two for later. I don't argue, because she takes her sweets very seriously.

"Remember when I ate your Reese's cup, and you wanted to stab me with your pencil?"

Midge laughs, turning to her side to look at me. "Who eats someone's candy, though? Like, we were just doing homework and you ate my candy."

"In my defense, I didn't know it was the last one. It was king-size, for Christ's sake! I thought I could take one."

"The last one."

I chuckle. "I didn't know."

"I was saving that particular one for when I was done, and then I go to grab it and it's gone. You're lucky you actually didn't get stabbed."

After we lay there for a little while, reminiscing about some of our times together when we were kids, we pack everything up and drop it off at the house, then grab the canoe and head out to the water.

"I can see why my parents loved it so much out here," she says, taking in all the scenery.

"Me too."

We spend the next hour out in the middle of the water, watching the sun drop lower and lower in the sky.

It's something I hope we continue to do for years to come. Even if I have to buy a house up here just for us. Just for moments like this.

MIDGE

I'M STARTING TO THINK MY MOM WAS ONTO SOMETHING. Maybe this place does have magic, because I'm starting to have urges to spill my guts to Cillian. And by that, I mean I've already nearly slipped and told him I love him.

Now I know it's not hard to believe. I mean, I've loved him for a while. Yes, it was as a friend, but doesn't that make the transition easier? I love Cillian, yes, but now I'm in love with him.

You may ask yourself if there's a difference. The answer is simple. Fuck yes there's a difference.

I love London. I love Jon and Daniel. I even love Royce. They are my family by choice. But I'm not in love with them. My heart doesn't react to them the way it reacts to Cillian. I don't crave their company the way I crave his. I'm not addicted to their laughter or the way their eyes crinkle in the corners when they smile.

And on top of that, Cillian makes me feel good about myself. He treats me well. I mean, come on, he came over with coloring books, ice cream, and medicine when I was sick and looking and feeling like trash. He took care of me.

He makes me laugh and he makes me want more. With him, I can look into the future and not be afraid. I can see a wedding dress and babies. I've never thought about that before. In fact, I thought I never wanted it, but with him, I look forward to those things. Because I know that life with him would be fun.

I've realized the way I was thinking before was wrong. I was incredibly stupid to ever try to put Cillian in a category with Matthew. Cillian creates his own category. I'm almost positive there's nobody else like him in the world. I was bitter about my past, but I've smartened up, and I want nothing more than to be with him and only him forever and ever.

After a while, we head back to the house and put the canoe away, but we choose to settle in the Adirondack chairs that face the water so we can watch the sky change colors as the sun dips below the horizon.

Cillian reaches over and holds my hand, stroking the back of it with his thumb. I love that with him, we don't always have to be joking and teasing each other. I love that these quiet moments are just as good. We don't have to fill the silence, because we're just as comfortable in the absence of conversation as we are when we're reminiscing about old times.

He squeezes my hand, stealing my attention. "You seem lost in thought over there."

I smile. "I guess I was."

"Anything good?"

"I'm with you, aren't I?"

His grin spreads across his lips. "So, you're thinking about me?"

"Yeah. You. Us. Just stuff."

He gives my hand another gentle squeeze. "Me too."

"Yeah? Like what?" I shift in my chair to get a good look at his face.

"Oh, lots of things," he replies with a crooked smile.

"Well, do you want to share?"

His eyes crinkle in the corners as his smile grows. "Do you?"

"I love the way your eyes crinkle when you smile."

Cillian laughs. "Wasn't expecting you to say that."

"I love your laugh, too."

He continues to watch me with amusement, his smile never faltering. "Keep going."

"I love being out here with you. I love that we have so much history to look back on and that we'll never run out of things to talk about, because we're friends. I love that my parents love you. I love the way you look at me when you're thinking naughty things."

We both laugh, and I'm very aware of how often I'm saying the word love.

"I love how close you are with your brothers. I love your talent. I love your kind heart and generous spirit. I love the way you make me feel." Once it seems like I've said too much, I stop, and say, "Now, you go."

Cillian blows out a long breath, resting his head on the back of the chair as he watches me. Our bodies are facing each other, and our hands are still connected, but his face no longer holds that smile I love so much.

I hold my breath, waiting to hear what he's going to say. Will he have a long list like me? Maybe he wasn't thinking as deeply as I was. Maybe he was just thinking about what we're going to do next weekend.

"I was just thinking about how much I love you." My eyes widen, my heart smashes against my ribcage, and my stomach tightens. Cillian grins. "It can't be that big of a surprise, can it?"

I shake my head, sweat pricking my skin. "N-no."

"God, Midge. I think I've always loved you. You've been such a good friend to me over the years. I was on the ledge of despair for so long, looking down and wanting nothing more than to plummet to a deep, dark place where nobody could find me. But you didn't let that happen. You tied yourself to me and kept me anchored. Stable. I'll never be able to repay you for that."

I dab at a tear. "Stop."

Cillian gets out of his chair and kneels between my legs, grasping my hands. "No, it's true. You did things for me my brothers weren't able to. Not at that time. Not when we were all struggling. I'm sad that they didn't have someone like you in their corner. I know Royce came out with us after a while, and we did things together, but you were always mine. My anchor. My everything."

He pulls down on the collar of his shirt, and points to a tattoo. Even though it's dark, I can tell what it is. An anchor.

My heart swells, threatening to burst with emotion, and tears fill my eyes. I've never had a man make me cry through sheer happiness.

I trace the ink with my finger as he continues to stare into my eyes.

"On top of all of that, I love you for who you are. I love everything about you, Midge. Your open mind and warm heart. Your selflessness, and the love you have for your friends. I love how you're unapologetically you. And I love what we have. We've had years as friends, and now we get to start a whole different journey as lovers."

I smile down at him, biting down on my lip to keep it from quivering. I capture his face between my hands and pull him up to plant my lips on his.

"God, I love you." I kiss him again. "So, so much. I was afraid to say it. I was afraid you'd think it was too soon."

Cillian pulls away and presses his palm against my cheek. I nuzzle into it and place my hand on his.

"If anything, we took too long." He drops his hand and grabs mine, pulling me up from the chair. "Come on. Let's go inside."

"You got that naughty look in your eye," I say with a smile.

"I'm thinking very naughty things."

I giddily follow him into the house, ready for him to show him to show me the types of things he's thinking.

EPILOGUE

Midge

"It's party time!" I yell as soon as my parents have walked in. Everybody else yells Happy Birthday.

"Oh, my God," my mother cries, her hand going to her mouth.

I mean, she knew there would be a party, but maybe she didn't think it would be today, or that her friends would travel up here for her. She's still surprised, so that's good.

Mom greets a couple of her friends, her eyes darting around the room before she gets to me. She comes in for a hug, but as we're embracing, she says, "I'm gonna kill you for that sign."

I laugh. "Happy birthday, Mommy! I love you!"

She snorts and gives me a kiss on the cheek. "Thanks, baby. This is great. Really."

Cillian steps up and gives her a hug. "Happy birthday, Mrs. H."

Mom reciprocates the hug, then steps back and holds onto his hands. "I hear congratulations are in order."

Cill glances at me with a grin. "It was always bound to happen."

"I'm surprised it didn't happen sooner," Mom says. "But I'm happy for you two. Come over for dinner again soon, okay?"

"Yes, ma'am."

Mom smiles at us both, then moves on to greet the other guests.

After everybody eats, we move the party out back since the weather is nice, and Mom starts opening her presents.

"I feel like a six-year old." She laughs, going through the bags and boxes, and I'm there with a trash bag to collect the wrapping and ribbons.

She thanks her friends, ready to move on, but I stop her.

"Hold on, Mom. We have one more."

Cillian's already gone in to set up the three piece painting. When we go inside, he has them leaning against the wall.

I gesture toward them, and my mom stops mid-stride and mid-sentence. Her hand shakes as she brings it to her chest. "Oh my."

I link my arm with hers and stare down at the exquisite paintings. "I asked Cillian to paint this for you. I know how much this place means to you and Dad, and I know you don't come up here as often as you'd like, so I wanted you to always have this to look at."

Dad comes to a stop next to Mom and pulls out a hand-kerchief. She accepts it and dabs at her eyes. "This is...I have no words. It's perfect."

My dad whistles. "Doesn't look like a painting. You did this?" he asks Cillian.

"Yes, sir," he answers with a nod and smile.

Mom throws her arms around Cillian and then me. "This is absolutely perfect. Thank you."

The party goes on for another few hours, and then everybody starts to leave. Some of them plan to stay in the area for the night, others have to go back to Gaspar. I'm just glad my mom has friends that love her enough to make this trip, even if it's just for five or six hours.

Elijah spends some time talking to my mom before he leaves, and whatever he's saying has her a little emotional.

"He's thanking her for being there for us when Mom and Dad died," Cill says, his arm going around my waist. "He hasn't seen her in a long time, and he never got the chance to express his gratitude."

"Aww, that's nice."

"Your mom came to our house to talk to him. Did she ever tell you that?"

I shake my head. "No. When? Why?"

"It was back then. She would send over meals and check in. One day I saw her and Elijah in the living room. It was the one time I saw him crying. I think she was offering advice. Being motherly, you know? I snuck away, because it felt like a moment that was meant just for them. I'm not sure what all that conversation entailed, but it was after then that Elijah pulled himself out of his sadness and started really taking care of us and the house."

"I had no idea."

Elijah hugs my mom and then heads over to us. "I have to go, but thanks for the invite."

"Of course," I say, giving him a hug. "Thanks for making the trip."

He and Cill hug goodbye, then he moves on to talk to Royce and London. Soon after he leaves, Royce and London do too. Once everybody is gone, my parents head out back, and Cill pulls me into our room.

"I have something for you."

"It's not my birthday," I say. "But I do love presents!" I bounce on the balls of my feet. "What is it?"

Cill disappears into the bathroom then comes out with a twelve by sixteen frame. I arch a brow, but he holds it against his chest, hiding it from me.

"I thought maybe you'd like this."

He turns the frame around and I see myself. Actually, I see two of me. The picture is done in charcoal, and it's a replica of the one he did of me ten years ago, but this time, he's drawn a current depiction of me in front of the older one.

The current me is laughing, my head slightly tossed back and to the side, as if I was looking at someone. My hair is flying every which way, but I look extremely happy. The version of me from ten years ago is a bit similar in that I'm smiling and looking deliriously happy. My lips are parted, my teeth showing, but back then my hair was longer, and I was wearing a hoodie. My dark locks partially cover my face as I hold my hands together under my chin.

"You've always been so carefree. Your smile and joy is infectious, and to be around you is to be hypnotized completely. I loved you then and I love you even more so now, and I'll keep loving you until we're old and retired, living in one of these houses out here."

"Cill." My voice cracks.

"It's happening, babe. You and me were made for each other. I told you that. You're not getting rid of me."

I smile as a lump forms in my throat. "I never want to be rid of you."

He places the picture on the bed. "Good."

"I have a question for you," I say, reaching up to wrap my arms around his neck.

Cillian wraps me in his arms, hugging me tight. "I may have an answer for you."

"Truth or dare?"

He chuckles. "Hmm. Dare."

"I dare you to take me to the nearest hotel and make love to me all night long."

He picks me up and my legs tighten around his waist. "My lovemaking is likely going to turn into fucking."

"Mm. Then let's hurry."

Cillian throws his head back and laughs. "I fucking love you."

"And I love fucking you. Let's go."

PREVIEW OF ON THE ROCKS

KINGSTON BROTHERS NUMBER ONE

Royce

"You break up with your boyfriend for me yet?" I ask London as she wiggles into the barstool across from me.

She purses her pink lips and tilts her head. "Sorry to disappoint," she answers, placing her wallet down in front of her. "You know what I want."

I smirk at her. "You know what I want, too."

She rolls her eyes, but a smile plays on her lips. Her head turns toward the stage where the band is setting up.

"New band?"

"Yep," I answer, pulling the Johnnie Walker bottle out and then pouring it over ice. "They're pretty good."

"Gonna be hard to fill the last band's shoes," she says, raising her brows at me.

I chuckle. "Yeah, I'd say so. But we can't keep doing karaoke every Saturday night. It's been months of that shit, and the last thing I want to hear is a bunch of drunk asses getting up there and screaming the wrong lyrics into the mic." I slide her glass over to her. "Black Label. On the rocks."

"Thanks, Royce."

I give her a nod and quick smile before moving down a few seats and serving another customer.

It's only six-thirty, so it's not too busy yet. The place usually starts filling up around nine, and it doesn't slow down until about one.

Gaspar is a small town and it isn't really known for its nightlife, but we get plenty of business throughout the week, regardless. In fact, we're probably the number one place people choose to spend their time after work or on the weekends.

"Same thing, Jim?" I ask one of our regulars.

"You bet," he answers, knocking on the wood before going back to a conversation with his co-worker, Craig.

Because I've lived in Gaspar my whole twenty-seven years of life, I know most everyone who comes in here. Craig and Jim always come in after work on Wednesdays, and most Saturdays and Sundays.

I pour him a Jack and Coke, heavy on the Jack, and place it on one of our King's Tavern napkins.

"Craig, buddy. What are you talking about? The Bengals are way better than the Browns!"

"No they're not," Craig scoffs. "A Bud Light, Royce."

I grab a pint glass and begin filling it up, still listening to their conversation.

"What?" Jim exclaims dramatically, his hand slapping against his forehead. "We lead the overall series fifty to forty-one."

Craig waves his hand through the air, dismissing the stats.

I place his beer in front of him. "Good luck."

"You're not gonna help me out here?" Craig asks, gesturing to Jim before sliding me his credit card.

"Sorry, man. I'm staying out of this one." I leave them to their arguing and start their tab before I go back to London.

"Need me to fill you up?" I ask, my lips pulling up on one side.

"Why does everything you say sound dirty?" she asks, running her dainty pointer finger around the rim of the glass.

"Maybe you have a dirty mind. I'm just asking if you need a refill."

"You could just ask if I need a refill, and not if I need you to fill me up while you look at me like that."

"Like what?" I ask, leaning onto my forearms in front of her. My tongue briefly slides across my bottom lip as my eyes drop to her mouth.

London attempts to keep a serious face as I stare into her light blue eyes, but she falters after several seconds and dismisses me with a laugh. "You know what you're doing," she utters, taking a sip from her drink.

I stand up straight, raising my arms in surrender. "Hey, I'm just making sure my customers are satisfied. It's part of the job."

"Mmhhmm," she murmurs. "I've seen you in action. You don't have to tell me twice."

"What do you mean you've seen me in action?" I ask, leaning my hip against the bar.

"Oh please," she says with a laugh, pushing her long, blond hair behind her shoulder. "Everybody in here knows you hook up with some rando who laughs too hard at your jokes, which aren't even that funny, by the way."

"Rando? And what do you mean I'm not funny? Remember that joke I told you about how French fries weren't first made in France, but in Greece. You laughed!"

"I chuckled, maybe. But that was only because an eight-year-old had just told me the same joke the day before."

"Ouch," I say, placing a hand over my heart.

She laughs and shakes her head at me. "Anyway, you don't need lame ass jokes. Just ask them if they want to sleep with you. I'm sure that's all it'll take."

"Oh really?" I ask, placing my chin in my hand as I lean over the bar again. "And why is that? Because I'm the most attractive man in all of Gaspar?"

She rolls her eyes. "And the cockiest."

"But the most attractive too, right?"

"Anyway," she sings, changing the subject and gazing at her phone. "Midge should be here soon."

"Oh good. I like Midge. She gets you drunk and makes you dance."

"Oh shush. That was only like three times."

I look down the bar and notice Chad's taking care of a couple new people who walked in.

"Well, maybe tonight will be four."

"Don't count on it. It'll be an early night for me. Got plans for tomorrow morning."

I don't bother asking about them, because I'm sure it involves her boyfriend, Hunter. I've seen him once. He had to come pick London up when she got absolutely shit-faced, which was one of the nights Midge got her drunk and on the dance floor. But I've never talked to Hunter. He doesn't join her when she visits the bar, and I've never thought to ask why.

I point at the glass she has clutched in both hands. "You sure you don't need a refill?" I ask.

She grins. "I'm gonna babysit this one for a while."

"All right. I'll come check on ya later."

I end up getting sucked into Craig and Jim's fight while I'm at their end of the bar, but when I serve Curtis his Hennessy I tell him about the Bengals vs Browns argument knowing he's from Pennsylvania, and a Steeler's fan.

"Hold up, guys. The Browns ain't better than anyone," Curtis pipes in, moving over a seat to get closer to them.

"Oh, here we go," Craig responds, taking a drink.

I chuckle as I slip away, making my way to the other side of the bar.

About a half hour later, I spot Midge taking a seat next to London, so I saunter over to take her order.

"Hey, Midge. What can I get ya this time?" She wants a new drink every time she's here. She's not a creature of habit like most drinkers.

"A tequila sunrise sounds good. Thanks, Royce."

"You got it."

I pull the orange juice from the fridge under the bar, grab the tequila and grenadine, and place them in front of me.

"So, Royce. How's your brother?" She rests her cheek in her palm, her head tilting to the side as she stares up at me with a smile.

"Which one?" I ask, pouring the tequila and orange juice over ice.

"Any of them. Who's single?"

I laugh. "All of us are single except Cillian."

After I stir the two ingredients, I slowly pour the grenadine inside the edge of the glass, observing the red syrup settle at the bottom. I plop a cherry on top and put an orange slice on the rim before sliding it over.

"The Kingston brothers," Midge sighs, grabbing the glass. "Everyone wants a piece of one of you boys."

"Not everyone," I state, glancing at London. Midge laughs as London once again rolls her eyes.

"Hunter's not a bad guy," Midge says.

"Oh, God," I mutter in disgust. "If anyone ever describes

me as *not a bad guy* I want you to shoot me in the face. What a terrible way to be described."

"Hunter is kind, generous, and thoughtful," London defends.

Not really a better description, but okay.

"Anyway," Midge interrupts. "Merrick. How is he?"

"Not the one you should be interested in since he just left."

"I know. Damn. I should've put the moves on him a while back. Now I'm gonna miss out on the good life. How about Elijah?"

"Probably too old for you."

"He's what? Thirty?"

"Thirty-five."

"That's not too old for me, plus I love his sexy professor vibe."

I scrunch my face up. "Well, Elijah and Cillian will be by later."

"I'll be sure to say hi," Midge says with a grin, tucking her short black hair behind her ear.

"London? Need me to..." I stop myself and just gesture to the glass.

"Yes, please."

After I give London another drink, I go busy myself with a group of girls who've approached the bar. Two are pretty hot, but neither have anything on London.

When London first walked into the bar, my dick twitched, wanting to say hello immediately. She strutted in wearing a black shirt tucked into a white skirt with a white blazer to match. Her long legs were on display, showing off a slight tan, and her black heels click-clacked across the hardwood floor as she made her way to me. Her blond hair fell well past her shoulders in waves, and all I could think was that she didn't belong in this small town. She belonged in Hollywood or on a runway. More importantly, she belonged in my bed.

However, that was also the day I found out she was off limits. Hunter called her shortly after she settled in in front of me, and I heard enough to know she wasn't single.

So, while I still like to flirt with her, I mainly focus on the people who are available.

"Hey ladies. How can I serve you?" I flirt.

"Service me?" One of them asks, flirting back. "I can think of some ways."

I throw her a smile and take her order first. She orders a Long Island iced tea, two of the other ones get margaritas, and the last one orders water since she's the designated driver.

"You guys here to check out the band?" I ask.

"They are," the flirty one states. "I'm here to check out the bartender."

Midge and London's high-pitched cackle floats across the room.

"Is that right?" I slide the drink across the bar, allowing my hand to linger for the briefest moment. "You hear something about me?"

Her tongue snakes out and runs across her top lip. "Maybe."

Small town means big gossip. I've had my fair share of women, so I don't doubt they tell a friend, and that friend tells a friend, so word gets around.

"Must've been good."

Once I get the other girls' their drinks and gather their money, they wander off, leaving their friend to me.

"Oh, it was good."

"What's your name, sweetheart?"

"Olive," she answers, batting her long, dark lashes at me.

"Well, Olive. It's nice to meet you. I'm Royce."

"I know who you are," she states, before sinking her teeth into her plump bottom lip.

I take my time to look study her as she ogles me. She's got a pair of black, skinny jeans on, a white top that shows an inch or two of her flat stomach, and her perky tits look like they want to bust out of the tight shirt. Her big brown eyes pin me in place, waiting for my response.

"I'll be here all night, darlin'. If you're willing to wait around for me."

She nods her head. "Okay."

"Okay, then," I say, giving her a parting wink.

"Just that easy, huh?" Craig says.

"What can I say?" I remark with a shrug.

"Did you tell her one of your hilarious jokes?" London inquires as I walk past her.

"I didn't. You think I should?"

"Pretty sure you already got that in the bag," Midge giggles. "Or bed."

"Well, London told me all I needed to do was ask them to sleep with me. You know, since I'm the most attractive man in this town."

Midge's eyebrows shoot up right before she gapes at London. "That's what you said?"

London scoffs. "Definitely didn't say he was the most attractive man in town. I said he was the cockiest."

I shrug. "I heard what I heard."

"You are pretty good-looking," Midge admits, giving me a once over. "You and your brothers definitely have the top four spots sewn up. I'm not sure in which order I'd rank you, though."

"Well, for the sake of my ego, and since you're right in front of me, please say I'm number one."

"Oh whatever. Get back to work," she jokes, throwing her cherry stem at me.

I glance at my watch and notice it's almost nine. The band is about to get on stage soon, so it's time to get things ready.

"Well, ladies. Time to see how these new guys measure up."

I adjust the lighting, making it even darker throughout the room, while lighting the stage up. I cut off the music that's already blaring through the surround sound and head to the stage to introduce the new band.

"All right, people. It's time to introduce an up-and-coming band. They have big shoes to fill, but let's give 'em a shot, okay? Welcome to the stage, The Remington Six."

As I make my way back to the bar, Olive stops me by grabbing my forearm. I chat with her for a minute before getting back to work, but it doesn't go unnoticed that London was watching me the whole time.

ACKNOWLEDGMENTS

There's always a group of people I have to thank when it comes time to write these, but the first person will always be my husband. Will, thank you so much for your constant support and unwavering belief in me and the books I write. I'm so grateful you were around this time to help me with edits. I don't know what I'd do without you. Thank you, thank you, thank you! I love you so much.

Robin, gah! I'm sure I've said this before, but this cover might be my favorite! You always work your amazing, magical skills and create a masterpiece. Thank you!

Megan Cooley and Mia Orozco, thank you for being my first beta readers and for your wonderful words that let me know how much you loved it. Kizzy, Lindsey King, and Lyndsey Wharton, thank you for your kind words regarding this book. I'm so happy you all fell for Cillian.

Candi Kane, I'm so thrilled to work with you this time around. I can't thank you enough for all the time and effort you put into getting the cover of my book, an ARC of my book, and teasers from my book, to bloggers who then get them to readers. So appreciative of you.

Kay, thanks for your time and effort into making sure I have the best manuscript I can have. I'm always learning new things because of you.

To the readers, you are why I keep writing. Thank you for choosing my book to read. I hope you enjoyed.

Bloggers, your time and dedication to reading, reviewing, and posting doesn't go unnoticed. Thank you for everything.

ALSO BY ISABEL LUCERO

The Secrets That We Keep

WAR

Resurrecting Phoenix

Think Again

Darkness Within

The Escort Series

Living in Sin

Unforgivable Sin

Sins & Mistrust

Sinfully Ever After

The Kingston Brothers Series

On the Rocks

ABOUT THE AUTHOR

Isabel Lucero is a bestselling author, finding joy in giving readers books for every mood.

Born in a small town in New Mexico, Isabel was lucky enough to escape and travel the world thanks to her husband's career in the Air Force. Her and her husband have three kids and two dogs together, and currently reside in Delaware.

When Isabel isn't on mommy duty or writing her next book, she can be found reading, or in the nearest Target buying things she doesn't need.

Isabel loves connecting with her readers and fans of books in general. Keep in touch!

Sign up for my newsletter.

Join my reading group.

And find me on the sites below.

Made in the USA
Coppell, TX
16 March 2021